All Hat
and
No Cattle

Murder, Drugs, & H2O:
Nowhere Else But Texas

Nick Sibelius Series, Book 2

by R.W.Hacker

All Hat and No Cattle

R. W. Hacker

Copyright © 2017 by Richard Hacker
All rights reserved
LifeJazz Media

ISBN: 0-9982030-1-7
ISBN-13: 978-0-9982030-1-0

Dedication

To my beautiful, intelligent daughter, Anna.
May your creative spirit continue to blossom in the world.

R. W. Hacker

Acknowledgments

Over time I have come to understand a novel is not the work of a lone writer, but really the work of a small village of creative people. Of the villagers involved in the creation of this book, I'd like to especially thank Chip Locklear and Stephanie Cole for their careful reading and editing of the manuscript. And I also want to thank Chip for adding his expertise in the sciences in an attempt to keep my fiction from going too far astray from reality. You didn't always succeed, my friend, but then that's why it's called fiction.

I also want to give a shout out to the state of Texas—a character in these stories, my home for several decades, and a place close to my heart.

R. W. Hacker

Table of Contents

R. W. Hacker

ALL HAT
AND
NO CATTLE

All Hat and No Cattle

Target #5

Charity's universe demanded blood for the pain she endured.

She sat in her black Nissan Leaf, silent but for the sound of the impatient tapping of her fingers on the steering wheel. Her eyes fixed on a terra cotta roof-tiled Spanish revival number in the cul-de-sac of Island Palms Cove, a street lined with multi-million dollar mansions along a custom-built peninsula on Lake Austin. Ignoring the opulence, she watched a fire red Ferrari 430, license plate number HNJ 793.

Her hopped up, speed addicted, hacker of a cousin Larry had provided, as usual, the required critical information. She'd handed him her standard envelop with his "medication" and a license plate number. Several hours later, he emailed an encrypted file with all of the particulars, including a code for the security gate. Charity would make Daniel Hoyt pay for his disrespect of cyclists.

She pondered the idea of sticking a gun in Hoyt's mouth. She'd pull the trigger, watching his brain matter splatter across the mirrored surface of his fucking Italian supercar. The thought of how sun-baked blood and brain would absolutely eat right through the clear coat, destroying his its mirror finish, gave her a visceral pleasure. Charity took in a deep breath. *Balance.*

Sitting in her carbon zero car, she downed a non-fat latte, one power bar, and an electrolyte- packed coconut water. Her hip ached and the need to take a piss rose with some urgency. For a moment she considered packing it in for the day, knowing she could come back tomorrow. Tapping an iPhone strapped to her arm, a high energy male voice filled her ear buds.

"Are you haunted by demons? Do you find your plans faltering? Do you let your fear of failure stop you from achieving your goals?"

Charity spoke out loud to her demons—the lazy, fat, loser demons who always haunted her whenever she "hit the wall" during a race or a workout.

She shouted within the confines of her car. "Come on, Charity! Push it! Push through it, goddamn it! Let's go. Let's go!"

The podcast continued. *"How do you approach life? Fire, ready, aim? To live with intention, to live consciously in the world, you must rearrange your mindset from fire, ready, aim to ready, aim, fire!"*

Charity stepped out of the car into a warm, humid summer morning. She scanned the area, then pulled down her black tech fabric riding shorts. Squatting, she kept her legs far enough apart to avoid the splashing stream of urine. While peeing felt good, the indignity of the moment set off her ongoing anger at a patriarchal God. Men had pricks they could just hang out at will to pee. If God was a woman, then women, whenever the mood or necessity warranted, would be able to yank a man's prick right off, like the tail of a chameleon, who scurries away nub-butted while you hold the still twitching member in your hand.

The energetic male voice pulled her back to the task at hand, *"What is Ready? You are ready when mind, body and spirit, when your whole being is a coiled spring for action. Can you feel your creative, life spirit tension about to explode?"*

Charity repeated her mantra. "Yes, I am ready. I am a coiled spring. I am a creative explosion."

Finishing, she pulled her shorts up over her long and freckled muscular legs, watching her quads flex as she smoothed the leg band. As had been the pattern for the last three days, Hoyt had not left his house before 6:30 am. She checked her pink GPS enabled training watch. 5:05 am. Plenty of time.

"Readiness is not sufficient. To be powerful you must AIM. A for Attitude, the attitude of a winner. I for Intention, intending with heart, mind, and soul the reality you will create. And M for Manifestation, making your power real in the world."

Charity summarized the teaching reverberating around her. "I am ready. I am a winner. I will manifest my power to create life *exactly* how I want it. Let's go, Charity!"

Pulling the trunk release, she reached for her Iron Divas black and pink workout bag with a white skeleton riding a pink road bike, the skeletal rider's long flaming hair trailing behind, teeth gritted ferociously. She took in a breath and slightly bent her knees, feeling the strain of her triceps flexing under the load of the bag. Her focus on Hoyt had taken her off the daily workout regimen. Just one more reason she hated this sonofabitch. Opening the bag, she pulled out a one liter, brown, glass bottle filled with butyric acid, which she had stolen from high school chemistry lab the day before.

"I am a winner. I will prevail."

Moving quickly, she jogged the two blocks to an expansive home with a terra cotta roof and her target red sports car in the driveway. She crept to the driver's side of the Ferrari, checking the door. No alarm. Even though she had a "smash and go" plan if needed, it pissed her off the egotistical jerk assumed no one would dare mess with his ride. She worked fast. Placing a gel pack on the driver's side door to dampen the sound, she punched a quarter inch hole through the carbon fiber door with a titanium drill bit. She slipped a plastic hose fitted with a tiny spray nozzle on the end through the hole, then connected the free end of the hose to a small, battery-powered pump, which in turn connected by a hose to the chemical-filled bottle. She flipped the switch. A stench of soured gym socks filled the morning air as liquid flowed through clear plastic tubing, disappearing into Hoyt's sports car's door. A fine mist sprayed out the nozzle onto custom red and black Italian leather racing seats and hand-fitted wool carpets. Her pump strained, having emptied the container. She pulled the hose out, causing some liquid to dribble down the door, splashing onto the drive. Charity took a breath in through her nose, an odor of diarrhea and rancid curry causing her to gag, acidic vomit coming up in her mouth.

Be strong. Be confident. Be courageous.

Closing her eyes she regained her focus, put the equipment back into her bag and twisted a bullet-shaped tampon into the hole, its pale blue string dangling in the air.

She ran back to her, tossing her gear in the trunk, then drove to the Laguna Gloria Museum parking lot to put on her cycling shoes, helmet, gloves and riding glasses. 5:55 am. She lifted her pink, carbon road bike off the roof rack, checked tire pressure and brakes, then clipped in, heading back to Hoyt's house. Her legs burned as she conquered the gradual slope of Mount Bonnell Road. She was strong, powerful, in control. Hoyt had begun his crucible of becoming her fifth target. But as she shifted through the gears, Charity reminded herself that while Target #5 would be fun, she had come to Austin with a singular purpose: to kill her brother's murderer.

Yes, the Universe demands a balance of blood for pain.

~*~

Dan Hoyt awoke on his back, drool running down his cheek, and a woman's leg draped uncomfortably across his crotch. He turned his head to see a red 5:33 floating in the darkness. He tried to squirm out from under the leg. "Gotta get up."

He couldn't remember what the woman's leg had been attached to. Julie? Janice? Didn't matter. He pushed the leg aside, turning to get out of bed. The leg spoke up.

"You getting up? Come on back to bed, baby."

Jenny? Janet? The name associated with the talking leg just would not come to him. Knowing her name wasn't a big deal, but women seemed to get a bit bitchy in the morning if you couldn't remember their names.

"No, I've got to get up. Lots to do today. But you stay right there. After last night, you definitely deserve some extra rest."

He had absolutely no idea what had happened last night.

The leg's drowsy voice spoke in the darkness. "You weren't so bad yourself."

Whatshername must have been lousy, given he couldn't remember having sex with her. Telling her the truth wouldn't get him out the door any faster, but lying to her would at least keep her quiet. He leaned over in the darkness, finding a breast to kiss, which he assumed belonged to the leg.

"Mmmm. You leaving so soon?" The breast spoke, but with the voice of a different woman. The night was coming back to him. Two very hot women, tequila shots, short black dresses pulled up to panty level as the smaller one sat on the lap of the taller one, miraculously stuffed into the passenger seat of his Ferrari. They were undressed and all over each other almost before he could get them to the bedroom. He hadn't been able to find the damn Viagra. Hoyt figured with two he'd get it up, but once again his cock had let the team down. He kept the lights off, feeling a bit exposed for not being able to perform, especially under such optimal conditions.

"Yeah, lots to do, girls. Make yourselves at home. I'll leave some money for a taxi."

He closed the bathroom door, flipping the light switch. Hoyt stared at a squinting, naked, thirty-four -year- old man without an erection in the full -length wall mirror. He showered, shaved, pulled on a pair of creased jeans, a white starched shirt with silver and turquoise cuff links, a pair of handmade quill ostrich skin boots, and a Stetson hat with a diamond encrusted headband. He opened the door to the two women, one spooning behind the other, in the middle of his bed.

The stress lately had really taken a toll on his sex life. When, at first, he couldn't get it up, he panicked a bit thinking it might be prostate cancer or some other horrible malady his money couldn't fix. The doctor ruled out all the usual suspects, which left him with stress.

Stress. Yeah, I'm stressed 'cause of the deal I've got in the works, but Jesus. He shook his head in disgust. *Be a man, Hoyt.*

Fortunately, the Viagra worked, when he could find the goddamn bottle. But this seemed to be the way his luck fell lately. He manages to hook up with two cute darlings, get them home, and then nothing. His balls chimed in. *They must be lesbians, otherwise…*Hoyt liked the way his boys thought.

Going downstairs he stepped into an expansive kitchen, all granite, stainless steel, hardwoods, and glass. Flipping on the flat screen suspended under a cabinet, weatherwoman Samantha Fox in one of her typical bright primary colors--red this morning--stood by a map devoid of clouds with temperatures in the 100's. A message ran below pronouncing water rationing in effect. He pushed a couple buttons on the espresso machine, cursing when he realized he had forgotten to place his cup under the complicated contraption's nozzle. Coffee splashed into

4

a drip pan until he shoved his cup in place. Leaving the kitchen, he made his way to the front door with a partial mug of steaming coffee. While the morning so far had been a bust, he couldn't help but smile thinking about his drive out to the project south of Austin in his Ferrari. He loved his Ferrari like a man loves his woman. He loved the smell of her, the sounds she made as he ran through her gears, the thrust of clutching her, the scream of her tires as he stretched her around a corner. He loved the envious expressions of all of those people who could never be him, who could never sit in her black and red racing seats, know the feel of her shifter, the rush of air flowing over her sleek, graceful body.

He pressed the button on his key fob to open the door and, with a flash of lights, the alarm set. While wrangling two semi-inebriated randy women out of the car, he managed to lock the doors, but had failed to set the alarm. Fortunately he lived in a cul-de-sac of million dollar homes with an aura of security, so accidentally leaving the alarm off was not a big deal. He pressed the button again, hearing the locks release. With a coffee mug in his right hand, he opened the door with his left, looking up the street as a woman in black and pink lycra on a pink road bike rolled by silently. He wondered how he had missed seeing her in the neighborhood before. Watching the curves of her athletic body, he vowed to get several bottles of Viagra placed strategically in his homes, offices and vehicles before the end of the day.

As the door opened a thick putrescent stench solidified his brain into something resembling a lump of head cheese. His nostrils burned, eyes watering uncontrollably. His right hand, no longer responding to brain function, released its grip on the coffee cup, the ceramic object shattering on impact with the driveway. His bowels released while his stomach spasmed, simultaneously soiling his jeans and sending his morning coffee and all of last night's dinner spewing across the interior of his beloved Ferrari. The overwhelming odor of what he could only imagine was the shit of dead, rotting rats in a soup of blue-green chunky sick consumed him, voiding his lungs of air. He fell to his knees gasping, continuing to vomit uncontrollably until he had nothing left to give.

The woman on the pink bike had circled back around, he assumed to help him out. The thought of the two lesbians upstairs laughing at his limp dick and now another woman helping him because he shit his pants and projectile vomited all over his car really pissed him off.

She hadn't stopped, but Hoyt, raising a hand as if to repel her attention, preemptively called out. "I'm fine. No problem."

Willing himself to a standing position, he stepped away from the car, pulling out a cell phone, angrily pounding a phone number.

"Charlie!"

"Mornin' boss. What's up?"

"I'll tell you what's up. Some goddamn sonofabitch just destroyed my fucking Ferrari, that's what's up, Charlie! Get over here now. And didn't you tell me you had some kind of private eye friend?"

"Yeah, I keep his truck—"

"Well, call him. Now."

"It's awful early, Mr. Hoyt."

"I'd don't give a flying fuck what time it is, Charlie. Call him and have him meet me here in an hour. I don't know who did this, but they have no idea who they're fucking with."

"Want me to get a latte for you on the way over?"

"No, I don't want a goddamn latte. Just get your ass over here. Now!"

Business Opportunity

In hindsight, Nick would wish he had stayed in bed, dreaming about a naked woman sitting on a camel in a snowstorm. Instead, he sat on a lawn chair in front of his silver bullet-shaped Airstream trailer east of Pflugerville, a cup of coffee in one hand, a breakfast taco in the other, watching the sky gradually turn from a deep violet to orange and then a deep blue. Water restrictions left the grass surrounding his trailer, once a lush green blanket of St. Augustine, a crispy brown shag carpet. The turf crackled underfoot and bone dry soil split open crevasses like hundreds of little mouths agape begging for water.

This sad excuse for a lawn mimicked the sorry state of his life. After finding his anesthesiologist wife astride a trauma doc on her lunch break, Nick's life had taken a decidedly downward spiral, culminating in being fired from the Houston Police, punctuated with the rim shot of a nasty divorce. Then he fell in love, or maybe lust, with the sister of a murderer, which did not put him in a positive relationship with the local police department. To his horror she drove like a banshee into a raging forest fire, the locals pronouncing her dead. He thought he'd lost her too, until an anonymous email hinted at her survival. Alive or dead, he hadn't heard from her since the fire over a year ago. A year is a long time to hold onto a faint hope. Now he sat in front of his trailer just outside the same little town, staring at the sorry state of his lawn, and contemplating the equally sad state of his life.

His lawn needed, Nick needed, a long cool drink of life-giving water. He looked to a cloudless morning sky predicting the continued demise of his grass. Nick wondered if he'd be able to find the water that would bring him back to life before he completely dried up and blew away.

When his cell phone rang from inside the trailer, he poured the dregs of his coffee onto the parched earth and stepped inside to take the call.

"Nick, man I'm glad you picked up." Charlie Samuels. The mechanic who kept his pickup moving in a forward direction. *Why is Charlie calling me at 6:30 in the morning? Does Ford have a major recall for spontaneously combustive trucks?*

"Charlie?"

"Uh, morning, Nick. So sorry to bother you this early."

"Everything okay? Do I have a critical part missing from my truck or something?"

"No, no. I'm not calling about your truck. I just remembered the last conversation we had."

"Yeah, my clutch would probably be good for another twenty thousand miles."

"No, I mean the part about your business. Private investigations. You are in the private investigation business, right?"

"Yeah, that's what I do."

Nick's business plan demanded a swank address among the hills and million dollar homes of west Austin. His bank account, however, forced him to settle for a decomposing northeast Austin industrial park built in the early 70's on a plot of land contaminated by two decades of toxic waste-dumping. The new business bled cash as soon as he set up an office. Fortunately, Alice, his assistant, had agreed to come back to work for him part-time after he let the business slide over losing the aforementioned girl. Unfortunately, he had used most of his savings since leaving the police force in Houston and his few small investigation gigs. If he didn't get a client in the next week he'd need to start checking out cafe barista jobs and put the Airstream up for sale.

"I'm sure you're swamped with work, Nick, but I've got a client for you. Between you and me, he's all hat and no cattle, but I bet he'll pay pretty well."

Great. A poser. A con artist. Or worse. Nick decided to leave Charlie with the assumption he had clients falling all over themselves to use his services, especially after the word "pay" caught his attention.

"I might be interested. How do you know he'll pay well for the work?"

"I work on his Ferrari. Brand new. He won't trust it to the dealer, only to his personal mechanic."

"And that's you."

"Afraid so. Like I said, he's a bit of an asshole, but I've made a pretty good living off him. He drives a lot of high end stuff, so other than dealing with him, it's fun for me and I can charge premium prices."

"Do you know what this is about?"

"Tell you what. Can you be at 2002 Island Palms Cove in an hour? It's over by Mount Bonnell."

"That's the other side of town, Charlie. Don't know with the traffic, but I can give it a shot. So, you going to tell me what this is about?"

"Not sure myself. Something about his Ferrari being destroyed. Hell, I'd drive across town just to see what that looks like."

"Okay. Tell your guy, what's his name?"

"Hoyt. Dan Hoyt."

Nick had heard of this guy. Besides being a Texas tabloid playboy and a douchebag, he had made his fortune in commercial real estate before the age of thirty. Lately he had been on a bit of a losing streak. He started a controversial gated community for adults under fifty-five without children — kind of a little suburban City of Sin—which kept his lawyers continuously busy. In the middle of multiple lawsuits, he built a towering condo in downtown Austin with so many engineering issues the City Council finally had the building pulled down. Then Nick thought he had read something about the guy buying up land on the Gulf Coast in the last couple years. The speculation around his most recent activity ranged from a massive beachfront condo to an oil refinery.

"The commercial real estate Dan Hoyt?"

"That's the one. I'll meet you there." Nick shoved the phone into his pocket.

Well Nick, I guess it's time to dance with the devil.

~*~

Nick found time on the road provided a nice break from the ongoing challenge of finding a client. So driving toward a potential client offered a completely novel experience. He listened to the morning news about the Israelis and the Palestinians, China's influence on the world economy and increased water rationing due to a continuing drought in Central Texas. Between human avarice, global warming, and his deteriorating personal life, he figured he had about fifty years before the whole planet imploded.

Nick drove through rush hour traffic, only finding some relief after heading east onto Mt. Bonnell Road. Winding through the west Austin hills he passed a woman standing with a bike tire in her hand. He didn't want to miss the appointment, but he also didn't like the idea of a lone cyclist with a breakdown on the side of the road. He pulled off to the shoulder, then backed the truck down the hill to her. His rear view mirror framed a woman dressed in black and pink lycra, head down in concentration with a bicycle wheel. He stopped just short of her pink bike and got out of his truck.

"Morning. Need some help?"

The woman looked at him, her eyes obscured by tinted riding glasses. Wordlessly, she worked a tube around the wheel, pulling the tire into place with levers.

Nick tried once more. "Lots of construction going on in the area. Probably ran over a nail or something. Can I help you out?"

She worked her hands around the rim to seat the tire firmly in the wheel, speaking with an Australian accent. "I'm good." She looked past him. "You've got a pretty old pickup truck. Must get horrible gas mileage."

She stepped over to her bike, laid down on one side, and pulled out a CO_2 cartridge and nozzle which she then screwed onto the tire's valve. He noticed an almost imperceptible grimace revealing a pain accompanying her limp when she moved.

"Yeah, I live out in the country and a truck comes in handy pretty often. But you're right. I do wish there was something out there getting better gas mileage. Maybe a hybrid or an electric."

Tilting her head, she parted her lips into a slight smile, which turned to a frown when the CO2 failed to inflate the tube.

"Damn."

"Something the matter?"

"The valve must be bad and I don't have another tube."

Nick stepped beside the woman who rose to five foot nine or ten, the top of her head almost even with his nose. He guessed she must be in her forties or early fifties. Whatever her age, she had an athletic beauty about her. "How about I give you a ride?" The woman had been riding a steep, almost impossible gradient. "I don't think I'd want to walk a bike up that."

She lowered her glasses revealing green eyes, pale freckles, and wisps of red hair beneath her helmet. "I don't, as a practice, use hydrocarbon-burning vehicles." She scanned the incline ahead. "But I do need to get back to my car—electric, mind you—so I can attend to some critical business matters." She paused in thought. "Yes, I'll take a ride."

Nick helped the woman get her bike into the back of his truck, tied securely to her satisfaction, and then continued on his way.

"Where can I drop you off?"

"My car is parked over at Mayfield Park where Mt. Bonnell intersects Bull Creek. You know where it is?"

"Sure. I'm going your way."

They drove down the road listening to *Morning Edition* on the radio.

"Nice bike you have there."

"Do you ride?"

Nick occasionally got out on the backroads east of Pflugerville and usually had trouble walking for the next day or two. "Yeah, but I'm nowhere close to your league."

"Why do you say that?"

"I couldn't get up the hill you were on if my life depended on it."

The woman, lean and muscular with shoulder length red hair, laughed. "You'd be surprised what people will do when they think their lives depend on it."

Nick sensed a story between the lines, but he had pulled into the Mayfield parking lot. She stepped out of his truck and pulled her bike out of the pickup bed.

"Thanks for the lift." Limping away with her bike, she turned back. "Even though you drive a pickup, you're one of the good guys. Don't disappoint me."

Nick watched her limp away chuckling to himself about this woman's people skills. He knew she had just complimented him, but why did it sound like a threat?

Getting back on the road, he drove toward Mt. Bonnell. Approaching Island Palms Cove, the traffic gradually shifted from Toyotas, Fords and Hondas to Range Rovers, Porsches and Mercedes. He stopped at a green steel gate into the development, the property's perimeter surrounded by a high-dollar steel fence. Punching in a code Charlie had given him, the gate silently slid back. A well-maintained gate for a well-maintained gated community. At the end of the cul-de-sac a bow legged man with a beer gut paunch and grey, thinning hair stood next to a man in jeans and a cowboy hat right out of a *GQ* cover shoot. A perfect red Ferrari sat nearby. He pulled up to a house which, with its multiple roofs and chimneys, looked to Nick to be more of a resort community than a single home. His truck door creaked as he stepped out, causing Charlie, the bow legged man, to unconsciously cringe.

"Morning, Nick. Thanks for coming out."

"Morning, Charlie. Good to see you." Nick turned to the *GQ* guy. "And you must be Dan Hoyt." Nick extended a hand which Hoyt shook firmly, looking Nick straight in the eye. A musky aftershave mixed with an oddly out of place sour odor cloyed at the guy like LA smog.

"Charlie here tells me you're in the security consulting business."

"That's correct."

Hoyt released Nick's hand. "Well, I've got a security issue. Somebody's been fucking with my Ferrari and I want you to find the sonofabitch."

Nick glanced over at the sleek sports car which looked perfect, except for having something white sticking out of the driver's side door with a little blue string. "So, what's happened with your car? This Ferrari, right?"

"Yes, *this* Ferrari. I came out of the house this morning and when I opened the door... Jesus, the smell."

Broken shards of a ceramic cup and what appeared to be vomit near the rear tire and a bit on the roof offered evidence of a gut-wrenching reaction to something. He reached for the door, but Hoyt stopped him.

"I'd appreciate it if you wouldn't open the door of my car until I'm a bit farther away."

Nick looked quizzically at Hoyt and then to Charlie.

Charlie scrunched up his face as if a skunk had just walked by. "It reeks in there, Nick. I mean the most godawful odor you've ever smelled in your life. I've got a respirator in my truck tool box. Why don't you let me break it out for you before you go mucking around inside that thing."

The initial energy of facing a new challenge began to drain out of him. He'd been called out to deal with what amounted to a fraternity prank. Probably some of Hoyt's old buddies got drunk and then peed in his pretty Ferrari. Nick wondered how he had fallen from investigating homicides to sorting out overgrown boys with expensive toys. Hoyt must have sensed Nick's dissipating enthusiasm because he moved in quickly to close the deal.

"I imagine you spend most of your time on dangerous, high profile corporate espionage, Nick. You don't mind if I call you Nick?" Hoyt didn't wait for a response. "But you see, I'm in the middle of the deal of a lifetime and clearly, someone's trying to take me off my game. This is important to me, Nick. I'll pay you double your usual rates."

Nick replied, more out of pride than business savvy, "You don't know my rates. Maybe I'm too expensive for you."

Hoyt slapped Nick on the shoulder, laughing as if he'd just told an incredibly funny, raunchy joke.

"Whatever they are, I'll double them. And if you find this sonofabitch, there's a ten thousand dollar bonus. All I ask is that you play on Team Hoyt."

"Excuse me?"

He leaned into Nick as if they were old acquaintances sharing a secret, thrusting his hand out to seal the deal. "Once you get on the Hoyt train, you'll want to ride it all the way to station. Do we have a deal?"

"I'd figure a big real estate developer like you would have your own security guy."

Hoyt frowned. "Yeah, well, the sonofabitch decided he'd make bigger bucks in the Middle East and left me cold." He smiled, giving Nick a pat on his shoulder. "But I always like to see my people advance in their careers. That's what Team Hoyt's all about."

Nick had no idea what the hell this real estate huckster was selling, but he also knew he didn't have anything going to bring in revenue. And this guy seemed anxious to part with his money. Tracking down a stupid prank could hardly be called work, but getting some money in the bank would make room to develop new clients and some real security work. Charlie had it right. Hoyt was an asshole, but he did have cash. He shook "Team Hoyt's" hand, forcing himself to say, "I guess I'm on the Hoyt train. Yeah, we've got a deal." Why did he feel he had just bent over to have a gleaming red Ferrari shoved up his ass?

~*~

Once Hoyt had driven off in a big white Dodge Ram truck and Charlie, before leaving, had handed him a respirator, Nick looked over the Ferrari in more detail. A breeze moving a dangling blue string caught Nick's eye. He knelt, inspecting the object sticking in the side of the door.

"A tampon?"

Twisting the tampon out, a searing whiff of rotted clams in a bucket of puke sent him reeling back, landing hard on his butt. He heard a giggle and then a woman's voice.

"Hard night cowboy?"

Two barefoot young women in little black dresses and holding their high heels , stood a few feet away. Even with his olfactory system in chaos, his mind recognized they both had amazingly long legs. The brunette must have mistaken the bizarre sensory confusion long legs and rotting clams will have on a man for inquisitiveness.

"House guest," she offered, to explain whatever question she must have thought Nick had on his mind.

The blond looked him over. "And what happened to you?"

Nick got to his feet. "A bit odd to explain. Mr. Hoyt's car has a rather foul smell to it. Knocked me right off my feet."

The brunette turned to the blond. "I told you it was Dan Hoyt. The real estate guy?" The brunette, perturbed at her friend continued. "Jeez, Laura, don't you even read the news? Dan Hoyt."

"You ladies know Dan then?"

The blond cocked her head, fondling a strand of sun bleached hair. "Sort of friends of his. We just met last night, actually."

"So you were with him all last night?"

The brunette shot back, "I don't think it's any of your business. Besides, our taxi just arrived."

"No, don't get me wrong. I didn't mean anything by it. Mr. Hoyt, Dan has hired me to find out who damaged his car."

The blond placed a manicured hand on the hood. "The Ferrari? Looks okay to me."

"The smell I mentioned? Apparently the interior of the car has been covered with it."

Her face scrunched in disgust. "Gross."

"Did either of you hear anything unusual, like a slamming door or an odd sound earlier this morning?"

The two women looked at each other, a conspiratorial smile forming on both, then the brunette replied, "No, nothing really unusual. We were both dead to the world. A little too much tequila, if you know what I mean."

After the women left, he finished looking over Hoyt's Ferrari, this time with a respirator firmly affixed to his face. He soaked up some of the liquid on a cloth, placing the evidence in a plastic bag, hoping to God the foul smell wouldn't be able to permeate polyethylene. Then he packed his gear and headed to the office. He had a new client. Finally.

Lane Change

Nick drove away from Hoyt's red Ferrari with a renewed sense of confidence about his business. Yes. He finally landed some serious work. Merging into three lanes of fast moving traffic, doubts crept up on him. Wasn't this the way things always played out? He agreed to some proposition and then discovered too late he had made the wrong decision, aligned himself with the wrong people, found himself in an awkward and usually dangerous situation? Of course, he definitely needed the money, but Hoyt had a reputation for being a bit of a sleaze and a con man. Did he really want to get himself involved with this guy? However, he had only agreed to find out who trashed Hoyt's Ferrari. How bad could things get?

Don't be stupid Nick. Of course things could get a lot worse.

Before he could get too deep into a conversation with himself, he answered his ringing cell phone. Quentin Matthews. Quen worked for the Pflugerville PD, but had been on a one month leave to help his wife sort out an inherited cattle ranch in south Texas. He imagined Quen sitting on a horse, cell phone in one hand, lariat in the other.

"Hey Nick, how you doing this morning?"

Somehow Quentin had a knack for calling him in the middle of his internal wrestling matches.

"Doing okay. Just coming back from seeing a new client."

"New client? Fantastic buddy. See, I told you this private investigation thing would work out for you. Persistence man. Persistence."

A large semi followed just a few feet off the back of Nick's small pickup. A car on either side, he had no escape route. Something about this situation felt very familiar.

"Quentin, I'm thinking about turning this guy down."

"What? You've got to be kidding me. Why would you do that?"

Given Nick had been complaining about not having a client for the last several months made Quentin's reaction understandable. Annoying, but understandable. However, Quentin didn't have all the information.

"Ever heard of Dan Hoyt?"

"The real estate guy? Thought he went to prison for fraud or something."

A sedan on Nick's left changed lanes right in front of him and then slowed, forcing Nick to brake. The semi rig's chromed grill topped with a red oval Peterbilt logo filled his rearview mirror.

"Didn't go to prison, but I'm sure he'll make it there one of these days. With my recent track record, I just don't know if I want to get tangled up with a guy like Hoyt. Today I'm looking for whoever trashed his car and tomorrow..."

Quentin filled in the blank, satire dripping from his voice. "Tomorrow you're neck deep in terrorists and drug cartels?"

"No, Quentin, you know what I mean. I let my heart blind me to what was happening right in front of me before and look how that worked out."

He avoided answering the question, but the answer still crept into his mind. *I broke my heart, lost my job, and made a total ass of myself. That's how it worked out.* Peterbilt flashed his lights and the sedan slowed more as the driver tried to move into the right hand lane already filled with traffic. Nick thought about pulling into the passing lane, but before he could make a move, another semi pulled alongside him. *Great.*

"Will you listen to yourself Nick? How could you have known MaryLou was your murder suspect's sister?"

Nick wondered how they got into this conversation, the one conversation he didn't want to have with either Quentin or himself. "My point exactly, Quen. I didn't know. And because I didn't catch on until late in the game I almost let my suspect get away and MaryLou died." He didn't like keeping the truth about MaryLou from Quentin, but he had a feeling she needed to be dead. At least for the time being.

A loud air horn from the Peterbilt startled Nick. He could make out the shapes of dead bugs on this guy's grill. He looked left to see the wheels of a large blue rig hauling steel pipes and to his right another rig moved closer. He pounded on his horn, a David among Goliaths. Where the hell did all of these trucks come from?

"It's a new day, Nick. So you got played by the woman. Could've have happened to anybody."

"When was the last time you got played Quen?" Nick heard the flash of anger in his voice, but he knew his anger had much more to do with himself than anything Quentin could say.

"Well, you have to understand I'm a highly-trained law enforcement professional." Before he could respond with the expected "fuck you," Quentin laughed in the way a good friend who loves you embraces even your weaknesses. Nick never could stay angry at Quentin for very long. "No man, just kidding. So she was his sister, so she was undercover Homeland Security, so she killed two bad guys right in front of you— saving your ass both times if I recall. But maybe *you* played her. Have you thought about that? You ended up arresting the brother and getting two mean ass criminals off the streets."

Nick had just about had enough of these trucks and this guy in the sedan. Flashing his lights and honking he willed the car blocking his escape route to get out of the way.

"Are you trying to make me feel better Quen? 'Cause if you are, you're doing a lousy job of it."

"My point, Nick, is things are never what they seem and you made the best of a bad situation. Close the door and move on. Don't stand on the other side of the door and continually bash your head against the damn thing."

The sedan finally moved right, the driver taking the trouble to lower her window and shoot him the finger as Nick accelerated past on a slight incline, leaving the Peterbilt huffing and puffing behind him.

"So, you think I should take the work, even though Hoyt could be trouble?"

"Yes, take the work. Move on. Please."

Looking out his side and rear mirrors, the three lumbering trucks fell away as he crested the hill.

"Okay, Quen. But if this blows up in my face, I'll be coming after you."

"Right, I'd like to see that. Oh, and by the way, I stopped by your office earlier this morning on my way to Fort Worth. Very swank location, if you're a drug dealer or a porn shop."

Nick wished Quentin's tease wasn't quite so close to the truth. "Very funny."

"Sorry I couldn't hang around. Had to meet a bull up in Fort Worth."

"A bull."

"I'm a rancher now, cowboy. Anyway, I think you'll find something at your office which I believe just might be the thing to get you through this."

Nick tried to imagine what could possibly get him through a job with a guy known for being, as Charlie had put it, an asshole. A full-time attorney? A machine gun? A case of bourbon?

"What did you do, Quentin?"

"Let's just say you'll be surprised."

~*~

Nick pulled his pickup into the waste dump of an industrial park he had been occupying for over a year. The plan had been to move out when the EPA came to clean up the site. They hadn't shown up yet and he was beginning to think they never would. Given the high probability someone had been pouring solvents and who knew what else down his drains, he only used bottled water in his office.

He could see fluorescent light spilling out his front window. Given the budget constraints, he reminded himself to be more careful about turning out all the lights in the future. He needed every cent he could find. Putting his key in the deadbolt, he discovered an unlocked door. Nick knew for certain that while he might leave a light on now and then, he'd never fail to lock the door to his business. He went back to the truck, pulling his gun out of the glove box, then positioned himself to the side of the office door, slowly and silently turning the knob. The door opened inward a few inches. He heard tapping sounds from inside. *Damn. I take a job with Hoyt and within the hour he's got people breaking into my office!*

Nick, holding his gun in both hands, took a deep breath. He slammed the door open with his foot, taking a ready stance at the door, then scanned the room with his weapon. He honed in on a heart shaped rear-end, embraced by a pair of skintight jeans. The kind of feminine ass, full and curving, which makes a man forget why he's scanning a room with his Glock out.

The owner of the rear-end, hearing Nick's dramatic entrance, dove for cover. A furious, feminine voice called out from behind his desk. "Jesus Christ! What the hell are you doing?"

"What am I doing? Who the hell are you?"

The woman, athletic, Hispanic, in her late twenties with long, dark hair and deep brown eyes, stood, dropping a letter opener on the cheap, dinged up gun metal desk.

"Theresa Soliz."

"Where do I know you?"

She smiled, hands on her hips. Then it clicked. Theresa Soliz. Sgt. Theresa Soliz. Pflugerville Police Department.

"Mind putting the gun away?"

Nick lowered his Glock, flipping on the safety. "What are you...? How did you...?-

She offered a teasing smile and sat in Nick's slightly tilting desk chair. "What am I doing here? Remember when you asked Alice a few months ago to help you with your new business venture?" Al, who had become Alice, had been his office assistant until everything fell apart. When Nick pulled himself together, he offered Alice her old job, but she declined.

"Yeah. She didn't take the job."

"I know. John Mather's of Mathers, Smiley and Pritcher, Attorneys at Law, whisked her away to Jamaica. Love is a beautiful thing, isn't it? Anyway, she heard I left the department and thought you could use my talents."

He looked back at his door, the knob having punched a nice baseball-sized hole in the wall.

"How did I get in here?" Theresa anticipated Nick's next question. "I haven't picked a lock in a while, so I thought I'd have some practice.

Besides, since we're in the investigation business, breaking into our own office to check our security seemed like a good idea. And bad news, Nick. We don't have any security."

Nick closed the door. Could Theresa be the thing Quentin suggested he'd find at the office? "Now that you've made yourself at home, did Quentin drop by this morning?"

Theresa turned on a desktop computer. "He called me last week to let me know you finally got off your butt. So, here I am. And yes, Quentin stopped by this morning in mid-burglary. He looked a little surprised to see me, too. Said he'd give you a call on his way to Fort Worth."

"Theresa."

She looked up from the screen. He couldn't help but notice her. He used to tease Quentin about working with such a beautiful partner. Her outward appearance was pretty stunning, but Quentin had told Nick about the woman underneath the good looks, about her strength and resiliency. Given Quentin's description, she struck Nick as the kind of person who could take on any storm and come through the other side, not broken, but more complex, more refined for having been through the ordeal. Nick knew she had a couple of tours in Iraq and exceptional talents in small arms and hand-to-hand combat. Those skills had saved Quentin more than once. Nick would now be adding something along the lines of cat burglar to her resume. He wasn't sure how he would pay her, but Quentin was right, as usual. He couldn't think of a partner he'd rather have in this new business other than her.

"Theresa, thanks for coming."

"No problem, Nick. There's fresh coffee in the pot."

Nick took a cup, cautious from the burnt offerings Alice provided in the past. He poured hot, steaming brew from the carafe. She could handle a gun and make a pot of decent coffee? He took a sip, wincing at the thick, bitter aftertaste then set his cup on the coffee-stained desk blotter. Being good with a gun would have to do.

"Since you've decided to join this enterprise, I've got some good news for you. I do believe we have our first client."

"Really? Fantastic."

"Yeah, I know. I was beginning to think I—we—would sink before we got started."

Theresa came around to sit on the top of the desk in front of Nick. "So?"

"So...the client is Dan Hoyt."

"The real estate guy?"

"That's the one."

"I met him at a fundraiser last year. Definitely all hat and no cattle."

"Yeah, that seems to be the general consensus."

"And a bit on the dark side."

"Probably, but we're just doing a small job for him. Nothing shady. Some of his old frat brothers peed all over his brand new Ferrari and he's looking for evidence."

She crossed her arms. "You're kidding."

Nick pulled the plastic bag holding the foul-smelling sample out of his pocket and tossed it on his desk. "Not kidding. Here's a sample of the damage. Do you know anyone at the University we might get to take a look at this?"

Theresa reached for the bag, zipping it open before Nick could react.

"Holy mother of God!" The raw stench of vomit filled the air. She sealed the bag closed, taking in deep breaths to cleanse her system.

Nick had managed to get a handkerchief over his mouth and nose to avoid the brunt of the malodorous contents. "Sorry, Theresa. Didn't have time to warn you. So, do you know anyone who could tell us what the hell is in the bag?"

Still taking in gulps of air, she raised a hand saying, "No need."

"No need?"

She had recovered sufficiently to begin breathing normally and sat back on the edge of the desk, creating some distance from the putrid bag. "No need. It's butyric acid."

Nick stared at the bag, trying to connect the word butyric, which sounded a bit like buttery, with the foulness lurking within.

She shrugged. "I dated a guy who taught undergraduate chemistry. As you now know, it reeks."

Nick described the scene to Theresa and then produced his other piece of crucial evidence.

"I found this," he held a two inch long white tampon with a light blue string dangling off of one end. "In a hole drilled through the door."

She took the tampon from Nick. "I think we can rule out a guy."

"Why do you say that?"

"Come on, Nick. What guy do you know would plug a hole with a tampon? A hot dog, a wad of chew, a wine cork, his underwear, even a dog turd. But not a tampon."

He took a moment, doing a quick inventory of what he'd think to shove into a half-inch hole. She hadn't mentioned a dirty sock or some wadded up beer coasters. "You're right. Not the typical thing for a guy to use. Unless, of course, he's married or has a girlfriend. Maybe he knew he'd be tapping a hole into the car and came upon the perfect plug in the bathroom.

"Maybe. But my money is still on it being a woman."

Nick reached into his back pocket, pulling a ten out of his billfold. "Here's ten that says our perp is a man."

Theresa reached into her front jeans pocket, pulling out several crumpled bills. Unfolding them, she set a ten next to Nick's. "I do hate to take your money from you so easily, Nick. But if you insist."

Nick took the two tens and thumb tacked them to the bulletin board beside the desk just as his cell phone rang.

"Sibelius Investigations."

"Nick Sibelius?" A woman's voice.

"Yeah, this is Nick."

"I'm glad I caught you. I'm calling for Dan Hoyt. He would like you to attend a meeting with him at his compound later this morning."

"Out where?"

"The Compound. It's Dan's property southwest of Austin. We've gotten used to calling it The Compound and assuming everyone knows what we're talking about. Can I tell Daniel when he can expect you?"

Annoyance at this GQ Hoyt bossing him around crept into his voice. "Can you put your boss on for a second?"

"He's on another call right now."

"Well, if Dan wants to see me, I need to talk to him. Now."

Hoyt's secretary hesitated. "Yes, of course. I'll see if he can break loose."

A few moments passed and then Dan Hoyt's relaxed drawl filled Nick's ear.

"Nick, thanks for calling."

"I didn't—"

"I had my girl here, Virginia, set things up 'cause I think I might have more for you to do."

"Mr. Hoyt." How could a man be this perky in the morning?

"Dan! Please call me Dan."

"Dan, we've only just started on your Ferrari issue."

"I know. And I still want you to continue, but I've done some checking on you and I think you might be just the right man to handle my current situation."

"And what exactly is your current situation, Dan?"

"That's why I need you to come out to my compound, so we can have a heart-to-heart. I want you to be fully informed before you take me on as a client and I want to be sure you're the right man. Fair enough?"

"Yes, I suppose—"

"Excellent! See you at eleven. I'm looking forward to working with you, Nick."

Before he could respond, the phone went silent. Nick pulled the phone away from his ear to check his screen. No signal. Hoyt had hung up.

"Charlie, I hope I don't regret this."

Theresa, standing next to Nick to hear both sides of the conversation, stepped back. "Charlie?"

"Yeah. My mechanic. He's the one who connected me to this piece of work Hoyt."

"Are you going to his compound?"

"Well, if we didn't need the work, I'd tell him to shove it."

"While you're out falling on your sword for us, I'll check with a contact to see if any butyric acid has gone missing. Maybe I'll get lucky and find our tampon brandishing stink bomber."

Feeling the tug of her fan base, she looked at her phone as if the device somehow held the now thousands who waited breathlessly for her next anti-carbon action. Raising the phone to her lips, she pulled it away as she would a lover's head to look into his eyes. An intimate, discreet moment. *Well, if you liked chocolate man, you'll love what I'm going to do to #5.*

Los Diablos Tejanos

Driving the truck through rolling hills covered with mesquite and cedar, Hoyt considered who might be trying to screw with him in the middle of his deal. The governor had a vested interest in the desalination project getting water to Austin, so he doubted she would bother to try to intimidate him. If Frannie wanted to make him quake in his boots, he knew she had the resources to have someone rip his head off, literally. Besides, she of all people wouldn't mess with his car. Frannie loved it when he cranked the Ferrari up over 150.

No, someone who would put piss all over an Italian work of art on wheels definitely had to be an asshole. Izzy Zydeco. Had to be Izzy, the sonofabitch. The gaming entrepreneur had brought an evolutionary shift to the entire game industry with his virtual simulation software and gaming consoles, making 3-D look like a child's coloring book. Inside one of Izzy's games you were in the middle of the action—mind, body and spirit—or so Hoyt had read in one of the many blogs about the wiz kid. Izzy had been a competitor for the condo tower project and had lost the bid against him. The condo, about halfway built, had to be torn down because some twit in the city planning department had seen through the lead engineer's bogus certifications and the forty-eight building code violations uncovered during the inspection. Hoyt had assumed if he bedded a city councilwoman she would smooth the rough edges for him, but apparently the building inspector had worked on the campaign for an opposing city councilman with aspirations to become mayor in the next two years. God, he hated politics and politicians. No ethics whatsoever. Somehow, Izzy had managed to get to the city councilman and the building inspector. He didn't have any proof, but Hoyt knew in his heart Izzy had sabotaged the project. The upshot of the condo deal meant no one would talk to Hoyt about investing in his Next Big Idea, the desalination plant. They called him a con, a criminal, a felon, an idiot, a jerk—just about anything you can call someone other than business partner. When Izzy showed at his doorstep a few months later, Hoyt realized Izzy's plan all along had been to put him in a position where Izzy's would be the only offer on the table. Willing to be in business with the Devil rather than not be in business at all, Hoyt took Izzy's investment as a co-owner in the plant. The Ferrari was probably Izzy's way of reminding Hoyt he had him by the *cojones*.

Pulling up to the compound, a ten thousand square foot modern structure of steel and glass at odds with the surrounding semi-arid countryside, he drove into an underground garage. Once inside, he took an elevator to the main floor, stepping into the great room to see Izzy, a small, trim man in his late twenties with sandy blond hair and an almost imperceptible Louisiana accent, helping himself to a Bloody Mary at the wet bar.

"Hoyt. Great to see you. Bloody Mary?"

He hated how Izzy had the ability to pass through his security systems like a freakin' digital ninja.

"Do you ever knock, Izzy?"

His visitor chuckled. "Knock? Man, you crack me up. Knock. That's so, so…"

"Appropriate?"

"Analog. Very analog. We live in a digital world, Hoyt. No more secrets. What's yours is mine."

Izzy stepped up to Hoyt stirring his drink with a celery stick. At least he didn't have his side of beef bodyguard Puck with him. Puck was like a bull in a china shop wearing a blindfold. Something or someone always got broken with Puck in the room.

"Are you giving me a piece of your virtual game empire, Izzy?"

"No, Hoyt. Like I said, what's yours is mine."

Izzy had definitely shown up to push Hoyt's face into it, to flaunt his control over him. Hoyt pushed aside the antipathy he felt, realizing he had no leverage in this situation.

"I'm happy to see you, by the way."

"You're happy? You're never happy to see me, Hoyt." He took a bite out of the celery, tossing it in the direction of the bar. "Okay, I'm curious now. What about my presence in your little ranch house is making you so giddy with delight."

"Not giddy. Happy. I'm happy because I can ask you man-to-man if you fucked with my car."

Izzy sipped his Bloody Mary, spitting an ice cube back into the glass, then licking the spicy mixture from his lips. "See Hoyt, this is your problem."

"Just answer the question, Izzy."

"You think small. Don't get me wrong. You're good at thinking small. You make a lot of money thinking small. But you think small all the same. Imagine what your world would be like if you pulled your head out of your ass and saw the bigger picture for a change."

"So you messed up my car." Izzy, thin and wiry, looked to Hoyt like a little chihuahua, all bark and no bite. However, something disturbing behind Izzy's eyes gave Hoyt the suspicion that picking a fight with the dog-man would be like tangling with a rabid chihuahua. He wouldn't realize he was in over his head until the dog had taken off half his face.

"Of course I didn't mess with your precious car, Hoyt. Which one, by the way? I hope not the Shelby. I want to do some scans of it for *Road Racer: Ride Into Hell 3.*"

"The Ferrari."

"Oh, ouch." He said it like a guy in the crowd at a football game when a safety blindsides a tight end, the player's body crumpling to the turf. "But I'm not here to commiserate with you about your pathetic little life. I've got a business proposition for you."

"No."

"How can you say 'no'?"

"Let me think about it. You sabotaged the condo deal because you knew I was planning on using the revenue to start the desalination project. Without the condo I didn't have the capital, or the investors, to make the play. And so now, here I am in business with you, the way you planned all along."

"What did you expect me to do? Come on Hoyt. Business is a game. I simply won that level of play. Maybe you can still win something." He shrugged with a smirk on his face. "Miracles happen."

"Your 'game' almost took everything I had, you sonofabitch."

"For those who have much, much may be taken away."

"Fuck you."

"Now Hoyt, ease up. I'm sorry. I shouldn't pour salt into open wounds. Besides, I'm not here to dance on your grave. I want to help us both make a great deal of money."

Hoyt looked at his nemesis. Getting in the ring with Izzy always had risks. However, Izzy's 'games' often created opportunities to score large sums of money. And if he could position himself to throw the knockout punch, maybe Izzy would be the one in pain this time. He sat on an armrest of a large leather sofa.

"I'm probably going to regret this, but what's this deal you're talking about?"

"Heard of the Diablos Tejanos?"

"Sure, the drug cartel." The Diablos were known for killing anyone who got in their way, which included not only the Border Patrol and local police forces, but competing drug dealers, family members, dogs crossing the road—you name it, they killed it. "What about them?"

"They have a deep interest in the pipelines we're building across the state."

"Los Diablos Tejanos have an interest in water pipelines? I would think water might seem a bit too healthy for them."

"Not the water, Hoyt. The pipeline. With some modifications, the pipeline could be used to move merchandise all over the state without the feds and cops getting in the way."

"You want me to allow a drug cartel to move drugs and weapons around the state in *my* pipeline?" Hoyt rose to his feet, pacing the room. "You're out of your mind. No way. I'm not about to spend twenty years in prison when I get connected to the Diablos. Besides, you can't just flush drugs through a water pipeline, Izzy."

"It's *our* pipeline, Hoyt, not yours. And we'll use pigs."

"Pigs. You've lost your mind. You're going to feed pigs little baggies of heroin and then shove them into a pipeline?"

"Not the animal, Hoyt. Jesus, have you never seen a James Bond flick? A pig is an instrument used to inspect the pipe. We'll just co-opt the pigs to move drugs as well. Imagine it, drugs moving invisibly all over the state. Once they're dependent on us, we'll own the Diablos."

Hoyt hated this guy. He had cost him millions in the failed condo deal and now Izzy had made friends with some of the most dangerous people in the state. With Izzy everything was about acquiring as much power and money as possible at any cost. Hoyt definitely wanted power and money, but he also had a bias towards being alive to enjoy the spoils of his labor.

"No. No fucking way."

"You might want to think about this a little longer, Hoyt. Right now, I'm making a proposal. There's room for negotiation. The next time we talk I won't be negotiating."

Hoyt turned on Izzy. "Don't come into my home and threaten me, you little computer freak."

"I'm not threatening you. I'm telling you how things will be. Your call."

"Get the hell out of my house."

Izzy set the mostly finished Bloody Mary on the bar and walked toward the front door. He looked back at Hoyt with a wry smile.

"Sorry to hear you've once again chosen the path of the little man. We'll be talking again."

Izzy opened the door, stepping through as Hoyt shouted, "And knock next time!"

Wet Dream

The drive out to Hoyt's compound took almost an hour and a half as Nick turned off the toll road, to state highways, to four lane ranch roads, to two lane county roads, and now to a single lane roughly paved road cutting through hills of mesquite and golden grass covered limestone. On the way, he passed two grass fires, one by some rails, possibly started by a spark from a passing freight train and the other looked like somebody let a trash barrel burn out of control. If the sky didn't drop some rain soon, the whole place would go up in flames. Nearing Hoyt's compound, he stopped at a break in the high barbed wire deer fencing blocked by a large iron electronically controlled gate with a sign across the top proclaiming in large, bold letters, "Hoyt Enterprises, Inc."

Nick sat at the gate for a moment, in the process of dialing the number Hoyt's secretary had used to contact him early in the morning, when the gate opened. He put his phone away, driving through the gate and down a dirt track seemingly going to nowhere. After driving for about a mile, he crested a hill to see a huge house. Nick wasn't much of a real estate expert, but the structure below him looked like it could easily hold nine or ten normal three bedroom homes. He could make out a Land Rover Hoyt had parked in front of the colossal modernist structure. Nick figured Hoyt used the four-wheel drive vehicle to get around the ranch, since he was pretty sure the man had never been near an actual horse.

"Big ass house, ain't it?" Nick reflexively jumped at the sound of a man's voice. He turned to see a blue jeaned leg and a cowboy boot in a leather stirrup resting on the flank of a chestnut Quarter Horse.

"Crap. You scared the shit out of me. How did you..."

The cowboy leaned down so Nick could see his weather worn face under a sweat-stained cowboy hat. "Sheila here can move pretty quietly when she wants to." Nick figured he must be talking about the horse. "I take it you're here to see Mr. Hoyt."

"Well, yes."

"Lot of that happening these days. Lots of comings and goings. Hard to keep a herd calm with all this ruckus going on, but I guess it's the new millennium or some such crap."

"Hoyt's a cattle rancher?"

The cowboy laughed, spitting a stream of brown liquid out of his mouth. "I don't know if I'd go that far. He does own 'em. Tax purposes, I think. But I wouldn't know about his business now, would I. Nope, I'm just a good ol' cowboy." Sheila shifted, attentive her rider had decided to move along. The cowboy tipped his hat. "Keep on following this track and you'll end up right in front of the house."

Once at the house Nick walked to a massive oak door with hand wrought ironwork. Before he could lift the huge longhorn steer head door knocker, Hoyt's voice crackled from nearby speakers.

"Nick, good to see you. Just let yourself in and walk straight through to the back patio."

Nick opened the heavy door to a large sixty-by-forty foot room with a thirty foot ceiling. His shoes on the stained concrete floors echoed off walls covered with abstract paintings. Two glasses, one with a celery stick, sat at the bar. The other celery stick rested in a puddle of Bloody Mary on the floor. Either Hoyt was hitting it early or he'd already had some company. The far side of the room consisted of wood-framed glass doors folded against each other accordion style. He could see Hoyt sitting at a table, a large pool complete with waterfall in the background. The patio had an enclosed, secret place sort of feel to it, surrounded by desert grasses, yucca, and mesquite.

Hoyt looked away from his reading. "Nick, glad you made it. Drive okay?"

Hoyt apparently needed to chit chat, so Nick kept his impatience under control. "Just fine, Dan. Beautiful house."

Hoyt motioned to Nick to take a seat. "I'll give you a tour later, if you're interested. To be honest, I didn't figure you for an architecture guy. Iced tea?"

Nick nodded and Hoyt filled a glass with ice from a silver ice bucket and then poured the brown tea into the glass, passing it to Nick.

"Thanks. No, you're right. I'm not much of an architecture guy. Not on this scale. I've got a trailer I'm restoring."

"A trailer? Must be a pretty damn good trailer."

"Airstream. 1964. Sort of a hobby."

"That's good. It's good to have hobbies. Gets your mind off your problems, that sort of thing. From what I understand, you've had a need for a hobby in a pretty bad way."

Nick knew where this was going. Houston. Pflugerville. "How do you mean, a pretty bad way?"

"Come on Nick. If I'm going to trust you with my life, I think we need to lay our cards on the table. What I hear, you were a Houston cop. A pretty damn good cop by all accounts and then everything turned to shit. Am I summing it up correctly?"

Nick's gut tightened. He really didn't want to rummage through the garbage of his past with this guy. "Yeah, I suppose you could put it that way."

"You suppose? You find your wife humping her colleague in your bed and then let some psycho kill your partner right in front of you. Yeah, sounds like things turning to shit to me. Mind you, I have no problem with the wife fucking around. Mixed company getting in and out of hospital scrubs all the time, well hell, shit's goin' to happen. But then you come to Pflugerville and if I heard right, you did some intense undercover work," Hoyt raised his hands to mime quotation marks. "With that MaryLou woman. Man, and they say small town life is quiet."

Nick rose to his feet, his legs hitting the table and knocking the silver ice bucket to the floor. "Enough."

"Whoa, whoa there partner. I didn't mean anything. I just want to know who you are. Why you are, if you get my drift."

"Look, if you've got a job for me, fine. But I don't think we need to rehash my life history to get it done."

Hoyt, who had remained seated, calmly gestured for Nick to take a seat again. "I can understand the sentiment, but like I said, if I'm going to put my life in your hands, I'd just like to know who I'm trusting. A man who takes loyalty seriously enough to pretty much screw up his life because his wife cheats on him, well, I don't understand it myself, but I do value your kind of loyalty in my employees."

Nick sat back down, less certain if the money from this client was worth it.

Hoyt drank his iced tea, then set the glass back on the table. "So what exactly happened in Pflugerville?" Nick looked at Hoyt, trying to determine his game. "Come on, Nick. Did you really fall in love with the sister of your prime murder suspect or were your just doing her to get information?"

"What do you want?"

Hoyt stood, then leaned across the table. "I want your loyalty Nick. I want to know I can trust you."

Nick met his gaze. "You can trust me."

Hoyt smiled, sitting back down at the table. "I have a story too, Nick."

"Given what I saw this morning, your story involves lots of women and fast cars."

Hoyt laughed and Nick realized he had taken the words as a compliment.

"Yes, there are definitely lots of hot women and fast cars, and like you, I've made my fair share of mistakes. Hell, any successful entrepreneur has more failures than successes. Failure isn't the issue. It's how you rise from the ashes of failure that counts and I have definitely risen from the ashes several times."

"Like your high rise condo in Austin?"

Hoyt raised an eyebrow. "Ah, you know about it? Yes, that was definitely a low moment. Prior to the condo deal I had created a whole new business model for gated communities. No one over fifty-five, no children allowed, a town center with hot clubs, a community spa, a real playground for adults. I built one west of Austin, maybe you heard of it, Sin City, and before I knew it, I'm selling lots in Las Vegas and Phoenix. How many thirty-year-olds do you know selling pieces of dirt like they're candy. A real cash cow, except, of course, for all the damn lawsuits. Then the condo deal fell apart and I almost lost it all. But I gathered myself together and have created a whole new vision."

"So why do you need me? Sounds like you're doing just fine."

"And I am doing just fine, Nick. But the little incident with the Ferrari brought home the point that my current business venture might be threatening some of my competitors at a level I haven't had to confront to date."

"What, do you have operatives from the AARP after you?"

"Funny. But I'm not talking about the gated communities. That's the past. I'm talking about a grand vision of mine which is on the cusp of coming to fulfillment."

"Grand vision?"

"Yes, grand vision. I call it my Wet Dream."

Nick tried to purge his mind of weird pornographic images his brain was concocting to make sense of Hoyt's Wet Dream.

"We live in an arid land, Nick, and in increasingly arid times. Do you know what the cities of Texas, not to mention most of the Southwest, will be desperate for in the near future? Water. H2O. Yep, water is the next gold standard. And I'm on the bleeding edge of water distribution technology to bring the precious liquid to the thirsty masses."

"And how exactly do you plan to do this? Dam a river?"

Hoyt laughed. "Desalination, Nick. Desalination. You've seen the picture of the Earth taken from the moon's surface, right? If you look at a globe you'll see a planet with seventy-one percent of the surface covered in water. Do you get it? Water seems scarce, but the answer is right in front of us. So I'm building a desalination plant on the Gulf Coast as the first phase of a multi-phase business plan to solve the greatest threat to the continued existence of human life on this planet."

Hoyt paused, probably for effect. Nick let the time pass, working out how to respond to a man who thinks he's the savior of the entire human race. "I have to say, Dan, you do think big. But I still don't get what this has to do with me."

"Well a desalination plant, as you can imagine, is not an inexpensive thing to build, so I've had to bring in some investors. Now, whenever you have investors there's always a chance for drama. Take my high-rise you mentioned. How was I supposed to know the investor who insisted his brother get the engineering contract for the building didn't have the qualifications for that kind of work? So I was quite careful in my selection of investors for the desalination project, given prior experience. But when this catastrophe with my Ferrari happened this morning, it left me wondering if maybe one or more of my investors had decided to go rogue on me."

"So what do you want me to do? Be your bodyguard?"

"Certainly a bodyguard when we're together, but I don't expect you to be at my side at all times. No, I want to know who's after me and why. If it's one of these investors I need to know, for my own survival, as well as the survival of my vision. So will you take the job? I'll bump your retainer to five thousand dollars a week and if you find this bastard, a bonus of a hundred thousand dollars. What do you say?"

Nick figured Hoyt must really be spooked to be throwing that kind of money around, however he was pretty sure this was a prankster more than a gangster. He considered the very low odds of actually finding the party responsible for trashing the Ferrari based on the evidence, but getting paid 5K a week to do the investigation would definitely get Sibelius Investigations on its feet. He swallowed some of his professional integrity, thinking of all the good he'd be able to do once his business rested on solid ground. "I say yes."

"Then it's agreed." Hoyt raised his glass in a toast. "To my Wet Dream."

Nick tapped his glass to Hoyt's with a grimace. "To your...Wet Dream."

"Tomorrow we'll fly over to the Gulf Coast project so you can see my vision first hand." Hoyt took a long drink from his tea glass. "So the woman you fell in love with—Junior's sister—what happened to her?"

Nick thought she had died in a raging fire trying to escape from him. Hell, he had even gone to her memorial service. Then six months later he got an email with her photo at the Golden Gate Bridge saying she was alive. And then nothing over the last year. He kept hearing Sting singing the old Police tune on the radio, "If you love someone, set them free." She was either really dead, or for whatever reason, not willing to be in his life. And so while he loved her, he had decided a while ago to set her free. What he didn't know was if he could set himself free.

Draining the tea glass, he left it on the table as he rose. "See you tomorrow, Hoyt." He walked back through the house to the front door.

Hoyt called out, "Aren't you going to tell me what happened to her?"

Nick stood at the closed door. "She's dead." Then he opened the door and stepped into the summer heat.

Mujahid Deathmatch 1.1

Jonah Martin stood at the curb outside a small cafe in a neighborhood on the outskirts of Kabul, waiting for the appointed time, waiting for the killing time, waiting for death. Sweat burned his eyes, his mouth a dry wad of cotton. He desperately needed to take a shit, but then given the outcome of the next few minutes, a bowel movement was the least of his worries. Izzy had promised a moment of glory, a moment which would propel him to an eternal bliss. How the hell a Baptist boy from Lubbock finds himself on a Kabul side street with enough TNT wrapped around him to blow up the Fort Worth stockyards beat the hell out of Jonah. Standing before a somewhat dilapidated cafe, the sign worn and faded, the furnishings simple wooden chairs and tables, the clientele the usual assortment of bearded men robed in what looked to Jonah like baggy white pajamas, he wondered what glorious victory his death would bring and how a beer and some nachos would be just the thing right now.

Izzy's voice crackled in his ear piece.

"Let's go Jonah. Time to do Allah's work."

Jonah stood frozen in place. The vest of explosives wrapped with duct tape chafed him, setting off his skin allergy to vinyl. He thought of the red, itchy welts he'd have if he wasn't being blown into a million little bits in the next sixty seconds.

"Jonah! Move!"

He found his feet moving on command without his having consciously decided to cross the narrow street. Jonah stepped into the cafe, packed with men gathered after a day of work, some in retail, some in wholesale, most, he figured, in the black market version of both.

"Remember your training, Jonah. Move into the center of the cafe and then release the switch."

Since being placed in the allergy-inducing explosive vest, Jonah had been holding a button attached to red and yellow wires leading to a little box, the detonator, which would set off the explosives surrounding his torso. His thumb ached, but the fear gradually creeping up from his gut and now residing in his pounding chest, the fear of becoming a crater before his time, made him press the button with much more force than required.

"Now is the time my brother. Allah is great!"

Jonah wanted to release the switch, but his mind could not force the stubborn digit to relax. Several men near him who had been minding their own business, drinking strong tea and talking among themselves, looked up. Had they noticed him? His sweat-soaked shirt under the vest had mixed with the vinyls and glue of the duct tape, seeping into his pores, pouring toxins on his skin, the itch coming to an almost unbearable crescendo.

"Do it, Jonah! Do it!"

He looked to his left. The man behind the bar clearly knew he meant to destroy them all and was reaching for a sword, a knife, an AK47. He couldn't be sure. Two men to his right rose from their table, either to run or to tackle him to the ground. He couldn't be sure.

"Do it, Jonah! Now!"

A man in the corner looked at him with judgment or pity. He couldn't be sure. And the same man reached behind his back for what had to be a gun.

"Jonah!"

He was supposed to have walked into the cafe filled with the unsuspecting and then annihilate them all in one swift mighty act of jihad. But what Izzy didn't know was Jonah hadn't been able to take his dog Samson to the vet to be put down, he had run over a cat once and couldn't sleep for a week, and he had gotten a ranch hand job one summer and quit because he couldn't bring himself to press the red hot branding iron into big dumb cows with large brown eyes.

"Jonah, do it!"

With Izzy screaming commands into his head, the men around him wise to his purpose and the vinyl tape creating a chemical war on his skin, fear erupted from his mouth in a panicked cry, "I can't take it! I can't take the itching anymore! Aaaaahhhhhh!"

With his scream he fell to his knees. His thumb, having gone rogue, failed to release the button. Even though Jonah knew he would not be meeting the promised virgins, he would willingly forsake a virgin just to end the itching of the duct tape.

~*~

He felt nothing. He heard nothing. He opened his eyes to a large, windowless room with subdued lighting and black walls, ceiling, and floor. A little woozy, he struggled to shift from the virtual gaming reality to the sim-game room. He wondered how much not releasing the button would lower his overall score.

Izzy startled him with a slap on the back. "Well, you almost passed the tenth level of *Mujahid Death Match 1.1*. What do you think?"

"I passed?" He tried to pull himself back into reality.

"Almost. No virgins for second place, Jonah. Let's get you out of your sensor suit. We have business to discuss."

Puck, standing six foot nine with shoulder-length blond hair and dressed in black slacks and a skintight black tee shirt straining against his steroid enhanced physique, stood with his usual blank look by the game room door.

"Help him out, Puck."

Puck's large hands helped Jonah out of the black bodysuit consisting of a lightweight technical fabric laced with a fine mesh of micro thin sensor wires and released the virtual gaming visor wrapped around his head. The three stepped into a lounge area just outside the gaming room. Large angry welts had indeed risen on Jonah's chest, stomach and back. What seemed to be a thousand tiny people with pitch forks prodded and poked at his flesh. The need to scratch overwhelmed him. He sat on a bright red sofa, squirming in the seat to rub some of the little people off his back, but as soon as he stopped, more of them would join back in to torment him. As the itching intensified and the reality of the ordeal Izzy had just put him through came home, his anger rose.

"Izzy, what the hell, man! I could have died in there."

Izzy had a cigar in his hand, rolling the smoke between his fingers, breathing in the aroma, then snipping off the end with a cigar clipper. "You didn't. Quit whining."

"Whining? I thought I was going to die in there. Man, don't ever do that again." He hadn't wanted to play Izzy's latest game, but Izzy insisted. And when you owed a man like Izzy Zydeco $100,000 because you picked Pittsburg by 7 over the Packers, you did whatever the man asked you to do. Izzy lit the cigar with a gold butane lighter, the gas hissing just before ignition into a flame.

"I'm glad you appreciate the realism, Jonah."

Jonah forgot about the little people attacking his skin. "Appreciate? Did you not hear me? I could have died of a heart attack or something. You're lucky I'm not on the phone to my lawyer."

Izzy exhaled a thick cloud of brown smoke, staring at him with fierce, dark eyes. Jonah's need for a shit resurged.

"Izzy, I'm just saying the game is pretty damn real."

Izzy flicked the lighter repeatedly, the hot blue flame rhythmically hissing to life, then nodded to Puck. "I appreciate you beta testing the game for me Jonah." Puck slammed Jonah's arm down on the table.

"What are you doing? Izzy, man I didn't mean anything." Puck's huge piston-like arms pinned Jonah's left arm to the table. For a moment he thought Puck intended to simply snap his arm in two.

"Jesus, Izzy. What the..."

"I don't need to remind you our arrangement is confidential, do I?"

"Totally, Izzy. Totally. Come on, man. I didn't mean anything."

"I want to believe you, Jonah."

"Yeah, believe me. I'm your man, Izzy."

"You *are* my man, Jonah. I recognize acquiring untraceable radioactive materials requires some finesse, something which, by the way, you failed to demonstrate in Level 10 today." He took a puff of his cigar, the embers glowing. "Pathetic."

Jonah squirmed, trying to free himself. "But Izzy—"

"Shut up. I was supposed to have the material yesterday. Why don't I have what you promised me, Jonah?"

"I'm working on it, Izzy. I just can't conjure up a bag of nuclear waste. I'll have it. I promise. Come on, man. Let me up."

He tried to pull his arm away, but Puck held him firmly, twisting Jonah's palm up. Izzy stood in front of him now, his lighter poised over Jonah's palm. "When will I have what you promised me?"

"Ah, tomorrow. I'll have it tomorrow!"

"Don't disappoint me." Izzy's lighter hissed like some predatory snake. Intense pain erupted in Jonah's hand, so intense his scream caught in his throat. He tried to pull away, but Puck kept him pinned, the searing pain punctuated with the sickening smell of burning flesh. Everything happened so quickly Jonah's mind raced to catch up. Released from Puck's grip, he staggered back, grabbing his forearm. The center of his palm had become a black, charred hole surrounded by red, blistered skin. He thought he could see bone. And the pain ripped into his hand, racing up his arm. He cried out, then sobbed uncontrollably.

"Jonah."

Lightheaded and queasy, he heard Izzy speak, but he couldn't find the part of his brain responsible for language. His cerebellum had turned inside out.

"Jonah."

"Yeah. Izzy…" He broke into sobs again, which only made the throbbing anguish of his hand pound harder.

"Jonah. I expect you to deliver on your promise. So here is my promise to you. The materials are due tomorrow night. Every night they are delayed I will burn another hole in your body. Not enough to kill you. Just enough to leave you in torment, until you come begging me to put a bullet in your brain."

"Oh, God!"

"God will not help you. And if you run, know I will hunt you down and make your death a lingering, excruciating ordeal."

Jonah took in large gulps of air, tears streaming down his face, his charred hand shaking. Izzy slapped his cheek.

"Do we have an understanding?"

"Yes. Yes, Izzy."

"I've got business to attend to. I'll look forward to seeing you tomorrow night with the package. Leave the back way."

"Sure, Izzy. Anything you say." He slipped away like a small wounded animal looking for refuge.

Izzy pressed an intercom button on a wall phone by the door. A woman's voice responded.

"Yes, Mr. Zydeco."

"Have the gaming equipment in the lounge sanitized, Heather. The place reeks. Our guest sweat like a pig and left the room smelling like someone burned meat in here. Disgusting."

"Yes, Mr. Zydeco. Do you want me to make any weekend plans for Mr. Martin?"

"No thanks, Heather. I think *Mujahid* wore him down. I imagine by the weekend he'll be dead to the world."

Surf'n Turf

Walking out of the compound later in the day left Hoyt a bit depressed as his truck brought home the reality of his trashed Ferrari. He thought about having his insurance total the car—his adjuster happened to be an old frat brother—and then get another replacement from the dealer. But bringing home a new Ferrari to replace the soiled one seemed a little to Hoyt like replacing your dead dog the next day with a new puppy. Yes, you had another dog, but she wouldn't be the same. His mind rambled through potential replacements: McLaren, Maserati, Lamborghini. Maybe he could get an older Aston Martin DB5 and have it kitted out just like James Bond's. He imagined taking his super spy car deer hunting, the guns blazing as bucks dropped all around him.

When he finally got to the house on Island Palms Cove, he had settled on a demo Lamborghini Murcielago to hold him off, at least for the rest of the summer and early fall, until his special order McClaren P1GTR arrived. As he thought about leaving the cops in the dust with the 1000 hp engine hurling the sleek British work of art over 200 mph, he came to the decision to place the order for both cars in the morning. Hoyt parked his truck in the spot once held by the Ferrari. Charlie must have hauled it away earlier in the day, as directed. Looking at the sad, empty expanse of driveway, he vowed to always park his sports cars in the garage, no matter how many women he had stuffed in the seats.

He locked the truck, went in the house, and made a gin and tonic with extra gin. He then flipped on the flat screen which took up a large portion of the wall in the great room, mostly because he didn't feel like slogging his way across the house to the theater room. The Texas Rangers were playing the Chicago White Sox and he was determined to watch at least one game in the series. The camera zoomed in on the owner and Hall of Fame pitcher, Nolan Ryan, looking nervous without the ball in his hand. Around the fifth G & T, or what baseball fans would call the seventh inning, he nodded off, to wake two hours later, a lone lime wedge sitting in the melted ice of his long since emptied drink. Jimmy Fallon had some girl maniacally dancing to knock socks and a stocking cap off her head in record time. He made his way to the bedroom, took off his clothes, and passed out again as soon as his head hit the pillow.

Hoyt stood at home plate. Nolan Ryan, who unexpectedly had come out of prolonged retirement to pitch specifically against Hoyt, kicked dirt at the mound. The crowd, somewhat sparse, consisted of his mother, the brunette from the previous night, and himself. Oddly, while standing at the plate, he also sat naked in the stands holding red and blue pom poms. Just as Ryan went into a wind up, Hoyt realized he had a yellow Fred Flintstone bat in his hands, the barrel of the plastic bat as big around as a pie pan. The ball, released from Ryan's grasp, moved towards him with such ferocity, it caught on fire, flames and smoke trailing behind. He momentarily thought he had the situation in hand until the fireball suddenly looped and spiraled, diving and ascending, twisting and curving. He swung the mighty yellow plastic Fred Flintstone bat with all of his might yelling, "yabba dabba do!" when the ball paused in mid-air, took careful aim and then shot at his foot with the crushing force only a Hall of Famer could put behind a ball.

"Aaaahhhh! Shit!" Hoyt sat bolt upright, his dream brought to an extremely painful conclusion. Someone must have put his foot in a pair of vise grips. He pulled his foot toward him, which seemed a bit heavier than usual, while at the same time throwing his bed covers back.

"Crap! Oh Jesus!" Hoyt flipped on the light to discover the weight on his foot was a three pound live lobster with a death grip on his instep. Two other lobsters stood facing him, pinchers raised, ready for battle.

"Jesus!"

He wanted to get the lobster off his foot, but his attacker flailed his other pincher threateningly. Hoyt's imagination took hold, as an image of a lobster rushing directly as his dick swept over him, sending his flight reaction into hyperdrive. He fell off the bed, all the while kicking his leg, desperately trying to dislodge his attacker. He rolled, some tape in his head about drop and roll repeating in the panic. The lobster held fast and when he looked back to the bed, the other two crustaceans had taken a position on the edge of his bed as if ready to jump into the fray. He knew he was going to be killed by a trio of hit lobsters. The cops would find the three lounging in his bed and the only evidence of his existence would be his gold fillings. He crawled across the room, his instep feeling like someone had sliced it open with a knife. The lobster hung on, nipping at him with the free pincher. Hoyt looked at his prized autographed Pete Rose baseball bat on the wall. The other two lobsters were no longer on the bed.

"No, oh God, no!"

Despair almost overwhelmed him, when in one last do-or-die act, he leapt for the Pete Rose bat, the killer lobster clinging to his foot. Pulling down the bat, as well as the entire rack in which the piece of white ash had been installed, he fell to the floor, rolling over to a seated position. In desperation, he pounded away at the killer crustacean, his foot, and anything else which might be moving in the room.

The ring leader lay dead, its pincher still firmly gripping Hoyt's foot.

He corralled the other two hit lobsters into a closet using the bat as a prod. Then Hoyt hopped down the hallway, his foot, swollen and quickly bruising from his batsmanship, opening a closet where he kept a small tool kit. He hopped back to his bathroom and sitting on the toilet seat proceeded to used screwdrivers and a hammer to remove his enemy's death-gripping claw. Finally succeeding, he drew a cold bath, placing his damaged foot in the cold water, which tinted pink from the bleeding claw wound. Sitting on the edge of his tub, he speed dialed Nick Sibelius on his cell phone.

"Nick."

"Who the hell is this?"

"Hoyt."

"It's three in the morning, Hoyt. Are you out of your mind?"

"I've been attacked again. The goddamn motherfucker broke into my house and attacked me!"

"Okay, okay. You're calling, so that's good. Did you get a good look at him?"

"There were three of the bastards. And yes, I got a good look at 'em alright. I smashed the holy shit out of one of the fuckers with my bat."

"Whoa. Hold on Hoyt. Are you telling me you killed one of them?

"Damn straight. And the other two bastards are locked in my closet."

"Have you called the police yet?"

"Police? Hell no! We're going to deal with this, Nick. Whoever is fucking with me is going to feel the hurt."

"If you killed one of them, you need to call the police. You can't hide something like that from the cops, Hoyt."

"Why the hell not? Shit, I ate one of those bastards for dinner just last week."

The line went quiet, then Nick spoke again, "Wait, Hoyt. I can see you doing all kinds of crazy things, but cannibalism? What exactly did you kill?"

"A lobster! A fucking psychopathic hit-lobster from hell. I mean this sonofabitch and his compadres had it in for me. Jesus."

The silence on the line lasted long enough for Hoyt to wonder if Nick had hung up on him.

"A lobster. You woke me at three in the morning about a lobster."

"Don't you think its an odd coincidence to have my Ferrari soiled with God only knows what and then somebody plants killer lobsters in my bed? Those bastards could have taken the family jewels."

"I don't think lobsters can open safes, Hoyt."

"Not those jewels, *my* jewels. So here's the plan. I want you to come out right now. I'll have my pilot ready with the plane. There's no way I'm staying here like some duck at a county fair shooting gallery. No fucking way."

"Hoyt, don't you think you're overreacting a bit. It's three in the morning and all that happened is you've had a run in with some seafood."

"Am I not paying you a retainer to be on the job 24/7? Now get over here!"

Hoyt hit the off button on his phone. He didn't know which investor had decided to screw with him, but when he figured out who it was, the bastard was going to pay. He gingerly dried off his foot, put on his clothes and, carrying his boots in his arms, limped toward the wet bar. On the way, he picked up an ice bag and some Advil. Eventually he'd need to get his foot in a boot, but he'd wait for the anesthetizing power of bourbon to numb his wounds. Opening a bottle at the bar, he poured three fingers of the golden elixir in a glass. An orange object behind the counter of the wet bar caught his eye, some portion of his brain connecting the color to lobster sent adrenaline bolting through his system in a fight or flight response. Reeling back, he put his full weight on the injured foot, a bolt of pain shooting up his leg.

"Goddamit."

He hopped on his good foot around the bar, his need to know outweighing his need to run.

"A towel. A damn towel."

Hoyt tried to rip the towel savagely in two, letting the piece of cloth know who was in charge, but the fabric wouldn't cooperate. He threw it on the counter, but the soft material landed silently, lying there with no ill effect. He picked the bar towel up by a corner, putting a lighter to it, but the damp towel resisted bursting into flames. Finally, he slammed the towel into a small trashcan behind the bar with as much force as he could muster. He stood over the can pointing at the errant, and in Hoyt's mind, broken and defeated towel.

"Don't ever fuck with me again you, you fucking towel!"

Having vanquished the enemy to his satisfaction, he drained the bourbon, then poured another. The warm, numbing sensation of alcohol moved through his body. He filled an ice bag with cubes from the bar refrigerator, grabbed a putter leaning on the wall behind the bar, hopped over to a large leather chair with a clear view of the entire room, and waited for Nick to arrive.

The Search Begins

Driving east one hundred fifty miles to Huntsville from Austin proved a challenge to Charity's electric car, but more critically, to her conscience. On the one hand, she felt bound by a sacred oath she had taken two years before to forsake all carbon-based energy sources which poisoned the earth and made cycling treacherous. On the other hand, her dead brother Barry needed her. She thought about renting a car, maybe a hybrid as a compromise, but she knew as soon as the gas engine kicked in she would be poisoning the planet with volatile organic compounds. So instead, after completing the next phase of her work with #5, she drove to Navasota. The small town on the way to Huntsville was bound to have at least one unoccupied house. To her delight, her plan worked flawlessly, as she broke into a small two-bedroom bungalow and plugged her 100-foot long 220 volt extension cord in the socket for the washing machine. As a bonus, she took a four hour nap, enjoying the sleep only afforded to those who haul live lobsters through darkened mansions. She awoke in a quaint iron bed with a beautiful quilt of tan and peach on a blue background, woven like the rush seat of a chair. She decided to take the quilt with her. The late morning sun rose higher into the sky, as Charity had a glorious lunch of toast with peanut butter washed down with one of the sports drinks she kept in the ice chest used to store the lobsters for #5 in the trunk of her car. She would have to review the video feed from the bedroom cameras she installed at #5's house to see how her little crustacean lovelies managed with the carbon-burning pig.

From Navasota she drove on to Huntsville. Arriving at the prison, she soon found herself peering through a glass at a rather haggard looking man in his forties with several gold teeth and a clean-shaven head. Feeling his eyes searching her, she played nervously with the top button of her blouse. The man on the other side of the glass, Earl Pendleton Jr, known as Junior, sat with a black phone handset to his ear. He motioned with his head toward the handset for her to pick up. She could feel her nipples hard and erect against the silk of her blouse. There was something about a man in a cage which really got her going.

"Do I know you ma'am?"

"My name is Charity."

Junior let out a deep sigh. "God knows I can use some of that."

"Use some of what?"

"Charity. I could use some charity, you know, as in a helping hand."

She cooled a bit. While she liked a man in a cage, she couldn't abide whiners.

"Oh. I see. As I was saying, my name is Charity. I want to ask you a few questions."

The man paused, looking at her with suspicion. "You a reporter?"

"No Mr. Pendleton."

He relaxed his shoulders slightly. "Call me Junior."

"Okay, Junior. Did you know a man named Barry Swenson? He was a dentist."

"Did I know Barry? Shit, the crazy fuck just about killed me and my sister too. A real nut case. See these gold fillings?" Junior turned so Charity could see his open mouth. "Well, Barry drilled holes in my teeth to try to get me to kill people. Can you believe it? I mean what kind of a crazy fuck does a thing like that?"

"He sounds like an interesting man." Charity meant it.

"Interesting if he's not after your ass, I suppose. Look, what do you want?"

"I understand you might have been present when my broth—when Barry met his demise."

"You mean when he got shot? Yeah, sure, I was there."

"Why did Nick Sibelius kill him?"

Junior paused, pulling the handset away for a moment as if gathering his thoughts. "Lady, Barry was about to kill my sister."

"So you know this Nick Sibelius."

"Sure. He's the sonofabitch who put me in here."

"I've heard Nick is a violent man. He killed several of your associates and gunned down Barry."

"Aw, he's not so bad. He can definitely scare the crap out of you, but I suppose if he's good enough for my sister, he's good enough me."

"Your sister?"

"Yeah, MaryLou. Man, they loved each other."

"Where can I find your sister? I'd love to talk with her."

"MaryLou? Well, for one thing, she's dead. And anyhow lady, even if she was alive, you don't find MaryLou. MaryLou finds you. And if you've got ill intent, and I have a feeling you do, trust me, you don't want to fuck with Lou Lou, dead or alive."

"Junior, one more thing."

Junior stood. "No, I think we're done here."

"Wait." Charity's mind raced to devise a way for him to keep talking to her. What could she possibly use to get this Neanderthal to talk? Before she could stop herself, she blurted out, "I'll show you my breasts if you'll tell me where to find Nick."

He sat back down. "You'll what?"

"You heard me. Do we have a deal?"

He leaned back in his chair, tilting his head, clearly imagining the possibility. "Sure, let me see those titties and I'll tell you anything you want, lady."

"Here's the thing, Junior. Once I reveal myself, I imagine I will be physically removed from the premises."

Junior sat nervously biting his lower lip. "Okay. Under normal circumstances I wouldn't trust you as far as I can spit, but I'm hoping, given your name is Charity, I can trust you to do the right thing here."

"Absolutely, Junior."

"Okay. Nick lives in one of those silver Airstream trailers on a parcel of land east of Pflugerville. Don't know the address, but my nephew Carl has a place on the road east out of town. Big two-story white farmhouse with a barn. Can't miss it. Tell Carl I sent you and he'll lead you to Nick." Junior leaned forward. "And now, the titties."

Charity offered Junior only a wily smile and began to stand, but Junior put a hand on the glass.

"Hold on there, little lady. I believe you need to complete your part of our agreement."

"I don't have to do anything. Thanks for the information. Goodbye, Junior."

"You do if you want Carl to tell you where Nick lives."

Charity sat back down. "What do you mean?"

"I mean if you don't show the titties I'll tell Carl to play dumb. And believe me, playing dumb is one of Carl's best things."

Charity stared at Junior for some time, wondering how many stars her fans would award her on the Facebook page for tormenting this jerk. Then it occurred to her exposing herself in a prison visitation room was bound to rate five stars. Easy. And having not only Junior, but the guards, the inmates and their wives and girlfriends watch, made her blood run hot. All of the horny desire, the wanton sexual lust, simmering just below the surface once she had entered the prison, now boiled over. Attitude, Intention, Manifestation. On fire, her toes tingled, each breath increasingly shallow until she suddenly ripped open her blouse, small white buttons arching in all directions, then slammed her molten-hot breasts against the cold glass.

She screamed, "Oh Jesus. Yes!"

Junior, startled by the two dark nipples surrounded by creamy white mounds of flesh coming directly for him fell back over his chair. She could see the guard on Junior's side of the security glass standing frozen, then begin digging in his pocket for his phone to take a picture he would probably one day show his grandson on the occasion of his eighteenth birthday. Charity rubbed her breasts against the glass making the sounds of a herd of wild animals in heat. Nearby visitors yelled expletives at her while others sounded like Joe Buck at game three of the World Series calling the play by play to their imprisoned loved ones. The hands of two guards pulled her arms behind her back, cuffing her wrists. The exhilaration of being bound, of men behind glass, the shouting crowd ogling her bare breasts, overwhelmed her. She fell into the guards' grasp and as they dragged her out of the visiting room, moaning with a deep pleasure only multiple orgasms and the location of your brother's murderer could provide.

Hoyt Enterprises

Arriving at Hoyt's house, Nick found him fully dressed, with an ice pack tied to one foot resting on an ottoman, holding a golf putter defensively in one hand while nursing a bourbon with the other. Hoyt's housekeeper, who he must have also awakened demanding her immediate attention, muttered about God and the Virgin Mary, and something probably a little less religious, over and over again from somewhere upstairs.

"Tough night, Dan?"

"Tough night my ass! Somebody's got it in for me. First the Ferrari and now a goddamn herd of killer lobsters."

Nick had been considering one-liners the entire drive to Hoyt's house. "Did the, uh, hit lobsters get away or do you have them in a holding tank?"

"Yeah, go ahead and laugh, Mr. Security. Looks to me like you're not getting the job done."

Nick struggled not to laugh, at least a little. "First of all, the Ferrari happened before you called me in. But you're right about this most recent...incident." Nick couldn't bring himself to call marauding lobsters an attack. "I'll need to go through your home security to make it more difficult for someone to get into your house in the future."

Hoyt waved him off with his bourbon. His slur inferred the glass in his hand had been refilled at least a couple times. "I already called the security alarm people to get out here and fix this. No, I need you to go with me to the plant. If they're attacking me in my home, then the plant has to be the next target."

"What about the lobsters?"

"Took care of them. Told Maria, my housekeeper, the lobsters are hers as long as she cooks them alive, the bastards. Nobody comes into my house and fucks with Daniel Hoyt. Nope, the Garcias are knee-deep in lobster tonight." He refilled his glass with bourbon. "That's right. Mess with me and you're a fucking seafood dinner."

~*~

They arrived at the Alamo Flight Center via limo, walking directly onto an awaiting corporate jet. Hoyt, his lobster-nibbled and baseball bat battered ankle back in a cowboy boot, slept off the bourbon while Nick pondered why he was flying with a lobster bitten drunk in a jet to the coast.

Money, he reminded himself. Babysitting this guy would give him the revenue he needed to get his business afloat and pay Theresa a salary. Under the white noise of jet engines he mumbled a mantra, "The money, Nick. Remember the money."

Landing in Houston they transferred to a helicopter which took them to the desalination plant situated on the coast between Texas City to the north and the Brazoria National Wildlife Refuge to the south. Nick had imagined something like a small refinery on a couple of acres. The facility, the size of a football stadium, sat on a vast expanse of land. The desalination plant itself did resemble a refinery with a tangled mass of pipes twisting and turning in all directions, interrupted by large steel containment vessels. White smoke or steam, Nick wasn't sure which, billowed out of several tall stacks. They landed on a helipad inside of the plant security fence and were greeted by a man with a yellow hard hat and a pocket protector stuffed with mechanical pencils and emblazoned with Hoyt Enterprises, Inc. tucked into the chest pocket of his short sleeve shirt. Hoyt and Nick stepped out of the chopper, ducking under whirling blades with Pocket Protector in the lead.

"Welcome back, Mr. Hoyt." Pocket Protector shouted the words over the loud thumping of the helicopter's blades.

Hoyt turned to Nick, shouting, "Nick, this is my lead engineer on the project, Nathan Donaldson."

Donaldson, a tall, angular man who looked more suited to branding cattle than working a slide rule, jutted his hand out, shaking Nick's. "Call me Nate. Good to have you on board."

"Thanks Nate. You know why I'm here?"

"Sure. Mr. Hoyt has some security concerns. Makes sense to me."

They walked away from the helicopter, the machines blades gradually slowing. Nick had a sick feeling seeing the size of Hoyt's plant. This project, which started with a sports car prank, had shifted to some serious large scale corporate security. He needed the money, but only if he could actually do the job.

"Dan, we need to talk."

"Absolutely Nick. I'm going to leave you with Nate here to show you around." Hoyt limped away from the pair toward a two-story building. "Nate, bring him by my office when you're through."

Nick stood beside Nate watching Hoyt's back. "Hoyt, we need to talk."

Hoyt hobbled along without turning back. "We will, Nick. We will. Just take a look around first."

Resigning himself to the tour, he let Nate walk him through the plant as the engineer explained the desalination process. Whenever Nate would digress into the fine details of specific engineering challenges, which happened often, Nick would use the time to look over the security infrastructure—camera placement, sensors, security doors, and locks. At first glance his assessment was somewhere between worthless and pathetic. Nick, bored and fatigued from the mind-numbing mix of engineering jargon, pipes, and computers, perked up when a few anxious words from Nate caught his attention.

"Aw hell. Are these numbers correct? Have you double-checked them?"

A young woman, probably an undergraduate intern for the summer, looked intimidated by Nate's sudden interest in the sheet of paper she held in her hand.

Nick looked over at the sheet with columns of numbers. "Is there a problem?"

Nate walked quickly in the direction of the plant offices. "Problem? No, no problem. A plant this size with this level of complexity has many challenges, but nothing we can't handle. Now let me take you to the conference room. Mr. Hoyt had a video produced to give prospective investors an overview of the process. I think you'll find it quite educational."

After walking across numerous steel gangways and then into a building with fluorescent lit hallways, Nick found himself in a conference room. The modernist space of stainless and glass looked more like something you'd find on the penthouse floor of a corporate office building than in a factory or a plant. Within minutes, Nick had a cup of coffee and a private screening of *Adam's Ale: Bringing Life to Texas.* The film started in the Garden of Eden. Adam and Eve, who looked like porn stars on steroids drank the "water of life" in Paradise. After some allusions to the Almighty, the film quickly outlined a brief history of water in Texas, beginning with Native American tribes, to the Spanish conquistadores, to struggles over water between farmers and ranchers and the ongoing challenges of meeting the needs of agriculture, ranching, manufacturing and municipalities across the state. With dramatic flair and a sound track provided by the top band from last year's South by Southwest Festival, Death Scum Rotting, Hoyt's voiceover offered desalination as the great technological solution to the problem vexing humankind since the First Man and Woman drank Adam's Ale in Paradise. Rivers may be polluted, aquifers may run dry, but the Hoyt Enterprises Inc AquaTex Desalination Plant would always provide a dependable, clean source of drinking water for Texans. The film ended with a couple walking a Texas beach hand in hand, the desalination plant in the distant background, as a buxom bikini clad woman, who looked very much like Eve, held a silver tray. The camera zoomed in on the tray's two crystal clear glasses of water. The couple picked up their respective glasses and with the sun glinting through the prism of water and a hypnotic techno beat in the background, a deep male voice proclaimed, "Adam's Ale of the Future: Desalinated water. Water for the people. Water now. Water for Texas. The dream of water realized for the twenty-first century."

As if on cue and Nick thought possibly, actually on cue, Hoyt opened the conference room door.

"I see you've been viewing our little video about the plant. Pretty impressive wouldn't you say?"

"Yes, very impressive. And that's what I need to talk with you about."

Hoyt went over to a wet bar and poured himself a cup of coffee. He sat at the far end of a long table. "Okay Nick. What do you want to talk about?"

"I want to talk to you about the scope of this project, Dan. We started off with your Ferrari and now the work has expanded to providing security for a very large operation. I'm a private investigator, not a corporate security firm."

"And I don't want you to be. I want you to find out who's after me. Like I told you, I thought I had picked my investors carefully, but somebody's definitely got it in for me. I mean, what kind of a nut case covers a brand new Ferrari in piss and then puts live lobsters in your bed?"

Nick had to agree. "Yeah, what kind of a nut would do that? I don't think you've got someone trying to kill you. If you did, they would have accomplished the goal by now."

"Well, what do you think they're doing if they're not poking around, looking for weaknesses in my security?"

"Dan, if I was going to kill you I would have planted an explosive device on your car or waited with a scoped rifle on the hillside and shot you dead in your driveway. And I definitely would have popped you in the head in your bedroom and taken the lobsters home for dinner. No, this isn't about killing you. Someone's trying to rattle you, maybe get you to make a mistake. Sound like anyone you know?"

"Do you have any idea what's at stake here?" Hoyt waved his hand implying what the plant and all the facility meant in terms of business and politics. "I'm going to undercut water districts and put municipal governments at my beck and call once this plant is operational. Do you see the dynamics here? If one or more of the players is not trying to kill me outright, intimidation would certainly be a possibility."

"You really think a municipal utility district is after you?"

"Who do you think sits on those district boards, virgins and naive taxpayers? Hell no. More like people with a vested financial interest in development. And you don't think state politicians know how to play hardball? I'm telling you, one or more of those bastards are trying to take me down."

Hoyt had worked himself up, splashing coffee on the conference table. Nick didn't doubt the possibility of Hoyt's claims, but he still knew he couldn't handle something this large on his own.

"Like I told you, Dan. I'm a small firm. I don't have the resources to implement a complete security set up for an operation of this size."

"I don't need you to Nick. I've got security at the plant and while they did a pathetic job, I do have security at home and the compound as well. No, I want you to find out who is trying to intimidate me. Check out my investors, utility district members, everybody—including the governor. I would not put it past the governor to get nasty in order to coerce me into lowering my price for water. I will not negotiate from weakness. Ever."

"You really think the governor of the great state of Texas would put lobsters in your bed?"

His face flushed red with anger. "That crazy bitch once shoved a live goldfish down my pants at a sushi bar. Of course she'd put lobsters in my bed!"

"Why would she shove a goldfish down your pants?"

"I don't think it's important to our conversation. Look, I'm asking you to do one thing. Find this sonofabitch. Do you want the work or not?"

~*~

Flying back to Austin on Hoyt's corporate jet, Nick knew his mechanic, Charlie, had completely understated the situation when he called Hoyt an asshole. He didn't like Hoyt's attitude. He didn't like the way Hoyt spoke to him. He didn't like having to chase down some tampon-stuffing, lobster-tossing nutcase instead of doing real investigative work. But most of all, he didn't like the bad vibes his intuition kept sending him about this whole arrangement. He stared out the window, watching the sun-dried East Texas landscape pass thirty thousand feet below, mumbling to himself over and over, "The money Nick. Remember, the money."

Proposal

The first time Izzy had approached Tigre, the self-proclaimed head of the Los Diablos Tejanos cartel, he knew his work would be easy. Tigre, in his thirties, immaculately dressed in a tailored suit, with handmade boots, a meticulously trimmed jet black beard, slicked back black hair and manicured hands, spared no expense in his lifestyle. He rode the streets in a chauffeur-driven bulletproof Rolls Royce, traveled in a corporate jet, sailed on a seventy-five foot yacht, and generally lived like the king he had become. Izzy imagined having some rich white guy enter Tigre's dangerous world to sell him on the idea of allowing him to research a game must have struck the drug lord as odd, if not hilarious. But once Izzy got Tigre into the game room, the cartel leader wanted more. Within a year, Izzy had built a game simulation room, including the necessary computer systems for Tigre to play all of his games, including *Guns n' Drugs*.

Today he would take the relationship to the next level. While he didn't need the Diablos for his plan to work, having them in the mix would certainly create a level of turbulence which would help his plan come to fruition. Puck at his side, they had flown to Tigre's private airstrip in southwest Texas. A black Hummer picked them up as the engines of Izzy's jet wound down and deposited them in the courtyard of an expansive hacienda, complete with red tile roofs and a large fountain in the middle of a manicured courtyard. Two men with machine pistols checked them for weapons, inspecting the box Puck held in his hands, then escorted them into the main foyer and over to a large living room furnished in leather sofas and Mission style chairs and tables. Tigre, dressed to the nines even at home, turned from looking at a window with a view of the Guadalupe Mountains to greet his guest.

"*Buenas tardes*, Izzy. I trust you had a good flight."

"Yes, thanks." He took the wooden box from Puck, presenting it to Tigre. "A small gift to honor our friendship. Hoyo de Monterrey Doblo Coronas."

Tigre took the offered box. "Cuban. Yes. How did you know?"

"I make it a point to take care of my friends."

Tigre opened the box of cigars, lifting one out, swiping the seven inch cigar of Cuban tobaccos under his nose slowly, taking in the aroma. He closed the lid and set it on a side table by a large leather sofa.

"And what is your business with me today, Izzy?"

"I have a proposal for you, Tigre. A proposal I think you will find very attractive."

Tigre looked to Puck, suspicion in his eyes.

"Puck's okay. He's very loyal."

"Where does one get a name like Puck?" Tigre spit the name out.

"It's Mayan."

"Puck is Mayan?" Tigre laughed. "Listen white boy. Suck. Fuck. Puck. Whatever his name is. Definitely not Mayan."

Izzy looked over to Puck, narrowing his eyes, willing Puck to stay cool.

The large bodyguard spoke in an even, controlled tone. "Ah Pukah. The name is Ah Pukah, the Mayan god of death. It was my stage name when I wrestled." He turned to Izzy. "I should go out in the courtyard, allow the two of you to talk." He nodded his head toward Tigre. "Very good to meet you, Mr. Kitty."

Puck retreated from the den under Tigre's glare.

"Insolent little…"

"My apologies, Tigre. He's a little sensitive about his name. However, in his defense, I have found his name to be very accurate. He is definitely the god of death."

Izzy retrieved a cigar cutter from his pants pocket. "So what's this proposal you have for me, Izzy? You want me to finance one of your games?"

"Tigre, first of all, let me be clear. You're not simply an investor to me. No, I see us—and I hope you agree—I see us as business associates. The proposal I'm bringing to you will definitely expand your business and provide a nice revenue stream for me as well."

"And what is this proposal?" He clipped the end of his Cuban, slipped the cutter back into his pocket.

"I am in the process of completing a network of water pipelines throughout the state designed to move water from the first of several desalination plants on the coast. Those pipelines, beyond transporting water, provide a secure path for the movement of drugs and other product you might want sent to various parts of the state without the prying eyes of the DPS, ATF or the FBI."

"Interesting. I'm listening."

Tigre put the freshly cut end of the cigar to his lips. Izzy stepped forward, his lighter hissing to life. Tigre leaned in, Cuban tobacco burning to a red ember with brown smoke, a leathery aroma filling the room.

"The pipes use PIGs, pipeline inspection gauges, which I will modify to carry product. You get exclusive access to the pipeline and I get twenty percent off the top."

"You get five percent because of your boy, Puck. When will this be operational?"

"I can set up a test run for you in the next few days. There is a Pig insertion point outside of Zapata near the border. We'll pick up the package outside of Austin. And I think fifteen percent will offset the cost of building the infrastructure, as well as ongoing maintenance."

"Ten percent, Puck gets to live and we continue to be business associates."

"Sounds fair to me, Tigre."

Tigre smiled, motioning for Izzy to sit at a game table. "Please, have a seat, Izzy. I'll have Alegria bring some tequila to seal our agreement." He picked up a phone from the table beside a large sofa. "*Alegria. Tequila y dos copas, por favor.*" Tigre sat across from Izzy. "So how is *Guns n' Drugs* doing?"

"Thanks to you, *GND* is the number one game in the world right now. We've even started *GND* clubs in several countries. Quite the phenomenon."

A young Mexican woman in her early twenties walked into the room, in spike heels and a blue bikini, looking very much like an actress Izzy had seen on a Latina porn site a few days ago. She stepped behind a wet bar on the far wall, placing a bottle, two shot glasses, a salt safe, and a ceramic bowl with lime slices on a silver tray. She walked across the room, Izzy and Tigre both enjoying the show as she set her tray on the table.

"*Algo más, Señor?*"

Tigre placed his hand on the woman's rear end. "Later, my dear. *Gracias.*"

As her heels tapped on the clay tile floor Izzy decided once he was really in charge of everything, he'd have bikini clad girls serving him drinks too—which reminded him to get back to business.

"Tigre, one more thing. I need a car stolen in the next day or two."

"Practical joke?"

"Just a loose end."

"If I can help, I will Izzy. Where is this car?"

"It will be in Austin. Do you have a number of someone I can call, someone reliable who will steal the car, break it down, and sell the parts off? And as a token of appreciation, I'll waive my ten percent fee on our first pipeline test."

"Sure. We get some nice cars out of Austin. All those techies love to buy exotic sports cars. I'm sure stealing one more car won't slow things down at all."

Carl

Charity spent the afternoon in a prolonged counseling session with the prison chaplain playing the distraught redhead who had exposed herself to an indeterminate number of wives and girlfriends, attorneys, guards, and inmates. Having fulfilled the chaplain's need to heal her, she drove away from Huntsville to find Junior's nephew, Carl. She once again had to stop for a recharge. Tying up an entire family, including their dachshund, had been a bit of a bother, but she had worn a Conan O'Brian mask and rubber gloves. They would only be able to say a late night ex-talk show host had held them at gunpoint for a bed, some disgusting Fruit Loops cereal with whole milk, and a four hour charge on their 220 volt outlet.

Late in the afternoon she drove through Pflugerville, pulling off the road down a dirt track where a white two-story house sat, just the way Junior had described. Across the yard from the farmhouse the legs of a man protruded out from under a blue tractor. The antique looked to her like something Henry Ford would have driven, if he had been a farmer. She walked up to Junior's tractor, but before she could say a word to whoever lay underneath the iron beast, the man spoke first.

"You must be Charity."

"Yes, I am."

The young man, in his early twenties with blond hair and blue eyes, wiped grease off his hands with a dirty rag as he crawled out from under the tractor.

"Junior told me to expect you." He smiled with the hint of a wink. "Said you kind of made his day."

"He tells me you can direct me to Nick Sibelius' place."

"Well, yeah."

Charity felt Carl's eyes doing a full-body scan. He tossed his rag on the tractor seat. "And I guess, I'm thinking maybe you could make my day too."

Even though she imagined this farm boy might be a good roll in the hay, her impatience to get on with her revenge won out. "Where is Sibelius, Carl?"

"Just a little peek, darling. Then I'll tell you anything you want to know."

God, men were all the same. Since her little prison adventure she realized she could get them to do just about anything if she showed them some leg or some cleavage. And vagina? Given the power of her breasts, Charity imagined she could get men to empty their bank accounts and kill people. But a deal is a deal. Fudging deals which had been negotiated in good faith destroyed efficiency. She stepped toward Carl, a smile on her face and a tease in her eyes.

"So you want a bit of what I gave Junior?" Charity reached behind her back for the taser she had tucked into her waistband. In one smooth motion she brought the unit into direct contact with Carl's crotch.

"Yeah, that'd be great. Then I'll..."

She could tell from the initial expression of joy on his face he had misinterpreted her action as foreplay. Once Charity had pressed the button on the taser, sending eighty thousand volts through Carl's balls, his look of joy turned to one of a man going into a seizure just before he hits the ground. Charity watched Carl jerk about for a bit, waiting for the effects to subside sufficiently for civil discourse. Before he could rise to his feet, she sprayed his face with pepper spray. He fell to the ground, his hands over his eyes, moaning.

"Carl. Carl, can you hear me?"

"Uhh."

"Good. Now Carl, your uncle told me I could rely on your directions to Nick Sibelius' trailer. Is that true?"

"Uhh."

"Excellent. Here, let me help you sit." Charity pulled Carl to a sitting position, leaning his back against the large rear wheel of Junior's old tractor. "I know I can always think better when I'm in an upright position. Don't you Carl?"

Carl rubbed his eyes with one hand, the other between his legs. "Uhh. Shit."

"So where do I find Nick?"

"Uhh."

"Carl, do you want me to zap you again?"

"Uhh, no, no. Shit. No. Uhh. I. I. I."

"You what, Carl?"

Charity realized she may have zapped Carl a bit too much, so she gave him a few more minutes to recover. Then she loaded him into her car and had him show her where Nick lived using "eeff" for left and "rriii" for right. He held his crotch with both hands, as if cradling an injured bird, rocking forward and back. Sometimes he would stutter or get a little disoriented, but eventually Charity found Nick's silver Airstream trailer on a parcel of land east of Pflugerville. By the time Charity dropped Carl back off at his house he could put several words together into sentences.

"Why…you…zap?"

"Because I had a deal with Junior, not you. I'm not paying twice."

"Zap me?"

"Quit complaining, Carl." Charity got out of the car, walking around to the passenger side and then helping Carl out. "I could have done a lot worse."

"Worse? What?"

"I could have shot you in the kneecaps; tied a bale of hay around your balls and tossed the bale off the barn with you standing on the roof; knocked you unconscious, covered you in honey and tossed you on a fire ant mound…"

"Okay. I get. I get, uhh."

"So here's the deal Carl. If I ever learn you have told anyone about our little conversation today, I will personally come back here and I promise, I will not use a taser. Do you understand?"

"I, uuh, yeah."

~*~

Since her quarry was not at home, Charity decided to go back to the trailer and learn more about the man who had murdered her brother. She left her car on the road, walking cross-country to the gleaming Airstream. She quickly picked the door lock and stepped inside, closing the door behind her. The interior looked tired and worn, the upholstery a faded beige and blue-striped fabric, tattered and threadbare in places. The counters and appliances were a combination of actual and faux wood, plastic components yellowed and cracked. However, to her surprise, the murderer Sibelius kept a tidy home with only a dirty coffee cup in the sink. She looked through the drawers hoping to find some kinky twist she could use to make him squirm, but all she found was a photo tucked in a sock drawer of a woman in jeans sitting on a rock wall with the Golden Gate Bridge in the background. "MaryLou" had been written in cursive on the back.

Stepping back outside, she spotted a propane tank he used for cooking and hot water. He hadn't built any kind of surround to prevent animals or cunning assassins from easily accessing the bottom of the trailer. The obvious approach would be to simply blow the bastard up, but Charity told herself to take a breath, to let her creativity flow.

She drove back to Pflugerville, stopping by a little Chinese restaurant for the Buddha's Vegetarian Delight. Changing into her riding gear, she checked her tool bag, making sure the Philips screwdriver she had sharpened to a razor point was ready, then rode out to Nick's house. The ride felt good. She pushed herself up hills and made a point of passing a young guy on a Trek racing frame. About a quarter of a mile from the single lane track leading to Nick's trailer, Charity got off her bike. She checked both directions to be sure no one was in view, then pulled the small phillips head screw driver from her seat bag. Squatting, she removed one of her derailleur adjustment screws, apologizing to her bike while reminding her machine the screw had been removed for a good cause. She gave the peddle a turn flipping the chain off its cassette. Then she took the same screwdriver, and with a swift downward motion, punctured her rear tire.

Her trap set, Charity relaxed with a bottle of electrolyte packed sport drink and a power bar. Two hours of daylight left. She realized for the first time, the hunt would end in the death of her prey. Hyper-alert, Charity's heart raced, colors seemed more saturated, sounds clearer, her mind finely tuned. More than the usual high she always got when tormenting her quarry, adrenaline pulsed through her system. She felt fully awake, alert and alive. She liked the feeling.

Troubled Waters

Hoyt, deep in discussion with a contact in Miami who had a line on a great condo deal, didn't notice Nate standing by the door of his office until Nate cleared his throat. He turned around to see his plant engineer, looking like a kid who had been sent to the principal for shooting spit wads, holding a printout and rocking nervously back and forth.

"Excuse me a second, Michael." Hoyt held a hand over the phone. "Something the matter or are you just trying to annoy the hell out me, Nate?"

"We need to talk."

"Can't you see I'm conducting—"

"Now. Mr. Hoyt, we need to talk now."

Hoyt quickly and smoothly got off the phone, ushering Nate into a chair across from his desk.

"So what's so damn important?"

Nate handed the printout to Hoyt. "Let's just say we're screwed."

Color drained from Hoyt's face as he set the print out back on the desk. "Did you check these numbers? Those are the right numbers?"

"Yes sir. We're not going to be able to produce the volume required by the contract in time. No doubt about it."

"How the hell did this happen? You're the lead engineer. Didn't you account for this?"

"We're on new ground here, Mr. Hoyt. A plant this big, being built so quickly and coming on line so soon..."

Hoyt stood, tossing the paper at Nate. The sheet floated erratically, finally coming to rest on the floor.

"I don't want to hear your damn excuses, Nate! Don't you understand what's at stake here. If we don't get this place generating water by the deadline we're dead in the water. Dead-in-the-water. Do you understand what I'm saying?"

"Yes sir, it's just, well, as your engineer, I've got to tell you the truth."

"Do you now? Okay then, Mr. Engineer. What *is* the truth?"

"I know you don't want to hear this, but there's no way we'll be generating sufficient water by the deadline. No way."

"No way? In my experience, there's always a way."

"But Mr. Hoyt—"

"Shut up, Nate. No better yet, you're fired. Get out!"

Nate sat in his chair, looking something like a condemned man expecting one hundred thousand volts to be running through him at any moment. Hoyt leaned over the desk, looking directly at his engineer.

"Hello? I said get out. Now."

Hoyt couldn't believe this. He had everything, everything tied up in the plant. But before he had an opportunity to move into a full panic, the phone rang. Governor Francis Adamson, a handsome woman of fifty-six and an ex-cheerleader for the University of Texas Longhorns still had the perky energy of a pep squad captain, yet tempered with the menace of a great white shark.

"Daniel. You haven't been avoiding my calls now, have you?"

He should never have slept with the woman, who used the intimacy between them like a vise grip on his balls.

"I'd never avoid a call from you, Franny." His pet name for her. She insisted. "What can I do for you?"

"I think it should be obvious, Daniel. I need to know the water's flowing." Franny had way too much experience to be stupid enough to mention the money he was supposed to put into her designated account now that she had delivered the necessary votes to support his water project.

She had loved the idea from the beginning when he explained how the desalination plant would create fresh water, while painting her toenails as she sat back on the chaise lounge, smoking a cigar, her bikini top dangling from a towel hook on the other side of the deck at a discreet beach house near Galveston.

"Water. Now that's definitely a dog that'll hunt in the State of Texas, Daniel. How can I help you bring this life giving resource to the thirsty masses?"

Hoyt did not have much practice with painting toe nails, so he struggled to maintain his focus on the gubernatorial toes while pitching his deal. "You see Franny, building a plant near a protected wildlife area and then running a pipeline across the state to Dallas, San Antonio and Houston—"

"Would meet quite a bit of opposition. You'll need some serious assistance to get past all of it."

"Assistance I am more than willing to reward appropriately."

She exhaled, a smoke ring floating away from her mouth. "Hmmm. I imagine your pipeline will need to be built quickly, so you need someone to help push the easements through, as well as obtaining the consent of landowners for the right of way. I should think you'd want to sweeten the pot by paying them a percentage of revenues."

Franny had gone on to have her people set up a series of difficult-to-trace holding companies which owned property along the pipeline's path. Even though she was twenty years his elder, something about her political savvy and killer instinct made him want her badly. Besides, in his lovemaking with her, he had discovered experience definitely counts. No need for Viagra with Franny.

Hoyt tightened his grip on the phone. "We do have a little technical glitch, but we're still on schedule as planned." Why had he said anything about a glitch? Franny had a spell over him which seemed to make him almost tell the truth way too often. Most distasteful.

"Technical glitch?"

"Don't worry yourself about it. I guarantee you'll have water on time and on budget." He hoped sounding self-assured might make her back off a bit.

"Be sure it does, Daniel. The State does have other options and I'd hate for you to miss your opportunity for public service."

Options. With water demand overreaching reserves, Texas cities were scrambling to identify and nail down water sources to the point of negotiating with a billionaire entrepreneur about selling them water from an aquifer in West Texas. If he didn't get a believable flow of water out of his plant on time, Hoyt knew he'd miss the window for water deals with the three largest cities in the State. He wished Franny would do the deal just for the incredible sex, but he soon realized her ambitions to be president were far greater than any orgasm he could provide. Scoring a new water source for the State would definitely increase her profile, not to mention all the voter rich, water poor, states of the Southwest. To get this deal to work, Hoyt knew he had to keep her thinking he would actually come through with the goods.

"As we've talked about before Franny, you and I know while those other schemes may provide a short-term solution, this desalination plant offers a permanent panacea to the state's water problems. After we're up and running—trust me—Phoenix, Oklahoma City, and Albuquerque will be begging to buy water from you. Water will be the oil business of twenty-first century Texas."

"That's what I like to hear, Daniel. So we're on track?"

"Absolutely. We'll be generating water in sixty days, as planned."

As the conversation continued, Franny clearly intimated she wanted to get laid, so before he hung up, he arranged to meet her for *dinner and drinks*. Why a woman who wanted to rule the world had to be wined and dined every time she wanted to have sex initially made no sense to Hoyt. But over the course of their relationship the last two years, he had discovered anticipation actually did make the sex better. Not that he ever wanted to take *loads* of time with a woman just so she'd put out. But with Franny, he had learned to enjoy the journey almost as much as the destination.

Getting off the phone, the panic he had begun to sip like a bourbon on the rocks, became great gulps of a full blown cocktail with little umbrellas and swizzle sticks.

"Donaldson, where the hell are you?"

"Mr. Hoyt?" He sounded surprised, as if he took the whole 'firing' thing seriously.

"Yes, it's me. Who the hell is do you think it is? Now I need you to get over here. Right now!"

"I thought I was fired."

"Will you grow a pair? I was just shaking things up a bit. Now get over here. I need you."

"Oh, now you need me." Hoyt did not like the taunting tone in Nate's voice.

"Listen here, you sorry excuse for an engineer. You know, as well as I do, the only reason you're on this project is because you couldn't get a job flipping burgers, much less an actual engineering job. Nobody wants an ex-felon engineer with a drug habit. So stop the whining and get your ass over here."

"I told you I was innocent. There's no way I engineered the building to collapse for insurance money."

"Nate. Nate. Think about who you're talking to here. I know the guy who bribed you." Nate made no response. "Now get over here so we can figure out what to do about this plant?"

"Yessir."

Hoyt and Nate brainstormed ways of mitigating the crisis confronting the business. The plant would definitely not be online in time to meet the expectations of the investors, the Legislature, and especially, Franny. And while he hadn't planned on running a desalination plant for very long, Hoyt had planned on running it long enough to elicit some significant concessions from the state for his next development, which would be built on some currently protected wetlands. His endgame also included rolling the plant over for a nice profit. However, if water didn't flow out of the plant on time and in the promised volume, there'd be a lot of negative publicity, Franny's political career and their sex life would be trashed, and worst of all, he'd lose a large infusion of cash and the piece of dirt he needed for his next big development.

Nate tossed ideas out, hoping against hope one of them would strike Hoyt as a creative solution to their problem. "We could hire an engineering firm to come in, fix our problems and get us online. They won't get us operational in time, but we'll only be maybe six months late."

Hoyt paced like a wolf in a cage. "Six months late? Nate, we need to be up in sixty days—period. There is no alternative."

"We could just pump saltwater through. It won't be desalinized, but it will at least look like we're on line."

"Nate, what a stupid..." Hoyt stopped in his tracks. "Wait. I think you may have something there."

"Really? Well, yeah. We just need to clean the sea water a bit so it looks okay."

"No, no, no. Not the seawater part. The thing you said about making it look like we're on line. We can't use sea water, but..."

"You want to use fresh water? Where are we going to get that much fresh water without showing our hand?"

"I don't know." Hoyt paced the room again tapping his leg nervously, then stopped in mid-stride. "Wait. Do you remember a story a number of years ago about some good ol' boy pumping hundreds of thousands of gallons of water from the Edwards Aquifer to support a fish farm?"

Nate had been standing in place watching his boss. "Yeah, I think I remember something about it. Didn't they shut him down?"

"Yes, but this is America. You might be able to shut down a fish farm, but by God, you can't shut down a good idea."

"You want to pump water from the Edwards Aquifer and make it look like we're producing the water at the plant?"

"Why not? We've got the pipeline infrastructure. All we need to do is tap the aquifer."

"How do you plan on getting the water? Buy the land the fish farm guy used?"

Hoyt looked at his engineer with the disdain he usually reserved for the homeless or attorneys. "You focus on getting the plant on line. I'll figure out how to get the water. Now get out."

"You do realize you keep throwing me out of your office?"

"Get out, Nate. Or I'll fire your ass again!"

As his semi-skilled engineer sulked away, Hoyt rested his forehead on the desk. A throbbing pain had been building from his shoulders, up his neck, and now had firmly taken hold right behind his eyes. He needed some bourbon, a massage, a blow job, preferably all at the same time. Hoyt had no idea how he was going to pump water out of the aquifer. Izzy, the principal investor in the plant, also wanted the pipeline for the drug cartel, so he could probably convince Izzy to find the water to make the plant appear to be running. However, doing a deal with Izzy meant doing the deal with Los Diablos Tejanos. Hoyt had no desire to spend the rest of his life looking over his shoulder for Diablos hit men. No, he needed to find another solution, but his brainstorming always came back to Izzy. He banged his head repeatedly, hoping the pain of the impacts would somehow cancel out the pain behind his eyes. Unfortunately, it only compounded the throbbing.

All Square

Wrapped in gauze and surgical tape he had picked up at a drugstore, Jonah's hand throbbed with pain each time he unconsciously rested his roughly bandaged palm on the steering wheel. He considered going to a hospital, but emergency rooms ask too many questions. First, he'd get Izzy his package, then he'd get the hand taken care of. He sat in his car by a convenience store searching vainly for the courage to offset his anxiety about looking like a lump of charred swiss cheese under the searing flame of Izzy's lighter. When the call came, Izzy's message could not have been more clear.

"Meet me under the 360 bridge at 10:30 tonight with the package. Come alone. And Jonah, do not disappoint me."

Jonah had no intention of disappointing Izzy. He had met him at a Game Developers Conference in Cologne, Germany the year before. Izzy attended the European GDC to publicly network and privately spy on his competitors across the Atlantic. Jonah, who had been creating battle-ready software for the Department of Defense, had also developed some advanced algorithms on his own time and hoped he could translate his skill and knowledge into a gig. They met by chance in a bar, Izzy playing the part of a hip entrepreneur excited to hear about Jonah's ideas. Next thing Jonah knew he was doing freelance work for Izzy, helping him develop cutting-edge games, and making more money than the DoD could ever pay him.

Jonah had always gambled a little, but with the funds he got from Izzy, he put more money on the line and took greater risks. Often his gambles paid off, but then he had a run of bad luck. So he borrowed from Izzy, hoping to win back his losses. The Packer-Steeler game had been a sure thing. No way the Packers were going to win and he got a great line on the game, dropping the hundred K he had borrowed from Izzy. If the Steelers had done what they were supposed to do, he would have walked away with several hundred grand, paid off Izzy's loan with interest and had enough left over for a down payment on a condo he wanted out in LA. But the damn Steelers lost, so he forfeited all the money, which put him in the position of owing Izzy big time in the form of acquiring a shit-load of illegal nuclear material for God knows what. And now the fucker burned a hole in his hand. In the damn hand! Every time he thought about Izzy torching his hand with the lighter, Jonah's insides recoiled, the impulse to vomit rising. *This is the last thing I'm doing for this guy. After this we're even and I don't want to see him ever again. Period.*

Jonah drove north on 360 through the hills west of Austin, past a nest of radio towers, a rest stop with a stunning view of the city and finally down a long hill towards the rusty brown arches of the bridge suspended over Lake Austin. Houses, lit up like Christmas luminarias, sat atop limestone cliffs on the other side of the lake. Taking an access road under the bridge, he pulled to the water's edge. The parking lot, which served the boat ramp by the bridge, stood empty, lit only by the moon's glow. Jonah needed to get to a doctor about his hand, which hurt like hell. He checked his radiation badge one more time. The guy who sold him the lead-lined case advertised the container as virtually leak free, but then, the guy didn't have to drive around with a case full of nuclear material. He reminded himself to stay calm and just get this whole ordeal over with.

Headlights appeared in the distance, moving down the access road and then turning directly into Jonah, blinding him. *Izzy always has to be so damn dramatic. Why couldn't I have just dropped the case off behind JVI and be done with it?* Izzy shut off his lights. He could see Puck behind the steering wheel. Izzy got out, walking to the front of his car . Jonah opened his door, hearing the rumble of traffic overhead as he stepped away from his vehicle.

"I'm glad you met the deadline, Jonah. Not that I wouldn't have enjoyed burning a hole in another part of your body, but your ineptitude has made me alter my schedule."

Jonah's stomach turned over and the pain in his hand throbbed as if responding to the frequency of Izzy's voice. A dank odor of lake algae carried in the damp night air nauseated him.

"Let's do this, Izzy. I just want to get you what you want and be done with it. I'm sorry all this happened, but I just want this to be over."

"I'm sorry too, Jonah. Not for punishing you. You deserved it, of course. No, I'm sorry you disappointed me. I had such high hopes for you."

They stood silently, Izzy's eyes penetrating through any facade Jonah had, his insides roiling, his heart pounding.

"Why don't you get me the case, Jonah."

"Right. Yeah. It's in the trunk. I'll need some help."

Izzy motioned to Puck as Jonah walked back. He opened the trunk and with Puck's help, lifted out a metal case the size of a footlocker. They carried it back to Izzy's car, the trunk lid popping open as they passed Izzy. They lowered the case carefully into the Audi's trunk. Jonah stepped away from the car, startled by Izzy's close proximity to him.

"You're a little jumpy tonight, Jonah. You need to take up yoga. Does wonders."

"We're done now, right Izzy? All square?"

Izzy nodded. "All square, Jonah."

Jonah's eyes burned from sweat dripping down his face, more from anxiety than from activity. "Good, good. Okay then, I'll be on my way." He lifted his bandaged hand in the air. "I need to get this checked out." He looked to Izzy, whose face gave no hint of emotion's face. Jonah took several steps away from Izzy, then turned to make the last few strides to his car.

Phut.

At first he thought he was having a heart attack, the pain erupting in his back and chest, a flash of agony going down his already injured arm. But then a second and third jolt of pain seared into him, blood and gore spraying out of his chest and abdomen. By the time his knees hit the ground he didn't feel the rough surface beneath. And when his head slammed on chipseal, gravel embedding in his face, he felt nothing at all.

Game Changer

Nick endured the ride back to Hoyt's house in the limo, as Hoyt wheeled and dealed over his cell phone. When he finally got back to the office, Theresa's sky blue MGB still sat parked out front.

"I figured you would have left by now, Theresa."

She sat at the desk, a notebook with tightly scribbled notes in front of her. "I tried, but my boy wouldn't start."

"Your boy?" Nick couldn't imagine what she was talking about.

"My car, Nick. It won't start."

"Battery?"

"No, sounds like something catastrophic. With MGs they either run or they're dead. And all my tools are back at my place."

Okay, make that good with a gun, a cat burglar and she's got tools. He was really beginning to appreciate this woman.

"Why don't you let my mechanic take a look at it?"

She shoved herself away from the desk. Nick guessed maybe money was an issue, especially since he had delayed getting the business up and running.

"I'll advance you some salary so you can cover the cost."

She stood, closing the notebook. "It's not the money, Nick. I drive an MGB because I like working on him. I just don't have much luck with other mechanics working on my cars."

Nick imagined Theresa, all covered in grease, under the little convertible, only her legs showing, calling out to him for a half-inch wrench. He willed himself back to reality.

"Yeah, I understand. But Hoyt wants more of our services, so I'd rather pay to have your car repaired and have you available."

"I don't know, Nick…"

"Theresa, my guy is good. Really good. He works on everything from my beater to high-end Ferraris. His name's Charlie."

She frowned. "The guy who gave us the lead on Hoyt?"

"Yeah, he's the one. Look, maybe he's not the best judge of potential clients, but the guy's a master mechanic. I'll call him right now."

After hemming and hawing a bit, Theresa finally agreed. While they waited for Charlie to swing by with a tow truck, they briefed each other on progress to date. Nick described the compound and the desalination plant.

Theresa came around her desk, then sat on its edge. "He wants us to provide security for a desalination plant?"

"No, he says he wants us to find out who's gunning for him."

"Someone took a shot at him?"

"Not in the traditional sense. We know someone sprayed butyric acid inside his Ferrari and now he says he was," Nick struggled to maintain a straight face, "he was attacked by a group of lobsters."

Nick could hear his watch tick in the silence between them just before they both burst out laughing.

Theresa held onto the desk. "Did they try to pinch him and collect the ransom?"

A wave of laughter rolled over them.

"No, but I think they danced the Lobster Quadrille."

Theresa howled, obviously a reader of *Alice in Wonderland* too, holding her sides as if trying to keep from exploding.

"Was it..." She struggled to take in enough breath to speak. "Was it a lobsta mobsta?"

They both erupted into fresh round of laughter, wiping tears from their eyes, holding on to each other for support, just as Charlie walked through the door. Nick, seeing Charlie, let go of Theresa.

"Hey Charlie. Thanks for coming by."

He cocked his head with a raised brow. "Have I caught you two at a bad time?"

"No, no. We were just..." Nick looked to Theresa for help. For a brief moment he thought he saw something in her eyes not related to work.

She stepped over to Charlie. "We were just laughing about something from earlier today. You must be Charlie." Theresa shook his hand, guiding him back out the door as she walked him through her assessment of her car.

Once Charlie had determined the MGB did indeed have a catastrophic issue requiring garage time, he loaded the car onto the tow truck, promising to call Theresa with an update as soon as he had done a full diagnosis. Nick offered Theresa a ride home. As they drove the winding curves of 2222 west of town, Nick glanced over to see Theresa looking at him.

"What? Did I miss shaving this morning?"

"No, Nick. I was just wondering."

"About what?"

"I was wondering when you were going to tell me what really happened in Pflugerville?"

Nick looked out over the rolling cedar and oak covered hill country, which seemed to go on and on for miles.

"We arrested Junior for a variety of crimes and two bad guys were killed in the process."

"I'm not talking about what I already know. I'm talking about the rest of the story, Nick. Who was MaryLou, really? I know we thought she was a reporter, but you and I both know her newspaper job was a cover. But a cover for what? And then to die like that...burning up in a fire. God. Why would she choose to run into a fire instead of trusting you?"

Very good question. Why did she run away when he could have saved her? MaryLou was alive. At least he thought she was still alive. And yes, she was a Homeland Security agent under cover and she's the one who killed both Jason and Barry, not to mention being Junior's sister. If she was still alive, Nick assumed he was the only one who knew. Even though she betrayed him, Nick could not bring himself to betray her.

"I'm not sure, Theresa. As you know, she was Junior's sister. Maybe she felt running away was the only way to save her brother. I don't know."

Theresa sat in silence as Nick navigated the twisting downhill road, hugging shear rock walls of limestone.

"Did you love her?"

Nick glanced over at Theresa, the question asked without emotional weight. Tossed into the air like 'do you want a beer?' only Nick had a clear answer about beer, but not about MaryLou.

"I guess I did, but we didn't really have much of a chance, did we?"

"No, I suppose you didn't. Sorry. I'm getting a bit too deep into your business."

"It's okay. I understand. We're partners and we need to have each other's backs. We've got to trust each other implicitly. I trust you, Theresa. I trust you to be there and to do the right thing."

"Thanks. Nick. I trust you too."

~*~

Nick pulled into a barbecue joint where they got a table and a couple Coronas topped with wedges of lime.

Theresa lifted her bottle toward Nick. "To our new venture."

After ordering some brisket and ribs, she excused herself, finding her way to the restroom. She wasn't quite sure how she felt about Nick. When he came to Pflugerville, an old friend of Quentin's, she looked at the square-jawed, broad-shouldered man with the nice, tight ass as a possible presence in her life. Then he got wrapped up with MaryLou and she realized, once again, she had fallen into her usual trap—tempted by a good looking slash train wreck of a man who would break her heart. She'd been down that road before and had no desire to take another trip. Now he says he's over MaryLou, which given the woman is dead, shouldn't be too difficult. But her intuition had no intention of letting down her guard so easily. Her intuition knew once he committed, Nick could not let go, which was a characteristic she loved about him and also one which worried her. Take Hoyt. Clearly the situation with Hoyt had moved beyond the realm of their small investigation firm, but Nick, having made an initial commitment to Hoyt and then sensing something amiss, would not—could not—turn away. And this thing about MaryLou. The woman lied to him and murdered two people. But all Nick could say was, "I guess I loved her, but we didn't have much of a chance." Maybe he just didn't like to speak ill of the dead.

She checked her make up, ran a brush through her hair, then washed her hands. As she opened the door to return to the dining room, she saw Nick's blue jeaned nicely proportioned rear end poking out from under a table as he crawled around on his hands and knees. Did he drop his fork? Was he helping someone find a contact lens? She walked toward Nick and over the country music could hear him talking as if he were five years old.

"Where did Teddy go? I'm sure Teddy's around here somewhere? Wait. There he is! He was just playing hide and seek."

Nick backed out from under the table, teddy bear in hand. "There you go sweetie." He handed the stuffed animal to a little girl who hugged her fuzzy friend with every inch of her being. "See? I told you Teddy was just hiding from us. Now let's go back to Mommy."

He moved over a couple of tables, handing the small child back to her mother. The hard, pragmatic, and she sensed, lonely man, apparently had another side. When Quentin first suggested she work with Nick, she knew Quentin was doing some matchmaking, in addition to supporting his friend's business venture.

"He's a good man, Theresa."

"I'm sure he is Quentin, but I'm looking for a job, not a man. Besides, I think your Nick has too many dark corners to illuminate for a relationship to work."

When Nick turned to see her looking at him, he half-grinned with a shrug as if to apologize for not being the man he had been masquerading as in the past. She smiled. Seeing him on his hands and knees with the little girl might just be a game changer.

Theresa sat down with him. "Congratulations, Nick."

"Congratulations? For what?"

She nodded, smiling at the little girl still hugging her Teddy tightly. "Looks to me like you have a very satisfied client of Sibelius Investigations."

"Yes, I suppose she is." He lifted his beer bottle in a toast. "To satisfied clients."

After dinner he stopped in front of her house, a little 1950's bungalow she bought when she had gotten out of the Army.

"You want to come in for a few minutes. I make a mean cup of coffee."

"I'd love to come in." He paused and Theresa imagined he was doing some calculus about getting involved with his business partner. So she relieved him of the burden.

"But you probably shouldn't."

He turned to speak to her. "I didn't say that."

"You don't need to. It's okay. I get it Nick."

Theresa stepped out, keeping one hand on the truck as she came around to the other side. She had teased Nick in the past, partly because he fit the two-dimensional stereotype of the kind of guy who found her attractive—all dick and no brains. She had the same problem in Iraq, until she busted a few heads. She also knew teasing Nick meant not having to let him near her heart. She thought she had him figured out. Now Theresa wasn't so sure anymore.

"Thanks for dinner and for connecting me with your mechanic." She gave him a gentle kiss on his cheek.

"You're very welcome, Theresa. Just give Charlie a call in the morning and he'll have one of his guys come by with the loaner for you."

"Thanks, Nick. Good night."

She stood on the sidewalk watching Nick's pickup pull away, tail lights finally disappearing into the darkness.

Yes, Nick Sibelius. Tonight was definitely a game changer.

Wormwood

Izzy sat at the absinthe bar, turning the silver nozzle of a tall glass decanter, adding water to the viridescent liquid in his glass. He liked coming here, talking to the women who sat nearby, letting the absinthe relax him. And he needed to relax. Jonah's incompetence had forced him to push his plans back. At least the idiot came through with the radioactive materials and killing him did provide some cathartic release. He hadn't intended to kill him so far from the dumpster, but Puck, never one to complain, easily picked up the body, tossing it like a sack of garbage into the green steel container. Having the Diablos steal Jonah's car was a nice improvisation, which meant the car would be broken down into parts by the morning. The only evidence would be the body and Izzy knew a garbage truck wouldn't be by there for another week. By then, no one would care.

Next on the to-do list was getting Hoyt on board with the narcotic packed pigs in the pipeline. He tasted the aniseed flavor of his absinthe, the liquid warming his throat. If he couldn't convince Hoyt to play along, then he'd just get rid of him. Of course, removing Hoyt would create its own complications, but he wasn't going to let a dim-witted frat boy screw up his plans.

The cartel play had been a brilliant move. He bought his way into the cartel initially to make his Spike award winning game, *Drugs n' Guns*, a more authentic virtual experience. Izzy found after a few months he liked the rush the drug business offered. Real life-or-death stuff. As with any business enterprise and in every other aspect of his life, his only point of reference was as the leader. So he put his plans to take over the cartel in motion, requiring him to surround himself with some serious thugs, who also doubled as grist for the character development mill at JVI. He discovered the sound of bullets ripping into flesh, the resulting blood and gore, and the priceless expressions of surprise, pain, and anguish caused by firing an actual, versus a virtual, weapon into Tigre's enemies, brought a thrill starting in his testicles and spreading into his chest, exploding like miniature fireworks in his brain. Those violent expressions also provided critical research instrumental in making *Mujahid Death Match 1.2* so compelling.

While he could have toyed with the Diablos for some time, he preferred to simply take over the entire operation, the pipeline deal being a cornerstone of his strategy. El Tigre thought of him as a weak business associate. He looked forward to the day when the gun exploding in Tigre's mouth would send a different message. Yes, for the sake of his plan and his domination of the Diablos, Hoyt was going to do business with him, one way or the other.

A feminine voice interrupted him. "Deep thoughts?"

He turned to a woman's face framed by dark, full hair, hazel eyes, and a mischievous smile. Taking his time, he followed the curve of her neck to her breasts and then back to her eyes. Maybe getting laid would be a good way to complete the day. He wondered how she liked it. "Do we know each other?"

"No, I just saw you here alone at the bar deep in thought. Sometimes I find it's helpful to talk things through with someone else."

"So you're offering me your services?"

"My fees are pretty reasonable. Martini, dry, twist of lemon."

"Very reasonable."

The bartender hovering nearby acknowledged the order as Izzy repeated her words. Ever since Izzy had become a rock star in the gaming world he had girls slipping room keys and panties in his pockets at conferences. They were usually younger, probably teenagers, and dazzled by his money. And he usually took them up on the offer. The woman beside him tonight, his age, maybe older, didn't look the type to tremble in his presence, but she did look interested.

She leaned toward him. "You here on business?"

"No, I live here."

She looked around. "At the bar?"

"Austin. I own a very successful high-tech company in town."

"Really? I pictured Michael Dell differently."

"Dell? Jesus." Izzy took a drink of absinthe to wash the name, both names, from his mind.

"So which is it? Dell or Jesus?"

He turned to face her, leaning one elbow on the bar. "Izzy Zydeco. JVI, Juego Virtuales, Inc. We create highly realistic virtual simulations. Spike award winners, Best of CES the last four years. I could go on."

"I'm sure you could. Lots of violence, I suppose."

"Never played?"

The bartender set her martini on a cocktail napkin, a yellow lemon peel spiraling in ice cold gin.

"I like living in the real world. You know, actual relationships, real consequences."

"No imagination then."

"Enough of an imagination to know a game responsible for making a kid shoot up his school with an Uzi…"

She obviously kept up with the news. Izzy's lawyers had the suit well under control.

"So you have heard of me. You *are* a naughty girl." Izzy moved closer. He liked the tension, the tease. "I like naughty girls."

She confessed, "Okay, maybe I knew who you were. Can't blame a girl for playing it a little coy."

"And you've never played a virtual game? As a living icon of the gaming industry, I believe I have a responsibility to help you experience the real thing."

"Real?"

"The real virtual thing. A highly realistic virtual gaming simulation experience."

She took a sip of her drink, licking her top lip with a sweep of the tongue. "Oh, I see."

"I think you will, once you find yourself in a life-or-death situation, a gun in your hand, and very few options. Most people, and I'm guessing you fit in with most people, don't know what it's like."

She set her glass on the bar. "And you do?"

"Of course. I developed the game."

"I might surprise you, Izzy."

"I'd like to see that, Ms.?"

"MaryLou. MaryLou Perkins."

"I'd like to see you surprise me MaryLou Perkins. Drop by my office tomorrow and I'll put you through your paces."

She rested her long, manicured fingers on his forearm. "Why don't you put me through my paces tonight? Strike while the iron's hot."

He pondered whether to do her in the limo or in the sim room. "Okay. Tonight it is."

Izzy got up from the bar, MaryLou following his lead as he guided her out to a awaiting limo. Ensconced in the back, he watched this beautiful, and more importantly, willing woman he had stumbled upon, as she stared out the window. Soon she'd be tied to his bed or maybe he'd have her tie him to the bed. In any case, the riding crop would be coming out for sure. Izzy took hold of MaryLou's hand, placing it inside his thigh. Their bodies pressed back in leather seats, as the limo pulled into traffic.

"I do love beautiful things and you are definitely beautiful, MaryLou."

She didn't move her hand, but looked to Izzy with a teasing smile. "Beautiful thing? A little on the misogynist side, Izzy, but thanks all the same."

"I've disappointed you."

"I'll recover. It's not every day a girl has Izzy Zydeco come on to her."

"I have the feeling you know more about me than you let on."

"I suppose I do." She removed her hand from his thigh. "I've disappointed you?"

"Not at all. Life can be so mundane. I have a premonition you'll bring some excitement to my life tonight. So tell me. What do you know about Izzy Zydeco?"

MaryLou turned to face him. "He's very bright. High School valedictorian, head of his class at MIT, dropped out of a doctoral program to create a startup software company which he sold and then used his wealth to take over, break up and sell off pieces of his father's conglomerate. Now here you are in Austin, Texas with a company called Juegos Virtuales, Inc., and accolades in the press about your virtual gaming software."

The tryst, which seemed so promising, now took on the look and feel of yet another business meeting. Some vendor wanting his business. His voice went cold. "I see you've done your research, which I assume means our meeting wasn't an accident. What do you want? You have sixty seconds. Make it good."

"Word on the street is you're gunning to take over the Diablos. Ballsy."

Izzy, who thought he had another wikipedia-fueled groupie or an overzealous vendor in the limo, perked up at the mention of the Diablos. She knew more than it was healthy for a young woman to know.

"Forty seconds."

"I want to work with you. I've got skills I imagine a man like you could use. If you're taking on the Diablos, you definitely have your hands full."

He forced a smile. "Congratulations, MaryLou. Great story and the bit about the Diablos provides a very realistic touch. But I think you're timing's a little too convenient. How do I know you're not a cop?"

"I thought you entrepreneurs were risk-takers. I'm legit, Izzy. You've got El Tigre by the tail and I want to take the ride with you."

"Your time is up." He leaned over to press the intercom. "Puck, pull off to the side of the road." The limo slowed to a stop on the shoulder. Izzy looked at MaryLou, trying to determine what game she played. If she really was a woman with skills, he could use her for at least one task. And if she was a cop, he could use that to his advantage as well. Either way, she'd be dead in a week. And besides, he really needed to get laid tonight. He pushed the intercom button again. "I've changed my mind. Continue on to JVI."

MaryLou smiled. "For a moment there, I thought you were going to do something rash, Izzy."

He took her hand, slipping it back between his legs. "The night's young, MaryLou. There's still plenty of time for us to be impetuous. Plenty of time."

Charity at Home

After dropping Theresa off, Nick drove home to his Airstream thinking about to ferret out who sprayed Hoyt's Ferrari with an malodorous chemical, how beautiful Theresa had been tonight, why the county never seemed to get around to filling in the pot holes, and what MaryLou might be doing right now. All he had was a picture of her at the Golden Gate Bridge from six months ago. He had hoped since she had taken the trouble to let him know she was alive, he would have heard something more from her. A card, a letter, an email, a text message, something. Maybe he had misinterpreted her last message, which he had memorized.

I'm sorry for all the pain I've caused you Nick. Maybe one day I can make things right. Take care of yourself.

M.

The note sounded to him like she would come back sometime in the future. But not a word for twelve months. *What are you waiting around for Nick? You only knew the woman a few days and for most of the time she was lying to you about who she was and what she was doing in Pflugerville. Her picture could have been taken anytime in the last three or four years. For all you know, someone in Homeland Security wants you to think she's alive. You need to move on, man. Get on with your life.*

About a quarter-mile from the turnoff into his property Nick caught sight of a cyclist at the side of the road in the arc of his headlamps. Cyclists liked the country lanes east of Pflugerville because they were relatively traffic-free, but he didn't often see someone training at night. He slowed down to check if this rider needed some assistance. As he neared, the cyclist looked familiar. Black and pink lycra, red hair, a woman, about five foot seven. This was the woman he had given a ride a couple of days ago. He pulled beside her, rolling down the passenger window.

"We've got to keep meeting like this."

She looked a bit startled to see him. Maybe being alone in the dark left her feeling spooked.

"It's me. The guy who gave you a lift a couple of days ago out at Mt. Bonnell."

"Yes, I know who you are."

"Have another flat?"

"Not sure. I need to take a closer look, but it's pretty dark tonight."

Nick looked around into the darkness. He did not feel comfortable leaving her alone on this stretch of dark road.

"Look, I live around here. Why don't you toss your bike in the back and you can at least work on it in the light. Or I'm happy to take you back to your car."

"You live around here?"

Nick nodded in the direction of his Airstream. "Yeah, I've got a trailer nearby. It's not much, but it is home."

The woman smiled and then placed both hands on the open truck window. "I apologize for my bad manners. Sometimes when I'm riding I get a bit, well, focused. I don't believe I caught your name."

"Nick. Nick Sibelius."

She stared at him, her green eyes going wide, then squinting, then wide again. Nick wondered if she might be suffering from dehydration.

"I'm sorry, I didn't get your name either."

"Charity Swenson."

"Charity. Doing okay, Charity?"

"What? No, yes, I'm fine. Just didn't expect…"

"It's okay, Charity. You're safe with me. Hop in and let's see if we can get your bike working again."

After placing her bike in the back of Nick's truck, she stepped into the passenger seat for the very short trip to the Airstream. All the while, Nick sensed Charity's eyes on him. He wondered if maybe she had fallen and had a concussion, although he hadn't seen any scrapes or other evidence of a crash.

"Did you have an accident?"

"What?"

"Did you crash your bike or did you have a mechanical problem?"

"Mechanical. I think it's the derailleur."

Once at the trailer Nick helped Charity get the bike off the truck, setting the machine by the steps with his headlights shining to give her sufficient light for work. She knelt by the bike, exploring her derailleur and chain, looking for the problem.

"A cyclist and a bike mechanic. Impressive. I never can seem to get those things adjusted right, myself."

She stood, wiping grease off her hands with a towel.

"When you ride the distances I ride, you pretty much have to be a mechanic or you end up taking long hikes with a bike strapped to your back. Come over here and hold the rear wheel by the seat for me. I'm going to run through the gears."

Nick stood behind the bike, lifting the rear of the frame by the seat, as Charity clicked through the gears at the handlebar. The chain whirred and then clacked into place on the cog, then clacked again as Charity seated the chain on the next gear. Then the chain slipped off the cog completely, the freewheel clicking as the wheel spun. Charity braked the wheel to a stop and squatted by the derailleur.

"So Charity, do you ride out here very often?"

She kept her eyes on the bike as she spoke. "I'm not from around here. Just visiting."

"Given the Australian accent, I figured you might not be from Texas. So you take your bike with you to train when you travel. You must be a pretty hardcore cyclist."

She glared at Nick. "Why do say that?"

"Didn't mean anything negative. It's a compliment. You don't meet many people who have a passion and are willing to do whatever is necessary to make it happen. Good for you."

Charity's tense look, which even to Nick looked a little scary, softened.

"Thank you. Sorry." She pointed to her head. "Red hair. A bit high-strung."

Nick laughed. "Funny, I met a guy once with red hair, last name was Swenson too and he was a bit high strung."

Charity picked up a screwdriver in her right hand, turning to face Nick. "What happened to him?"

"Why do you think something happened to him?"

"Come on, Nick. Something always happens, doesn't it?"

"I suppose so." He couldn't put a finger on it, but he got a weird vibe from this woman.

"Well, what happened?"

"He died a few months ago."

"Did someone murder him?"

Nick stepped over to put the bike between them, while keeping an eye on the screwdriver. "What makes you think he was murdered?"

"Just wondering. Thought maybe I read a story about him in the papers."

"Well, trust me Charity, he wasn't a very good person."

She grabbed the screwdriver by the end, repeatedly slapping the handle into her palm. "How can you be so sure he was a bad person? Did you know him very well?"

Nick wondered why this woman had taken such an interest in a dead sociopath. She was probably the type who liked to watch *When Pets Attack!* and *Sudden Death!* on the cable channels. "Maybe we better just drop it. I'd really rather not think about him."

"I'm just asking a question, Nick. You said he was bad and I just want to know how you go about deciding if someone deserves to die."

"I didn't say he deserved to die, Charity. Look, he dumped toxic waste illegally and dealt in meth, but more to the point, he was about to kill several people."

The screwdriver paused in her hand. "He dumped toxic waste?"

"Yes, and he attempted to murder a number—"

"But he had a permit, right?"

"No, he didn't have permit. He dumped it on open farmland. But you're missing the point."

She once again pounded a rhythm into her palm with the tool's handle. "So, the waste seeped into the water table."

"Yeah, I suppose that would be the end result."

"Sonofabitch."

She cursed slowly, as if letting her mind have time to come to some kind of resolution. Charity grasped the screwdriver in one hand, pressing the point into the palm of the other. Nick wondered if she planned on pushing the thing right through her hand.

"Did you know Barry Swenson?"

She refocused her attention on her bike. "No, no. Just curious. Like you said, I'm a bit too Australian to be from Texas. Ah, there's the problem. Just have to tighten this screw and fix the tire and I should be good to go."

Charity finished her repair, pulled lights out of her seat bag, and put her tools away. "Well I'll be off now, Nick. Thanks for the help."

"Are you sure you want to ride in the dark? I don't mind taking you to your car or hotel, for that matter."

The corners of Charity's mouth raised slightly and Nick thought she may have even blushed a bit at the mention of her hotel. He didn't mean anything more than a ride, but she looked more flattered than offended. "No thanks, Nick. You've done far too much already. I'm beginning to expect you to show up every time I break down."

"I can't promise, Charity, but if I'm in the neighborhood, I'll certainly help out anytime."

Nick watched her ride the dirt road until her lights disappeared. What an intriguing woman. If Barry Swenson did have a sister, she'd certainly have to be someone like Charity.

~*~

Charity rode away from Nick Sibelius confused and angry, arguing with herself all the way back to her car. She had failed in her singular mission to kill her brother's murderer. She deserved the Bunyips. How could she let a smooth-talking, evil bastard trick her into losing focus on the task? But what if Nick spoke the truth? Is it possible her brother poisoned the environment with toxic waste? Murder was one thing—she could forgive the occasional murder here and there. But dumping toxic waste? What kind of a sick animal does something like that?

Wait Charity. Just because Nick the bastard murderer tells you Barry dumped waste doesn't make it so. Think girl. He must have somehow gotten wind of your plans. He knew you were there to kill him and used his smarmy mouth to avoid your vengeance. He's a snake. He'll do anything, say anything, to keep alive.

"Maybe, but he also helped me out twice in the last several days. Not to mention he wants to drive a hybrid and agrees dumping toxic waste is bad. Besides, he's pretty good looking. Did you see his ass when he turned around? And if I'm not mistaken, he actually made a play for me back there. If he had his way, he'd be in my hotel room tonight making hot, passionate love to me."

Charity, get a grip. He didn't help you. He's a misogynist pig who gloated his superiority over you by stopping to help the weak little woman at the side of the road. And anyone can say they want to drive a hybrid or an electric. Only the committed actually drive one. And yes, I will give you the fact he's good looking and he wanted to fuck the bejesus out of you tonight, and frankly I'm a bit pissed you let the opportunity slide. Imagine plunging the knife into the SOB right in the middle of wild orgasmic sex. You'd have to change the rating system on your Facebook page just to account for taking your life's work to an entirely new level.

"Will you shut up? Okay, I get it. I did fail tonight and I let him use his suave manner and good looks to distract me. I never knew my brother, but it's not possible any brother of mine could poison the earth. Ever. I faltered tonight, but now I know the kind of adversary I face. I have to find a way to carry out my mission without being influenced by his words or his blatant sexual desire. I will not be thwarted again. Nick Sibelius will die. Definitely."

Oncoming headlights flashed toward her. She smiled, accelerating beyond her cardiac threshold. High beams blinded her, the car's horn blaring as she veered into its lane. Braking tires screamed across asphalt. Charity, maintained her speed while slipping to the side, passing the stopped car as if the vehicle didn't exist.

A male voice shouted behind her. "Hey, what the hell?"

The carbon-head may not have liked it, but he did yield to her. *In the end, they all will.*

Bang! You're It

Izzy's limo pulled to the front of JVI's corporate office under the glow of amber security lights. He guided MaryLou through glass doors. A night guard greeted them.

"Good evening, sir."

"We'll be in the sim room area, so I'll be shutting down security there."

"Yes sir."

The guard seemed used to Izzy's request to block off security in the sim room, leaving MaryLou wondering if he had a pattern of bringing women back with him. With all of the security shut down, there would be no witnesses, no camera footage. They made their way into the sim room lounge, the smell of new leather furniture filling the space.

"Would you like a drink before we begin?"

"What do you have in mind?"

Izzy had a bottle of gin and vermouth out on the bar.

"You wanted to play one of my games. Remember?"

"Of course. If I recall, you didn't think I'd be very successful."

He filled a shaker with crushed ice, then poured measured amounts gin and vermouth, finally shaking the mixture, looking something like a Latin percussionist. Izzy poured the clear liquid out into two martini glasses, placing a curl of lemon peel in each. He handed MaryLou one of the glasses, raising his in a toast.

"To your success."

MaryLou touched her glass to his, saying, "To success."

Izzy paused, closing his eyes as he took in the subtle juniper aromatics of the gin. "You seem like a woman who enjoys a challenge."

"What do you have in mind?"

"A simple wager. You win the simulation on points, you work for me, no questions asked. You lose, I decide what to do with you."

"As in, escort me out of the building?"

"Something like that. Are you game?"

"You might as well give me the job right now, Izzy. I don't lose."

"I like your spirit, MaryLou. We'll let the simulation sort things out."

~*~

MaryLou changed clothes into a body suit embedded with a sensory mesh, as well as a visor, and a gaming gun. Now she stood on a dark street, decaying brick warehouses to her left, a muddy, putrid river to her right and a bridge crossing the river about two hundred feet in front of her. The briefing told her she had manufactured a sizable amount of methamphetamines. Her buyer insisted on this time and place for the deal. Her car, a 1969 Dodge Charger, complete with flames painted along the sides, was parked behind her with a trunk full of meth. The buyer could be a legitimate drug dealer, a cop, or possibly someone intent on killing her and stealing the drugs. To optimize her points and ensure her place with Izzy, she needed to make the right decisions.

A black BMW drove under the bridge toward her, stopping fifty feet away, its lights on. The driver's side door opened and Izzy stepped out. "Got the goods?"

"Izzy?"

"Do you have the goods or not?"

"Yeah, I've got the goods." She walked towards the BMW as Izzy walked toward her. In her right hand she held a Glock with seventeen rounds, in her left hand, a brief case containing a sample of the product. Izzy and MaryLou stopped ten feet from each other. She tossed the case to Izzy, who had set a courier bag beside him. A second man walked toward them from the BMW carrying a small black medical bag.

"Who's he?"

"No worries. He's my chemist. I need him to confirm the product. Once I get his confirmation, we'll exchange cars. You don't mind a BMW with a trunk full of money, do you?"

MaryLou now had two men, one armed, but the other with a possible explosive device in the bag. She scanned the bridge and the warehouse for shooters. She hadn't thought about other players for her team. She was a sitting duck and she knew it.

The chemist opened his bag, pulling out a small test tube. He placed a sample from MaryLou's briefcase into the clear glass tube, then added a few drops of liquid, checking for a reaction. He turned to Izzy, nodding his head. As agreed, they each walked toward the other's car; Izzy and the chemist to the Charger filled with methamphetamines and MaryLou to the BMW. Twenty paces past Izzy, the hair on the back of her neck rose. Something wasn't right. Dropping the bag, she threw herself to the ground, rolling to face Izzy. Before she hit the ground, Izzy and the chemist had begun firing. Intense pain tore through her shoulder and leg. Real bullets? This was supposed to be a simulation. Rolling, she squared up and fired hitting the chemist in the face. He dropped to the ground dead. Izzy had moved behind the door of the Charger, continuing to fire in her direction. She tried to run but the fiery pain in her chest and leg left her crawling on the ground. Completely exposed, she emptied her clip in a last-ditch effort to kill Izzy, taking several more shots to her chest. She couldn't believe he had lured her into his trap and now he was about to kill her. Lying on her back, gasping through the pain, Izzy stood over her.

"Looks like I win."

She struggled for a breath. "Fuck you."

"I do like your spunk, MaryLou. Shot up and me about to take the *coup de gras*, you still manage to fight back. You do remember our wager, don't you MaryLou?"

"How about getting me an ambulance?" She swiped her uninjured leg in his direction.

Izzy hopped out of the way, saying, "I get to have my way with you."

"That wasn't the wager you...pervert."

"Wasn't it?" He cocked his head, smiling. "Yes, I think it was. Roll over."

"Fuck you."

"My plan exactly." Izzy's gun exploded again, sending a searing bolt of pain through her other leg. Struggling to remain conscious, she screamed as Izzy rolled her onto her stomach with his foot. He was astride her, his weight on her back shooting pain up and down her legs, the chest wound making her breathing labored. She wanted to fight, but she felt her life slipping away. Then he leaned over her, the muzzle of his gun pressed hard against her face, his other hand grasping a fistful of her hair.

"Maybe I should just kill you. You're a cop, aren't you? A fucking cop."

"No, Izzy. Please. I'm not a cop."

Izzy rose, firing into her right and then, left arm. MaryLou screamed in agony, sobbing from the excruciating pain.

"You're about to die, MaryLou. You don't want to die a liar now, do you? You're a cop. Admit it."

MaryLou, the overwhelming pain and broken and crushed bones leaving her unable to move, gasped, then mouthed the words, "Fuck you."

"Excellent. Guns 'n Drugs override, confirmation Izzy Zydeco 031544."

The dark street vanished and her pain diminished, though she lay on the sim floor for fifteen minutes before she could roll over and sit up. Izzy handed her a bottle of Perrier.

"You're one sick fuck, Izzy Zydeco."

"Maybe so, but you have to admit, my method is much better than a lie detector. Besides, I had a great time. The look on your face when you thought I was going to rape you. Priceless. And your defiance when you knew I was going to kill you. My God, it was fantastic. This is what virtual gaming is all about. Making it real."

MaryLou's body still reacted to the virtual brutality she had experienced inside Izzy's game. She gingerly rose to her feet, slightly nauseous, her head throbbing in non-virtual pain.

"So now that you've beaten the hell out of me, what's next?"

"You want to work for me, so I've got a job for you."

"Good, because you and I are not playing anymore of your damn games."

"Ever heard of Dan Hoyt?"

MaryLou shook her head, no. Izzy handed her a thumb drive.

"This file has everything you need to know about him."

"What do you want me to do? Follow him?"

"Heavens no. I know where he is pretty much 24/7. No, I want you to kill him."

"Murder him? Why?"

He leaned over, holding her chin tightly in his right hand. "Because I told you to."

Grabbing his wrist, she forced his hand away. "I'm a method killer, Izzy. I need a reason."

He reached out for her again, only this time her elbows flashed, smacking one then the other side of his face, followed by a knee in the groan. He crashed to the ground. Before he could ball into a fetal position, MaryLou, still holding her bottle of Perrier, sat astride her squirming, anguished victim.

"Touch me again, I'll kill you." She smashed the glass bottle on the floor, holding the jagged remains.

Between gasps, he said, "I see...you...have skills."

"Yes, I do. And if you want me to put those skills to work for you, then you better stop bullshitting and tell me what you're into Mr. Zydeco." She pressed the sharp glass to his neck.

Izzy took some deep breaths, shifting under her weight, searching for a vulnerability. "Let me up and we'll talk."

"Under normal conditions, yes. But you just simulated shooting me several times at point blank range. No, you're going to tell me what you're up to or I'm going to cut your jugular like a pig at the slaughter house."

"How very...graphic." He paused, closing his eyes as if taking in the image. "Okay. Do it."

She pressed harder, a trickle of blood flowing from his neck. "Do it? You want me to kill you?"

"No, I don't want you to kill me. But I've got to say, you astride me and not knowing if I'll live another minute, it's so...intense. Yeah, do it."

Killing him could bring her mission to a close, but she couldn't be sure what wheels Izzy had spun in motion. She had to find out about Jonah, the nuclear materials, and what Hoyt had to do with whatever Izzy had planned. She rolled off him, tossing the glass away.

Izzy remained prone, a lascivious grin spreading across his face.

"I feel like we've had this intimate moment together, you know what I mean?"

"Shut up."

"Better than sex. My God, I really didn't think you were bluffing. Fantastic."

"I wasn't bluffing. I need the work. So just tell me why you need this Hoyt guy killed."

Izzy stood, brushing dust off his pant legs and arms.

"He's my business partner in a water project that includes some pipeline I'm using to move narcotics around the state. And while he's a nice enough fellow, he's not comfortable with my entrepreneurial vision. So I need him out of the way. And once I pop my little surprise, I'll have a captive market and control the flow of water and the pipeline. Do you now have sufficient information to kill him?"

"Pop your little surprise?"

"I think you know enough. Certainly enough to make you far more susceptible to accidents. You told me you have skills, so show me. Otherwise we'll be playing *Guns n' Drugs* for real."

Finding Charity

The next morning Nick found Theresa busy on the office computer.

"Morning, Nick. Think I've got a hit on our butyric acid. Coffee?"

Nick, not already armed with sufficient caffeine to alertly decline, took the offered cup filled with a thicker than normal brown sludge he had never associated with the word coffee. Taking a sip, the astringent, gritty liquid chemically stripped his mouth of all moisture. Why couldn't he find an employee who made a decent cup of coffee?

"You know Theresa, isn't it a bit sexist for you to be making the coffee all the time?"

"What? I was here so I made some. You'd do the same."

"Well, maybe not exactly the same." Nick set the cup down casually, hoping to "accidentally" let the murky liquid get cold.

"No worries, Nick. Don't mind at all."

Nick hoped the bitter taste would ease soon. "I'm thinking of investing in one of those coffee makers with the pre-packaged ground coffee. Bit of a splurge, but I think we're worth it."

"You kidding, Nick? I'm fine with what we've got."

"Are you?"

"And those fancy machines always mean extra maintenance cost. You're the boss, but don't do it on my account. Don't forget your cup." She picked up Nick's cup, handing it back to him.

"Sure, not on your account. Uh, the acid. You had a hit?"

"Yeah." Theresa turned the computer monitor so Nick could see the screen. "Two days before the attack, this woman purchased a liter of the stuff from AusTex Lab Supply. The clerk remembered her because she asked if he had anything more foul than butyric acid, she paid cash, and the woman's red hair."

"Charity."

"Charity? No, she's not buying chemicals for a 501 3c Nick, she—"

"No, I mean her name is Charity."

"You know her?"

"I've met her a couple times now. The first time happened to be the same morning of the attack on Hoyt's car. She had a flat on her bike and I gave her a ride out by Mount Bonnell. I'd say it was a coincidence if it wasn't for the surveillance tape."

"And the second time?"

"She had a breakdown on her bike a quarter-mile from my house last night." Nick looked over at Theresa's raised eyebrows. "I agree. Pretty damn suspicious."

Theresa stepped over to the bulletin board, removing the two $10 bills they had wagered earlier. "Looks like we have a winner."

"Yeah, okay. I guess you were right about a woman using a tampon."

She pocketed the bills. "You think she might be one of Hoyt's old girlfriends intent on retribution?"

"She doesn't look the type, but maybe Hoyt's taste in women is broader than we think."

Theresa took a sip of coffee, making Nick unconsciously grimace. "What do you think she was doing at your place?"

"Good question. Maybe she knows I'm looking into Hoyt's Ferrari and decided to get a closer look."

"Maybe her mechanical breakdown didn't happen by accident. Sounds like a woman with a plan."

Nick set his thick brew back on the table. "Let's go see Hoyt and find out what he has to say about this Charity."

He moved quickly for the door, Theresa's voice trailing off behind him. "Want a travel mug for your coffee, Nick?"

~*~

Hoyt sat at his desk watching a large flat screen against one wall of his office. In the grainy surveillance tape a tall, redheaded woman stepped to the counter of Hill Country Outfitters. She spoke briefly to the clerk who then walked away from her for a couple of minutes and then returned holding several bottles. The woman, paying cash, walked out of the store with a bag containing the bottles. The image froze at a close-up side view of the suspect. Nick knew the woman in the video was definitely the woman who had introduced herself to him as Charity.

Hoyt frowned, leaning back in his chair. "So who the hell is this woman?"

Nick looked over to Hoyt. "You've never seen her before? Maybe a past girlfriend?"

"Nope. She's not anyone I know."

"A one-night stand then?"

"I've got video of most of those. So you could check if you like."

Theresa looked as if some foul smell had entered the room. "You're kidding. You have video of the women you sleep with?"

Hoyt leaned into his desk. "Don't give me a disgusted look. You wouldn't believe how many women want to have a night of wild sex with a successful entrepreneur, then the next morning, after consulting their attorneys, decide I might want to pony up some cash so they won't tell the police I sexually assaulted them. If you want to accuse me of assault, you're going to have to explain why the video shows you having such a good time."

Nick noticed Theresa's grip on her chair tightening, a tigress ready to rip out the throat of her prey. He pressed on. "Then maybe a friend of a girlfriend?"

Hoyt stood, walking around the desk pondering Nick's question. "A friend of a girlfriend? Hell, maybe…, but I've got to say Nick, I've never seen her before." He smiled slyly at Theresa. "Would you like to view my video archives? Maybe you can find her in there somewhere."

Nick stepped between them. "I think your word you've never seen the woman is good enough for us. Let's go, Theresa." Nick made sure to keep himself between their misogynist client and his indignant colleague until they had cleared the doorway and were walking back to the car.

"What a slimy, sick sonofabitch. I can't believe he's our client." Theresa mimicked Hoyt's voice, "Want to watch my videos?" She yanked the car door open. "I'll watch your videos you misogynist bastard, right up your ass until there's not enough light to make out the pictures."

Nick got into the driver's side of the pickup, Theresa dropping in the passenger seat, slamming the door behind her.

"You done, Theresa?"

"Done? How about we go to the AusTex Lab Supply so I can get a couple of gallons of butyric acid. I don't want Charity to have all the fun."

"So you're not done?"

"Yes, I'm done. Dammit! Don't I look like I'm done? That sonofabitch. Yes, I'm done. Damn!"

Nick drove silently, giving Theresa some time to cool down from her encounter with Hoyt. At every turn Charlie's assessment seemed on target. Dan Hoyt was definitely an asshole.

Theresa broke the silence. "So, what's the next move, Nick? We know who damaged Hoyt's car, but how do we find her?"

"For some reason she's found me twice, Theresa. I'm thinking she just might come right to us."

"And if you're wrong?"

"Well, I imagine our client will be pretty pissed at us."

"Excellent. Sounds like a win-win either way."

Dry Well

"Izzy, we need to talk."

Ever since his conversation with Nate about the state of the plant, Hoyt had been dreading this call. He knew Izzy would try to make him squirm, even beg a bit, to get his help in making the plant look like it was online. However, as a successful entrepreneur in his own right, Hoyt felt a renewed confidence. He needed Izzy, to be sure, but Izzy also needed him. Without the plant and the pipeline, Izzy's drug transport scheme was just an idea. Yes, Izzy needed Daniel Hoyt to make his idea a reality.

"Why hello, Hoyt. Decided to take me up on my offer?"

"Let's just say I can see the possibilities. Why don't you and I get together to discuss, Izzy?"

"Sure. I'll put you through to my assistant and we can meet in my office."

Hoyt almost agreed, his need for Izzy's help being so great, but then he caught himself.

"Yes, um, about that. I'd rather meet on more neutral ground."

"Neutral ground? I thought we were partners, Hoyt. What's all this about neutral ground?"

"Look, Izzy, I want us to work together, but every time we meet at your place I end up inside one those damn games of yours fighting for my life."

"Yes, they're loads of fun, aren't they?"

"Yeah, big laughs. But I don't have time for it."

"No time for some fun? What's happened to my carefree playboy of a business partner?"

"How about El Arroyo at 8 tonight?"

"El Arroyo? I suppose if we're not meeting at my office, slopping down a big plate of barbecued chicken enchiladas and a beer might be the next best thing. A rather public meeting place though. Do you feel the need for witnesses?"

Absolutely. The last thing Hoyt wanted was to be alone in a room with Izzy Zydeco. "Witnesses? Witnesses to me slamming down those enchiladas maybe. See you at 8."

Hoyt arrived at the restaurant, an old single-story wood-framed building straddling a dried up stream bed on 5th Street, a few minutes early to scope out a table where he could sit with his back to the wall and have a view of the whole patio. He realized, with some satisfaction, that all the time he had spent watching westerns and procedural crime dramas might pay off on this night. He anticipated where an attack might come from and scoped out all the exits. By the time Izzy walked onto the patio, Hoyt figured he had complete control of the situation. He motioned to Izzy, who came over.

"Hoyt, I told the waitress we want to move to the table by the tree. No sense being tucked into the corner like this."

Before Hoyt could protest, Izzy stepped over to a table under a large live oak tree. Hoyt, perturbed at how easily Izzy walked all over his best-laid plans, picked up his beer and sat down. Izzy now had his back to the restaurant, while Hoyt's seat exposed him to the entire patio and part of the street.

Dammit.

A cute twenty-something with a silver nose ring in one nostril and the hint of a tattoo above her right breast took their order, returning in a few short minutes with steaming plates of enchiladas.

"So Hoyt, you wanted to talk. Talk."

"I've been thinking about your proposal. The pipeline?"

"The pipeline wasn't a proposal, Hoyt. I told you what I was going to do. You're either okay with it, or you're not."

"So you think you can just tell me what you're going to do with my pipeline?" Hoyt immediately realized while he meant every word, he didn't mean for Izzy to hear any of it. "What I mean is…"

Izzy held a fork full of barbecued chicken enchiladas suspended in mid-bite, molten yellow cheese dripping in long threads back to his plate.

"What exactly do you mean, Hoyt?"

"What I mean is when I first heard your idea for the pipeline—you know—getting in business with the Diablos, I thought about it in terms of legalities."

"Legalities." Izzy swooped his fork to gather some of the cheese threads before placing the bite into his mouth.

"You can understand, Izzy. I spent the better part of two years in constant litigation over my Sin City developments and then when the condo had some structural issues, the city decided to take me to court, as well. So I'm a little gun shy of anything that might bring on serious legal issues."

"So what changed your mind?"

"Well, yes, the Diablos do have a reputation and what you're talking about doing, transporting drugs through the pipeline, is definitely illegal. However, I have a greater need, a greater good, if you will."

"Hoyt, can we just cut through the crap. Get to your point."

Hoyt hesitated while their waitress arrived with another round of

Coronas. "My point, Izzy, is that for the sake of the people of Texas I want to agree to help you in your use of the pipeline."

"Good."

"But…"

"Excuse me?"

"I need some assistance from you in order to make the pipeline functional."

Izzy squeezed a slice of lime into his beer, then stuffed the citrus into the clear bottle. "What are you talking about?"

"The plant. I just recently learned the desalination plant will not be online in time to meet our agreements with the state and our investors. If the plant is not online, then we don't have water flowing. And if there's no water, there's very little reason to send PIGs through the pipe."

"What?" Izzy's raised voice carried over a Stevie Ray Vaughn song playing in the background, quieting all the nearby tables as they reacted to his shout. He wiped his mouth with a napkin, leaned in and spoke softly. "How do you ever make a dime? You screw up everything."

"I'm an entrepreneur, Izzy, I—"

"Shut up. You're telling me the plant won't generate water?"

"It will. Eventually. Just not by the deadline. So I need your help."

"What do you want, a rain dance?"

"We just need a secure location where we can drill into an aquifer and pump water into the pipeline until the plant is online."

"Won't someone notice you're draining an aquifer?"

"We'll be in and out before they know it. Nate tells me we'll have the plant online inside six months."

"And what makes you think I can help?"

"Izzy, I'm aware of the land you own, some of it right on top of key aquifers. And, with your connection to the Diablos, we'd have a built-in security force."

"So we help each other. Is that the gist of your proposal tonight, Hoyt?"

"Yes, that's it. I help you with your package transportation idea and you help me with the water. Whaddaya say?"

Izzy took a long pull from his beer. "I say you're going to shut up and obediently go along with the Diablos arrangement. Since I'm providing the water to keep the desalination plant afloat, I will increase my ownership in the business to eighty percent."

"Eighty percent? Don't be crazy, man. No one in their right mind would agree to give away that much of the business."

"What would be reasonable, Hoyt?"

"I was thinking in exchange for my support of the pipeline deal you would solve the water issue. We're both doing what we need to do to keep the business afloat." Hoyt waited for Izzy's response, but instead he dabbed his lips with his napkin and precisely arranged his knife and spoon by the plate.

"Izzy, fair enough?"

Izzy slapped the table several times with a finger. "Of course it is Hoyt. I was just yanking your chain. You see, like you, I want to do something big, something really significant and water plays a key role."

"I'm glad to hear it, Izzy."

"Your house sits on top of the aquafer too, doesn't it Hoyt?"

"Yes, but—"

"Here's how it will go down. I'll send my man to your compound tonight. We'll drill from inside of your house."

"My compound? What the hell are you talking about? You can't drill in the middle of my house. That's crazy."

"Exactly. No one will ever look for a drilling operation in your house." "Izzy."

"You're either in or you're out, Hoyt. Which is it? I'm drilling through your house either way. I want that pipeline. And as you say, there's no pipeline without water."

"Shit. You sonofabitch."

Izzy smiled, standing. The meeting apparently had come to a conclusion. Hoyt rose, extending his hand, but Izzy had already walked past him toward the exit. His stomached churned from stress and a burning sensation crawled up his throat. He reminded himself the reason he made the big money was partly due to his ability to deal with people, unpredictable, dangerous people, like Izzy. Yes, he had involved himself with the most dangerous drug cartel in Texas. Yes, the evil sonofabitch was about to drill a hole right through his house. However, he had kept his vision of water for Texas alive. At least long enough to pull some cash out of this deal. He hoped.

Safe Cycling Association Fan Site

Broken headlight. When stopped by police, remotely shattered a fifth of bourbon in back of cab. #5 had to take a breathalyzer and walk the line: 3 Stars
Comments:
Jimmy Schmidt—an oldie but a goodie :-)
Tina Wong—nice, BTW go to my page to see new pics of my doggie in elf costume!
Olivia Darson—thanks for including pic of #5 walking the line. Makes a great screensaver.

Super glued wipers to windshield: 3 stars
Comments:
Amando Salvetti—how perfect is that!
Pete Wilson—sorry, but this one's pretty lame. You get half a star from me. That's OK. You can't hit a home run every time at bat.
Safe Cycling Association—Pete Wilson, effective immediately, you have been unfriended. The SCA is committed to promoting a carbon free world. You clearly, by your recent derogatory comments, have NO UNDERSTANDING OF GLOBAL WARMING, CARBON EMISSIONS, OR GOOD MANNERS.

Tied up a vicious dog in the bed of the truck: 3 stars
Comments:
Olivia Darson—There's no such thing as a vicious dog, only vicious dog owners. So I love the idea, but tying up the dog of vicious owner would be a better way to state it.
Amando Salvetti—I'll bet he peed himself! #5, not the dog.
Tina Wong—Was the dog in costume? And if so, do you have pics?
Pearl Schultz—New to the page, but I like where it's going. Some of these seem kind of mean though. :-(
Safe Cycling Association—We at the SCA have noticed an increase in criticism and lower scores of the actions taken against known carbon spewers. If you continue to not support the cause, admin will remove you from the list. And to the comment that some of our actions are mean, would you have us coddle carbon spewers? Is that the kind of world you really want to live in? Really?

Hung truck one hundred feet in the air from a construction site crane. See local news footage of the truck dangling in the air www.ktexnews/local/truckonastring: 5 Stars

Comments:

Amando Salvetti—Genius!!!!

Pearl Schultz—Wow. The SCA rocks!

Tina Wong—Talk about outing a carbon spewer! BRILLIANT

Olivia Darson—Would you like to fly in my carbon spewing truck, way up in the sky in my carbon spewing truck, we could float away together, you and I, we can fly, we can fly! Up, up and away in my carbon spewing truck…la, la, la, la, la

Jimmy Schmidt—I bow to your greatness o vengeful one!

Gus Garcia—Don't know what U got planned next 4 this guy, but its going 2 have 2 B pretty awesome 2 top this. You da best SCA!!!

Epic

Hoyt's irate Texas twang greeted Nick as soon as he opened the front door of the Compound.

"Goddammit, Sibelius. You're supposed to keep this crap from happening to me. I mean, what the hell am I paying you for?

As Nick walked through the foyer into the great room, he saw Hoyt in cowboy boots, burnt orange shorts with a white UT Longhorn emblazoned on one leg and a white straw Resistol cowboy hat atop his head. A gold chain slapped on his bare chest as he putted golf balls like a hockey forward making a slap shot to goal.

Hoyt didn't look up from his putter. "Do you know where I found my pickup this morning? Do you have any fucking idea?" He didn't slow down for a response. "Don't watch the local news? I found my pickup a hundred fucking feet in the air hanging by a cable on a construction crane downtown. Not only did this bastard damage my truck..." He toed another golf ball into position. "Do you have any idea what kind of a horse's ass I look like with my goddamn truck hanging by its *cajones* in the middle of downtown?"

Nick tried not to smile at the image of Hoyt's dangling truck, but failed.

Hoyt took another whack. The small dimpled ball ricocheted off the stone fireplace, sofa, a wall, and the coffee table, then disappeared under another sofa.

"You've had...what...how many days to find this bastard?"

"A bit over forty-eight hours."

Hoyt tossed his putter to the floor.

"Forty-eight fucking hours? I thought you were some big shot investigator. I'm beginning to think you couldn't find cow shit in a barnyard."

Nick sat on the arm of one of the leather sofas.

"When you decide to calm down, we'll talk. So go ahead and get it out of your system."

"No wonder your wife had her a well-hung trauma doc on the side. She probably had to stick a grenade up your ass to get a goddamn reaction."

Nick stood. His eye caught the putter on the floor, an easy reach away.

"Choose your words carefully, Hoyt."

"Oh, now I get a reaction. I get it. I've got to talk about fucking your ex to get a rise out—"

Hoyt clearly hadn't expected the right hook Nick landed on his face which spun him around and over a large lounge chair, wide-brimmed hat flying into the air. For a moment Nick thought he might have hit him a bit too hard for a client, given the lack of sound or movement. He hit bad guys at one hundred ten percent, but figured a paying client should be in the seventy to eighty percent range. Hoyt moaned and began to move.

"I think you've said enough today, don't you Hoyt?"

Hoyt crawled on all fours, shaking his head like a bull with twenty *banderillas* in his neck.

"Now let's talk about your situation."

Hoyt pulled himself up. "Are you out of your…"

Nick gave him a dead calm stare which had the desired effect of shutting him up.

"Let's be clear about what's happening, Hoyt. You're an asshole, therefore, most of the state of Texas wants to bury you. You've apparently got a serial stalker slash harasser who has made it their life's work to torment you. If you weren't my client, I'd be making a donation to the cause. Because you've refused my assistance in setting up any kind of meaningful security at your home, you have been repeatedly targeted by this person. Until I figure out who's after you, you'll be an active target. Do you understand what I'm saying?"

Hoyt had righted the lounge chair and now sat rubbing his chin where Nick had impacted him with his fist.

"Yeah, I understand. But what you don't understand is you're nobody to me." He spat the words out like small darts. "All I've got is a recommendation from my goddamn mechanic. I'm supposed to trust you because my mechanic likes you? Fuck that! And by the way, punching me in the face is not a trust-building activity."

"Then if not me, get someone else to secure your house."

"Pretty good punch, Sibelius. I wonder how you'd do if I expected it?"

"We can arrange it, if you'd like." Nick hoped Hoyt would say yes.

He looked at Nick, as if making an assessment before deciding. "Naw, at least not right now."

Nick, having been focused on Hoyt and his criticism, noticed chalk marks on the walls and the initials D. H. with an arrow pointing to a circle, about a foot in diameter, on the floor.

"What's with the chalk marks on the floor? Remodeling?"

"None of your goddamn business."

"Okay Hoyt. Then let's talk about what needs to happen next."

"What, you want to sucker punch me again?"

Nick let the sarcastic remark roll by. "I want you to come with me to your house on Island Palms, where I'll do a complete security inventory. Then you're going to stay in your house and only leave with body guards."

Hoyt stood, leaning over for his hat, which he placed back on his head. "I'm Dan Hoyt. I don't cower. People run from *me*."

"At least get your house secure, Hoyt. I can't be everywhere and as long as you're vulnerable, your stalker will find a way to get to you."

~*~

Since Charlie would have the Ferrari for at least a couple of months and the truck had axle damage from the crane-dangling incident, Nick drove Hoyt to his house in his small pickup. Hoyt kept fidgeting with his seat and seatbelt, as if he couldn't locate a comfortable position. Then having finally settled somewhat, he explored the glove box.

"Now we're talking a piece of iron." Hoyt held a Glock Nick kept in the glove box as one of his backup weapons. "So, you kill anybody with this?"

"Put the gun back, Hoyt."

"But you've killed with it, haven't you? I can tell." He put his nose to the corner of the muzzle, sniffing.

"Hoyt, if you're not happy with your nose, you keep it up. Otherwise, put the gun in the glove box."

"Okay, okay. But you have killed with it, haven't you?"

Nick looked at Hoyt's smirk of a smile, directed the gun into the glovebox with his eyes, then stared at the traffic ahead.

"It's been used. Only when necessary. And it's not made of iron." Nick looked forward again, this time more focused on when using his gun had been necessary, than the traffic around him. "Don't ever touch one of my guns again without my permission, Hoyt. Clear?"

"You've turned into a bit of a hard-ass, Nick. When we first met you were all puppy eyes and painful memories. You've gone all Clint Eastwood on me."

"Yeah, Hoyt. Make my day."

"See?" Hoyt turned, slapping the dash with enthusiasm. "That's what I'm talking about. Don't get me wrong now. I love it. Makes the bad guys piss their pants. So Nick, one-on-one, you might have the upper hand with me. But you fuck with me again and I'll have your ass pulled through a meat grinder by an honest-to-God butcher. And if you don't think I'm up for it, you just try me."

"I really don't know why I agreed to work for you, Hoyt. You are one of the most self-involved, nasty bastards I've known in a while—and I've known some nasty bastards."

Hoyt laughed, shaking his head. "Nick, Nick. You need the money. It's okay. Just say it. Hell, my entire professional life is based on the need of money. I need money, my investors need money, the government pricks I need to do my deals need money, we all need money. And I might be a nasty bastard, but I'm a damn successful nasty bastard. And after this next deal, you're going to be blown away with the vastness of my success. Epic. That's what it's going to be, Nick. Epic."

"Epic. Hmmm. The chalk marks have anything to do with your epic success?"

"You just don't let things go, do you? I've told you to drop it and you just keep coming back to it."

Nick drove down Island Palms Road towards Hoyt's house.

Hoyt pulled his keys from a pants pocket. "Park in the garage, I've got the remote on my key chain."

Hoyt raised the remote fob toward a large garage door…

The explosion hit them with a thud, followed by a roar, as the air pressure changed, blowing the truck backward, a sudden flash of fire erupting from the garage along with shrapnel of glass, wood, and metal pummeling the truck in what seemed like all directions. A two-by-four missile impaled the windshield, narrowly missing Hoyt, embedding itself in the upholstered seat back of the cab. Nick and Hoyt sat in shock, the the garage aflame, the lawn billowing white smoke and the smell of burning rubber and oil choking the cabin of air.

"We've…got…to…get…out." Nick looked at Hoyt, who appeared to be partially conscious, his ears bleeding. Nick opened the driver side door. Flames licked up from under the hood, blistering paint on its way to the windscreen. Getting out of the truck, reached over, releasing Hoyt's seatbelt, and pulled him across the seat and out the door. Then holding him under the arms, Nick dragged him into the street and away from the fire, just as the truck's fuel tank exploded.

Hoyt rolled onto his back mumbling something about Jesus. He took a deep breath and put several words together. "Find this…sonofabitch."

Nick looked at his burning truck. Sure, it was a beater, but it was his only mode of transportation. He'd have to get a taxi home and find another vehicle first thing in the morning, while he tried to find out who seemed so intent on killing Hoyt. He looked at his client, a little worse for wear. His intuition told him—hell, who needed intuition? Hoyt's "epic" venture had something to do with this.

"Yeah, I'll get right on it, Hoyt."

A Quiet Walk

After the firetrucks pulled away, the police finished questioning Nick about the explosion, and EMS bandaged his shoulder, he sat on the curb at the side of Hoyt's still smoldering husk of a house. Something about coming so close to death reminded him of Theresa. He needed to talk to her, to hear her voice, to feel grounded. Hoyt had a limo coming, so while they waited he dialed her number.

"Theresa, Nick. I'm coming back from Hoyt's."

"Any new leads?"

"You could call it a lead. Someone blew Hoyt's house all to hell and back."

"What? Really?...Figures."

"That's all you've got to say?"

"Well you don't have to get snippy about it, Nick. Why did you call again?"

"I just wanted tell you I almost got killed in a massive explosion."

"Oh, my God. Are you okay?"

"Yes I'm okay." Nick raised his voice in irritation. "We're talking aren't we?" He took a breath. This conversation had not gone where he had hoped and he wasn't altogether sure why. "I...I just wanted to hear your voice Theresa." Nick listened to her breathing, steady, slow, soft, wanting to hold the moment in time.

"Are you there, Nick?"

"Yeah, I'm here."

"Why don't we meet for a drink? Sounds like you could use one and I think I'd like to see you."

"A drink sounds good, but I don't want you to go out of your way." His voice dripped with sarcasm. "I'm sure you've got things to do."

"I think I'd like to be sure you're all in one piece."

"Hoyt's got a limo coming to take him to the Four Seasons. If you'll give me a lift home, I can meet you at the hotel bar."

"Sure, Nick. See you in a few minutes."

~*~

Walking into the bar, Nick found Theresa sitting on a bar stool sipping a margarita. He didn't know if the explosion had somehow heightened his senses, but she looked especially beautiful tonight in jeans and a tee. She motioned to him and then turned to say something to the bartender. By the time Nick made it to the bar, a bourbon on the rocks sat on a napkin waiting for him. Theresa's smiling face dissolved into concern as he approached. Nick hadn't looked in a mirror. He hoped he wasn't in as bad a shape as her furrowed brow suggested.

"Jesus, Nick. I didn't...Are you okay?"

Nick took a sip of Jack, letting the burn of alcohol slide down his throat. "Yeah, I'm okay. The medics said everything was superficial."

She very lightly touched his face, pulling back when Nick winced. "Sorry, Nick. Jesus. I probably sounded a little unconcerned on the phone."

"Well, you did sound a bit...objective."

"Yeah, sorry. I'd give you a kiss, but I'm not sure what part of your face doesn't hurt."

Nick looked into Theresa's dark eyes, concern etched across her face, a vein gently pulsating at the side of her throat. He touched his lips with one finger. "You're probably safe here."

Theresa cocked her head with a slight smile, then leaned over, gently touching her lips to his. He opened his mouth slightly, but she had pulled back. He felt like a man dying in the desert allowed to touch his lips to a cup of water, but not drink. She rested a hand on his. Her fingers traced his swollen knuckles.

"Looks like you've been punching hard objects."

"Hoyt."

"You hit our client?" She laughed, her eyes sparkling with delight. He loved the way a laugh poured out of her. "About time."

Nick took her hand in his. A large group of convention-goers several drinks into a party crowded around the bar, raising the decibel level high enough to make a conversation difficult.

"You up for a walk, Theresa? The idea of a quiet walk outside sounds really nice right now."

They left the bar and walked a lit path towards a running trail by Lady Bird Lake. Taking the crushed granite trail under Congress Avenue bridge, they crossed the lake on the 1st Street bridge, then made their way to the water's edge by a small pavilion. The city glistened across the lake's mirrored surface.

"Theresa, I..." He took in a breath. "Thanks for meeting me tonight. It means a lot."

"We're partners. Besides, you sounded like you could use a friend."

They walked together another fifty yards in silence, only cicadas rasping in the night air and traffic rumbling on the bridge. Nick stopped, taking Theresa's hand.

"Nick, what are you doing?"

"I want you to know I like you, Theresa. Very much."

In spite of the city's night rhythm of traffic, passing conversations and club music drifting across the dark water, Nick only heard her exhale.

"Theresa."

She took a step back. "Nick, when I first met you, I didn't want to be the rebound from your divorce. And to be honest, I stayed away because I didn't want to be the rebound from MaryLou."

"And now?"

"I'm not sure. You tell me. I know MaryLou is dead, but are you ready for a relationship?"

Nick wanted to tell her he was over MaryLou. How could he not be? She lied to him about her name and identity, threatened to kill him, made him think she was dead for months and after getting a one-line email message, hadn't seen or heard from her. He knew she was out there, somewhere, but he needed to get on with his life. Time to move on.

"Yeah. I'm over her."

Theresa put a hand on Nick's chest. He felt like she had some sort of direct connection to his heart, to his truth.

"I hear the words Nick, but something tells me you're not quite done."

Nick sighed, resigned to the power of her hand on his heart and the reality she was probably right. At least for now.

"Right. Well, I'd never tell you to ignore your intuition."

"Besides Nick, what about the business?"

"What about it?"

"I've got a girlfriend who started a restaurant with her husband. Soon all they had in common with each other was the job. And when the marriage fell apart, so did the business. Now she's a chef in somebody else's kitchen."

Nick, painfully aware of the vagaries of marriage and divorce had no rational comeback.

"There's always an exception, Theresa."

"Why don't we focus on making our business successful, while you get this thing about MaryLou sorted out. One day at a time."

They stood looking at each other, Nick wanting this woman, to kiss her, to hold her. Maybe he didn't love her—yet. But he wanted what he had lost when MaryLou punctured his solitude. He wondered if Theresa would still be patiently waiting for him if she knew he lived the lie of MaryLou's death.

"You're right. One day at a time partner."

He hugged her, then Nick felt her tense up and step away.

"I'm sorry Theresa. I'll back off."

"Looks like we have company."

"What?" Nick turned to see a figure duck into the shadows of the 1st Street bridge. A woman with red hair. "Charity? It's Charity, Theresa. I'll go follow the trail. Why don't you get on the bridge to keep her from leaving that way."

As Nick ran to follow her, he couldn't see into the shadows under the bridge, but footfalls rhythmically padded farther down the trail. Charity ran faster than he thought she would have been capable with her hip, but not fast enough.

He shouted after her. "Charity."

The woman kept running. Nick closed the distance, continuing to shout her name, only she ran faster. He knew he couldn't stay with her much longer, so he broke into a sprint, his legs and lungs burning. When he thought he couldn't go on, he leapt, a lunging tackle his high school football coach would have admired. The woman screamed, kicking and hitting as they crashed to the ground. He managed to get astride her, pinning her arms. Her knees pounded into his back as she tried to bite his arms.

"Get off of me, you son of a bitch!"

Nick realized within seconds the screaming, writhing blond-haired woman he held firmly to the ground was not Charity. He jumped up.

"I'm really sorry."

She screamed at him, fumbling for a pepper spray cartridge on her running belt. "Fucking pervert. Get away from me. Help! Somebody help me!"

Then Nick heard Theresa shout. "Charity. Stop. Charity."

Turning away, his jogger continued yelling. "Yeah, you better run you sick fuck. Help! Police!"

He ran back to the 1st Street bridge, finding Theresa sitting at the side of the bridge out of breath. "Are you okay?"

"Yeah, I think so. Sorry, Nick. I let her get past me."

Seeing a cyclist in the distance across the bridge, part of him wanted to continue the pursuit.

"Go on, Nick. I'm okay."

He knelt. "Let me help you up."

"But Nick."

Theresa's jeans were torn and an elbow bloodied.

"We'll catch up to her again. You okay?"

Nick helped Theresa to her feet and kept an arm around her, both to steady her and because he liked the feeling of having his arm around her.

Theresa kept her arm around him too.

"I saw her come up to the sidewalk with a road bike and ran across the street shouting her name, planning on tackling her to the ground. I was running behind her, almost had her, when she tossed what I think was a handful of ball bearings. Soon as I hit those I went down. Can you believe it? Ball bearings."

"Yes, with Charity I can definitively believe she would have ball bearings. She's a rather unusual woman."

By the time they got back to the hotel, then Theresa's car, she had shaken off most of the effect of her run-in with Charity. "If Charity is stalking Hoyt, why would she be following us?"

Nick closed the passenger door behind him. "For some reason, Charity decides to torment Hoyt, which culminates in her blowing up his house."

"So you think Charity torched his house?"

"I'm just trying to think this through. A big explosion doesn't quite have the touch of finesse she brings to her actions. Let's come back to it. So Charity keeps attacking Hoyt, then she shows up around me, twice."

Theresa pulled out of the hotel garage, driving through a mostly deserted downtown to the highway. "She made you."

"I'd agree, but the first time I didn't know I'd be working for Hoyt."

"So the first was an accidental meeting and then she discovers you're working for Hoyt, so she starts to stalk you."

Turning onto I35, a part of Nick's brain scanned a Tequila billboard ad. "But it's different, isn't it? She hasn't damaged anything or tried to intimidate me."

"I'm going to assume you're not ignoring the fact she threw a handful of steel ball bearings at me."

"Right, but just to escape. She hasn't taken the kind of actions against me that she has with Hoyt. But you're right. She's made us."

"What about the explosion? You said it didn't have her touch."

"Charity seems to like creating damage, but she hasn't been attacking victims lethally."

Theresa changed lanes, then took an exit at Airport Blvd to the Mueller neighborhood. "So, someone else is gunning for our boy Hoyt?"

"Yeah, and I think he knows who it is."

"Something to do with his desalination plant?"

"He called it his epic venture." Nick felt bone-tired. "I tell you what, Theresa. Let's sleep on it." She raised her eyebrows. "Separately. And then come back together in the morning. Maybe some of the pieces will begin to fall into place with a little rest."

"Sounds like a plan, Nick."

"One problem."

"What?"

"You've just driven us to your apartment."

She looked to her modern four-story condo, then sighed with a slight laugh. "I've got a sleeper sofa. You *can* handle being in the same space without going all crazy on me?"

"It will be touch and go, but I think I can manage."

"Good. That way we can both get a little more sleep and I'll swing you by your place in the morning."

The Meeting's A Hit

Nick didn't know exactly why he agreed to stay at Theresa's apartment. All night long he spent his time listening to her breathing, the barest hint of a snore, the bed spring creaking when she turned, her footsteps padding across the floor first to the bathroom and then into the kitchen. Cabinet doors opening and closing, coffee being made. He must have slept some, but all he could remember were her sounds, the sounds of her life all around him.

"Nick."

He opened his eyes to Theresa holding a mug of steaming coffee over him. He elbowed his way to a sitting position.

She pushed the mug toward him. "Good morning. How'd you sleep?"

"Great. Very comfortable sofa bed." He reached for the mug with one hand, touching her hand with the other. Nick noticed she didn't pull her hand away.

"Give me about thirty minutes, Nick, and I'll be ready to go."

"Sit with me for a few minutes. Can't have a guest drink coffee all by himself."

She cocked her head, as if assessing the situation, then sat beside him. Her warmth and something Nick could only equate with a spring garden enveloped him. He took a sip of coffee, girding himself against the bitterness he knew awaited him. Miraculously, the brew had hints of chocolate and deep-roasted beans.

"You made this? I mean, you made this...this really great cup of coffee."

She laughed, her eyes sparkling in morning light filtering through the windows. "Yes, I did. A new coffee pot. I'm a 'toss some beans in a saucepan and boil some water' kind of girl, but the sales guy talked me into it."

Nick wanted her, needed her. He wanted to turn the page on MaryLou and this beautiful, capable woman now sat beside him in a sleeping shirt, her long, smooth legs curled underneath her. If anyone could help him move past MaryLou, Theresa was the woman. "You are a lovely, lovely lady."

She rose from the sofa, the sleeping shirt clinging to her panties, then falling back to her thigh. She leaned over, kissing Nick's forehead. "What am I doing?" She wiped her kiss away with a thumb, awkward and nervous. "I'm really sorry, Nick. Habit, I guess."

He took her wrist in his hand, pulling her toward him. "You habitually wipe kisses off house guests?"

"No, I...I don't know. Nick."

Their lips touched, Nick running his fingers past her ear, through her hair. She leaned into him, kissing him on his lips, their mouths parting, tongues touching gently. Then she pulled away, her eyes searching his.

"I guess I better get ready."

He watched her walk away, in his mind, naked in heels on a windswept plain. In reality, barefoot in a yellow sleeping shirt with smiley face palm trees doing a dance with grinning dolphins. He needed to let the idea of MaryLou go. Theresa didn't strike him as the type of woman who would wait around for long.

~*~

After dropping by his trailer for some fresh clothes, they drove to a used car lot where Nick made the "deal of a lifetime" on a 1965 Chevy El Camino, complete with a Virgin Mother bobblehead on the dashboard. With one hundred sixty-five thousand miles and a rebuilt transmission, he figured he got a great deal for $500. If the business took off, he'd get Charlie to restore the car and if not, an old, broken-down El Camino would be the only thing he'd be able to afford anyway. Parting ways, Theresa went back to the office to do more research on Charity, while Nick went back to the Four Seasons to meet with Hoyt. Before he could get to the hotel, he got a call from Theresa.

"Nick, I think I've got something useful about Charity. I just found a Facebook page for the Bicycle Safety Association. The owner of the site posts actions taken against, and I quote, 'carbon spewers' and the most recent posting sounds exactly like what has happened to Hoyt right down to the Ferrari, the lobsters, and the dangling pickup truck."

"Charity posts her exploits online?"

"There's more. The posts definitely confirm we're right about her, but it's also interesting what's not posted. For example, nothing about Hoyt's house blowing up."

"Maybe she hasn't posted yet?"

"I thought that too, so I went back and checked the time gap between the events with Hoyt and the postings. She has consistently posted within a few hours. Waiting for the next day would not be her usual process."

"In other words..."

"In other words, your intuition may be right. Someone else may be gunning for Hoyt."

Nick walked down the stairs of the Four Seasons to the Riverside Cafe passing a couple on the way. Only when he got to the bottom of the stairs did his brain register something odd. He looked to the top of the stairs watching them walk away.

There's something familiar about the woman. MaryLou? No, couldn't be. Come on, Nick. You're working on four hours of sleep. You're seeing things. Besides, if she were in Austin, surely she'd let you know.

When he thought she had died he had done this—seeing her in a crowd, at the store, at a distance. He even pulled a Doctor Zhivago once, Yuri chasing after his lost love Lara. The woman, whose height and hair color matched MaryLou's, was a schoolteacher from Dallas with, considering the circumstances, an understanding husband.

He walked into the Cafe to see Hoyt in a very engaged conversation with a woman in her forties or early fifties. Definitively not Hoyt's typical female companion. The woman lacked the usual Hoyt-worship behavior, a behavior in young women Nick attributed to his money, since he never tried to hide he was an asshole. She had to be either his mother or the mother of one of the women he screwed over. Hoyt, seeing Nick approach, stood to greet him. Nick now had two pieces of dissonant information: Hoyt with an older woman and Hoyt with manners.

"Nick, good to see you." He stepped out from around the table. "And let me introduce you to the governor, Francis Adamson. Governor, Nick Sibelius."

The governor had the beauty of a woman who aged well and had a confident power about her. She shook Nick's hand firmly, looking him right in the eye.

"Good to see you, Nick."

"I don't believe we've met before."

She frowned doubtfully. "Possibly. In any case, I need to be on my way." She gave Hoyt a look which could have frozen molten rock, then turned back to Nick. "Very good to see you again."

Nick and Hoyt watched the Governor leave, as she paused at one table to shake hands then made her way out of the cafe. Hoyt motioned for Nick to take a seat and the waiter to come to the table.

"What'll you have, Nick?"

"Coffee is fine."

"Nothing to eat?"

"What's with the governor?"

Hoyt told the waiter to bring a french press of coffee and then turned to Nick.

"She's just concerned about the water project. Understandable. You know how politicians are. Anyway, I hope you have some good news for me this morning."

The waiter returned, setting a glass and chrome french press and a coffee cup and saucer next to Nick.

"Yes, I do have some news for you. Some of it good, some not so good. The good news is we have a lead on the woman who is harassing you. Her name is Charity Swenson."

"Do you know why she's after me? And more to the point, do you have a plan for taking her down?"

"I'm not sure why she's attacking you. Something about using carbon-based fuel."

"Like gasoline? Are you kidding? I've got some bitch screwing with me over some gas?"

Nick poured hot coffee into his cup. "I really don't know what motivates her, but I do know she's in Austin. We'll find her."

Hoyt wiped his mouth with a napkin, neatly folding the cloth on the table. "So what's the not-so-good news?"

"About the house last night. I believe someone other than Charity blew up your house. Someone who wanted to either kill you or send a very strong message."

Hoyt turned pale. "Really? What message do you think they're trying to send?"

Nick took a sip of coffee. Hoyt, typically cool, calm and collected, had a moist forehead and he kept wiping his hands on his napkin. "You tell me. Why would someone want to kill you, Hoyt?"

Hoyt laughed nervously. "I don't know what you're talking about. Who would want to kill me?"

"So you're saying no one out there wants you dead? Or at least wants you to hear a message loud and clear?"

He swallowed, his eyes darting away. He chuckled, re-folding his napkin. "I think you've gotten a bit paranoid, Nick. From what you've told me this morning, clearly this Charity woman is the one who blew up my house. So the sooner you find her the better."

Hoyt was lying, but Nick knew he couldn't make this guy want to tell the truth. Probably not a muscle he used much anyway. "Are you sure you want to leave it like this?"

"What? If you mean do I want you to stop Charity, the answer is yes." Hoyt wiped his mouth again with the napkin, nervously folding the cloth. "I've got a meeting today. A very important meeting with my principal investors. The last thing I need is for this Charity woman to spray paint my car or put stink bombs in the conference room. So I want you to come with me. A body guard of sorts."

"Okay Hoyt. But you need to know the longer you withhold the truth about who and what you're involved in, the less chance I have of being any help."

Hoyt tossed his linen napkin on the table. "I'm glad you're concerned, Nick. But you know everything you need to know to get the job done. My meeting is up the street at the Stephen F. Austin Hotel. Finish your coffee. I've got a limo waiting for us."

~*~

While the hotel was only seven blocks along Congress Avenue, Nick figured the one hundred degree weather and Hoyt's need for showmanship required the use of a limo to make the trip. Turning right on 7th the limo pulled up to the brass-and glass-doors under a green wrought-iron outdoor balcony. Nick got out of the limo first, looking around, but not really expecting to see any threat emerge. Hoyt followed, donning his Stetson as he exited the door.

Just as Nick reached across to shut the door, a bullet impacted the granite facade behind him with a thud, a gun blast from across the street, then a scream. *The roof?* He leapt toward Hoyt as a round hit the sidewalk, dust flying as a divot of concrete exploded. More screams, people in suits, heels, sandals diving for cover. Nick tackled Hoyt squarely in the chest. They crashed to the ground, Hoyt taking the brunt of the tackle, grunting and moaning in pain. Nick pulled his weapon, using the limo for cover, looking to the rooftop across the street. A puff of smoke from the muzzle of the shooter's gun accompanied the metallic thud of a round piercing the limo.

With Hoyt safely behind the limo, Nick rolled to a kneeling position behind the front fender, firing repeated rounds into the shooter's window across the street, but the gunman had already fled. Amidst the chaos, the screaming, Hoyt writhing on the side walk with blood streaming down his arm and sirens of approaching police, reality broke through the initial shock. The shooter, whoever he was, couldn't hit a side of beef in a butcher shop. This was either a bad attempt to kill Hoyt or a good attempt to scare him.

Of course, there was always a third option. What if the target wasn't Hoyt at all?

Hospital

Nick hated hospitals. Every one of his memories involving a hospital offered up some kind of pain and loss. His dad died in a hospital room. A friend who wrecked his motorcycle in college ended up dead in a hospital. He met his ex-wife in a hospital. Even his damn dog died in a veterinary hospital. And so here he was again, sitting in a fluorescent-lit waiting room of a hospital ER, waiting for something bad to happen. Unfortunately, he didn't think Hoyt would be the victim this time. The wound caused by fragments of concrete had been superficial and the doctor's prognosis suggested a quick and full recovery. All of which was fine. Nick didn't wish misfortune on anyone, even if karma had been failing to take care of business.

After Hoyt had been transported to a room for overnight observation, Nick dropped in on him. The room, to Nick's amazement, had been filled with plants and flowers, placed along the window sill and bedside table. Who would have thought Hoyt would rate anyone's best wishes? The man lay on a bed, his left arm bandaged, his right arm raised to point the remote in his hand at the flat screen across the room. The screen flashed with each flip of the channel as he mumbled to himself.

"You've got to be kidding me. Twelve channels? Who the hell has only twelve channels?"

Nick pushed through the door. "Maybe they don't want you to watch too much TV. Besides, it looks like it'll take awhile just to read all the get well cards."

Hoyt frowned. "Just vendors sucking up to the teat for some business.." He nodded to a large inflatable woman clad in a string bikini proclaiming "Get" on one breast, "Well" on the other, and "Soon" between her legs. Not the typical hospital shop item. "She's from Block & Sons Cranes. The flowering cactus by the window's from JJ's Porta-Johns."

"Good to be loved."

"Yeah, fuck you too. Anyway, .Thank God you're here. We've got to talk." He turned the television off.

"Sounds like your doctor wants you to rest. There's nothing to say that won't wait until the morning."

"No Nick, don't go." Hoyt gave out a small grunt from the pain in his arm as he sat up, grabbing Nick before he could move away from his bedside.

"Hoyt. You're okay. The doctor in the ER said you'll make a quick recovery." Nick locked his fingers around Hoyt's right wrist, breaking the hold he had on Nick's arm. "You're okay."

"No, I'm not. It was no accident at the house and the assassination attempt is the proof."

"Assassination? Hoyt, presidents get assassinated. If someone tries to kill you, the courts will call it attempted murder. And I imagine a few folks will call it even."

Hoyt fumbled for the bed controls, positioning himself into an upright position. "You think this is funny? You think having someone try to blow you into a million pieces and then shoot you is funny? I'm telling you, that crazy bitch is trying to kill me."

"Look Hoyt. I told you about Charity to keep you apprised of our progress, not to make you paranoid. She's not the type to kill. It's possible she blew up your house and took a shot at you, but if you'll notice, you're still here. The explosion was timed to damage the house, not you. And did you notice the spread of shots at the hotel?"

Hoyt adjusted the foot of the bed, going up and down, not quite satisfied with any position. "No I didn't see the spread of shots. I was dying in a pool of my own blood on the sidewalk."

"Hoyt, you weren't dying. You had a few pieces of concrete stuck in your arm. And you didn't die because the shooter was either the worst marksman in history or the best."

He stopped fumbling with the control. "What are you talking about?"

"A marksman who wanted to scare you would place one or two shots close to you and then spread a few shots around to make it look good."

"So you agree with me then. She is after me. She told me this morning, if I didn't follow through exactly as agreed, she would see to it this was my last deal." He pointed to a small pitcher on the bed stand which had been moved near his feet. "Could you get some water for me, Nick."

Nick looked at Hoyt's pleading eyes. The man was definitely going to bleed this whole victim of a shooting thing dry. He grudgingly moved the table into Hoyt's reach.

"You spoke to Charity?"

"Who's Charity?"

"The woman I told you about in the limo on our way to the hotel."

"No. I'm talking about Franny, Francis. The governor."

"The governor told you she was going to kill you?"

Hoyt shakily poured water into a plastic cup. "Finally. Yes! That's what I've been trying to tell you. She's after me and man, you don't know this woman. Once she gets the bit between her teeth there's no stopping her."

A male nurse dressed in blue scrubs stuck his head through the door.

"How you doing, Mr. Hoyt?"

Nick waited for Hoyt to move the nurse on down the hall.

"I'm okay. Do I have some pain medication coming soon?"

"Are you feeling some pain?" The nurse stepped into the room. Nick gave Hoyt a glare he hoped communicated this was not the time to have a nurse interrupt their conversation.

"A bit." He touched his bandaged arm lightly, then looked over to Nick. "But I need to finish up with my associate here. Could you check in on me in thirty minutes?"

"Sure. I'll come by again later." The nurse stepped back out of the room and Nick closed the door just to inhibit any more spontaneous visitations. He turned back to Hoyt.

"The governor."

Nick decided Hoyt must have hit his head on the sidewalk to think a sitting governor would put out a hit on a real estate developer.

"Yes, the governor. You've got to help me, Nick. I'm up for a fight, but not with bombs and bullets. Jesus, what happened to American capitalism?"

"When you could crush your opponent, leave them broken and penniless on the street, and not have them try to kill you?"

"Yes. Exactly. What's happened to this country?"

In Nick's eyes, the entrepreneur looked a little like Peter Pan in his hospital gown. "If you really think someone is out to kill you, maybe it's time to bring in the police."

"Police? No. No police. She's the governor. Don't you think she might have some influence over the police?"

"I don't know, Hoyt."

"Look, you're on my payroll. All I have to do is let Franny know you're an integral part of Team Hoyt and you'll feel the pain too. Like I said, she is nothing if she's not persistent as a bitch in heat."

"You think threatening me will buy my loyalty? I don't give a damn what you told her or how much evidence you think you have—"

"Alright. I get it." Hoyt's voice dripped resignation. "You can't blame me for trying. Look, I need your help. Okay? There, I said it. Does that make you happy? You've forced my hand. I'm begging you to help me."

While dumping this guy as a client had the feel of an ice cold beer on a hot, hot day, Nick knew he wouldn't turn his back on someone, even Hoyt, asking him for help.

"Hoyt, I need you to calm down. You're still my client. Nothing has changed. If you want to fill me in on your activities, especially if those details might help me stop the person harassing you, I'm happy to listen. No more bribes or threats from now on. Agreed?"

Hoyt shifted back into his self assured salesman voice. "Sure. You know the first time I saw you I knew you were alright. You had just started a new business and drove around in a heap of a truck, but I could sense the integrity, the professionalism."

"Hoyt, kissing my ass won't buy my loyalty either. Do you have something to tell me or not?"

"God, I love it. Right to the point. I like that."

Nick looked past the open shades to a view of a courtyard. A man walked tethered to an IV stand while a woman, probably his wife, held his other hand. He had met his ex at a hospital. She had been a surgeon working on one of his colleagues. They would often stroll in the hospital courtyard, stealing a few minutes together between their busy lives.

"So Nick, here's the thing."

He went on to describe his relationship with the governor, how the plant would not be going online by the required date, the contract with the city having a clause allowing them to purchase water from other sources if the plant failed to meet the deadline, and how pissed Franny was because missing the deadline would make her look bad only a few months from an election.

"So what have you done, Hoyt?"

"What do mean?"

"You're telling me Mr. Entrepreneur, God's gift to capitalism, doesn't have what I believe you business types call a mitigation plan? Hard to believe."

Hoyt looked quite pleased with himself, color returning to his face. "Ah, you know me too well, Nick. Yes, I've got a plan. I brought in an old friend of mine to help me pump water from the aquifer."

"The Edwards Aquifer? What makes you think the state will let that one slide by?"

"Well, the governor has a vested interest in delaying any crackdowns. I just need enough water to meet the deadline. Besides, I'm not going to let them know what I'm doing. As soon as the plant comes on line, processed water from the Gulf will be flowing through a pipeline to Austin."

"Who's this friend?"

"Actually, you just missed him. Izzy Zydeco, an old business associate of mine. And he's got a new girl working with him. MaryLou."

"What?"

"Yeah, a pretty hot-looking lady. MaryLou Perkins."

Nick walked down a hallway somewhere in the hospital. He didn't know if Hoyt had finished talking or not. People passed to his left and his right. A gurney cut across his path, someone in scrubs shouting, an old man using a walker staring straight ahead, two nurses chatting and laughing, a doctor looking grim with a stethoscope around his neck, two men in suits, a priest, a security guard by the door which slid open into the night.

Shit always happened in hospitals and tonight would be no exception. MaryLou Perkins had risen from the dead.

Chasing Shadows

Nick drove away from the hospital, his mind reeling in several directions. He had a wacko eco-terrorist attacking his client and now possibly the governor ordering hits on him as well. And now the woman, who in a single night had turned him into a love-struck idiot and whose secret about surviving the fire he had kept for a reason he couldn't remember, had shown up.

A quick Google search on his phone gave Nick the name and address of Izzy Zydeco's company. He had to know, to see her in the flesh. He had to know if his MaryLou Perkins still lived. And if, make that when, he found her, he would bring things to a conclusion. Either they walked out the door together or they parted ways for good. The idea of staying suspended between life and death, love and aloneness turned his stomach.

The JVI corporate offices sat on the shore of Lake Austin, which actually looked more like a river, except this body of water had no current. A drought-induced dead lawn sloped down to green water and a hundred yards across the water, white and beige limestone cliffs rose, topped with cedar and mesquite. Nick figured the building, an expansive five-story natural green-tinted glass structure, had probably been designed to blend into the surrounding terrain, if only all the vegetation in sight hadn't died from heat and the lack of water. A young woman, looking like the stereotypical sorority girl with a blond perm, the bronze glow of an artificial tan, and gold jewelry, sat behind the reception desk, thoroughly engaged in a conversation over her headset.

"I know. I told her he was trouble, but you know Jules."

Nick moved into her vision, distracting her from Jules' current life mismanagement. She looked at him, raising a hand in the air to acknowledge his presence.

"Got to go. Bye." She beamed a huge Miss Texas smile at him. "May I help you?"

"Yes, I'm here to see MaryLou Perkins. I believe she's a new employee."

The girl turned her attention to a flat screen on her desk.

"I'm sorry. We don't have a MaryLou Perkins on the roster. Is there someone else who could assist you?"

"Yes. Izzy Zydeco."

"Mr. Zydeco? Do you have an appointment? I ask because he's usually pretty busy."

"No, I don't. But if you tell him Dan Hoyt sent me, I think he may want to meet with me."

After a hushed conversation with Zydeco's assistant, Nick had a security badge and an escort, a guy in his early twenties wearing baggy shorts, Converse All Stars, a Los Lonely Boys tee shirt, gauged ears and tattoos running along both arms. They got in the elevator together and the escort/graffiti artist/surfer dude pushed the button for the fifth floor.

"He, man. So, what's your thing?"

"My thing? I'm a private investigator."

"No shit. Man, that's cool. Like stalking guys screwing around on their women, shit like that?"

"It's confidential."

"I hear that. Confidential. Man, you must see some crazy shit. So you're a 'smee' for Izzy's next game?"

"Smee?" The only thing Nick could conjure up were little blue and green furry creatures shooting rainbows out of their butts.

"Subject Matter Expert. SME. That what you doing?"

"Like I said, confidential."

Before his escort could press further, the doors opened and Nick found himself in a well-appointed Danish Modern reception area. Another attractive young woman greeted him, offering him something to drink. He chose a triple-filtered Icelandic snowmelt water called *Hreinleiki*, which he thought had something to do with liking rain, but the bottle informed him the word referred to the purity of the Icelandic snow melt. Just what Austin needed. A great big melting iceberg.

Nick walked into Izzy Zydeco's office, expecting to see an overweight thug, based on Hoyt's description. Something like a mafia boss. Instead he found a slender, young man, maybe thirty, in slacks and a silk short sleeve polo shirt and Italian loafers. Techno thumped in the background, as he scanned an array of flat screens on the wall across from his modernist glass tabletop desk. Seeing Nick, Izzy lifted his cell phone toward the wall. The music softened and the lights came up slightly.

"Nick Sibelius, have a seat. Dan's told me a great deal about you. Seems he's got someone pestering him and you're smoking out the bad guy. Good for you. Must be great for a small-time guy like you to have a wealthy client like Dan Hoyt."

Nick did not like the condescending tone of Izzy's voice, but he reminded himself he came to find MaryLou, not spar with some wet behind the ears high tech entrepreneur.

"I understand you're Hoyt's business partner."

"Yes, I am. I suppose Dan has told you about our project we've got going. Is that why you're here? To talk about security at the desalination plant? I don't think these things happening to Dan have anything to do with the plant. You see, Dan has a way of stirring up trouble. There's always a jealous husband or irate investor dogging him."

"I appreciate your perspective, but actually I'm here on another matter. I understand you have a woman in your employment named MaryLou Perkins."

Izzy moved to a leather and chrome chair, motioning for Nick to have a seat in the chair opposite him. "Before I respond, let me ask you something. What's your business with this Perkins woman?"

"It's personal. We have something of a past and when I learned she worked here, I wanted to come over and surprise her. For old time's sake."

"Personal, huh? You can't slide something like that past me, Nick. You're not talking business, are you? You had a relationship with her. Girlfriend? Wife? No, you don't look the part. I'm guessing girlfriend at best, a one night hook up at worst. Am I getting warm?"

"Like I said. It's personal."

Izzy raised a hand. "Say no more, Nick. I understand. I've lusted after women myself. Hell, take my assistant out there. I want to get inside her panties so bad I can hardly stand it sometimes. I mean, did you see my girl when you came in? But my damn VP of HR keeps telling me I'd be looking at the sexual harassment lawsuit from hell if I even breath lightly on her neck. I don't know. Sometimes I think it might be worth it anyway."

"About MaryLou. Does she work for you?"

"MaryLou Perkins. You know, the name doesn't ring a bell. But then, I've got thousands of employees in several countries. I tell you what...I'll get my VP of HR to do something constructive instead of harassing me and see if he can find her. Fair enough?"

"Thanks. I'd appreciate a call."

"If he finds her. I'm guessing it's a dead end, but we'll definitely look into it." He leaned back, putting his feet on the desk. "Somebody really drilled a hole in Hoyt's Ferrari and sprayed chemicals all over the interior?"

"Yes, they did. But I think we'll have the perpetrator soon."

"I should hope so. I told him driving around in a bright red Ferrari invited trouble, but he's like a peacock. Got to wave his feathers all over the place."

Izzy's assistant knocked, opening the door halfway.

"Mr. Zydeco, your next appointment is here."

He got to his feet. "Thank you, darling. Now Nick, if I hear anything about this MaryLou Perkins woman, we'll be in touch. But one word of advice. Don't be chasing shadows."

"Shadows?"

"Yeah. Ever try to catch your shadow? Can't be done. But you strike me as a guy who's chasing a shadow. And you and I both know it gets you nowhere. None of my business, but I'd suggest you move on. Life is short."

"Yeah, well, like you said. It's none of your business."

~*~

By the time he arrived at the office he hadn't sorted out how many people were after Hoyt, or how he would play this MaryLou thing with Theresa. He knew he should have told her about MaryLou when he had the chance. He just needed to find her, have a conversation with her. He needed to end it.

Nick walked into the office, seeing Theresa's back to him as she poured herself a cup of coffee. She turned, then stepped over to put a hand on his arm.

"I just made some coffee. Would you like some?"

"Sure, that'd be great."

Theresa, who had turned back to the pot, stopped pouring.

"You okay Nick? I ask because I've never heard you be so interested in a cup of my coffee. In fact, I know you've been dumping it in the plant by the door."

Nick could feel her eyes searching him. Her damn intuition had the volume turned all the way up.

"What's going on? Are you okay?"

Nick looked away, stepping toward the desk, fumbling with some papers in a file.

"I'm fine. What have you found out about Charity?"

"Quite a bit. In fact, you're currently flipping all of the pages of my research out of order."

"Sorry."

"Nick, what's going on?"

"Look Theresa. It's nothing. It's just, well…"

He wondered how he could face a gun pointed at his head, but couldn't face Theresa with the truth.

"Nick, just tell me what's going on."

"Do you remember MaryLou?"

"Of course I remember her. We were talking about her last night. Is this about what happened last night?"

"No. Yes. Sort of."

"Well, which is it?"

He looked into Theresa's eyes, her face hovering somewhere between concern, fear, and anger. "I need to tell you something. You see, MaryLou isn't dead."

Theresa sat down, resting the cup on the desk.

"I see."

"No, this doesn't change what we talked about last night. I still, I—"

"It's okay Nick. She's alive and you think you might still love her."

"It's not that, Theresa."

"Come on, Nick. You were crazy about her. I remember when you thought she had died. You were devastated for months. You're trying to tell me she shows up alive and a part of you, maybe a big part of you, doesn't want her?"

"There's more."

"More? How can there be more?"

"I knew she survived the fire. I knew she was alive."

"What?"

"About six months after I thought she died, I got an email with a note and a photo of her at the Golden Gate Bridge. It could have been a fake, but I guess I believed in my heart she was still alive."

"So let me get this straight. You lied to me about her being dead for months and you lied to me about your feelings for her. Have I just about got it right?"

Nick's mind raced to come up with something, anything he could say to heal the abyss which had ripped open between them. "I don't know what to say."

"Well I know what to say. I like you. Hell, I might have even fallen in love with you. And I think I've been pretty clear and upfront with you. I even told you to take your time getting over her death. Only to find out you've been lying to me. Playing me."

"Theresa."

Theresa stood, her hands shaking. "I'm nobody's fool, Nick Sibelius—ever. So let me put this as honestly as I can. Something, by the way, you seem incapable of doing. We're business partners. Period. And frankly, I need to think about whether I want to be in business with an asshole who left his *cajones* in a jar somewhere. Jesus, Nick. How could you? How could you string me along, you sonofabitch?"

"Theresa, please." Nick reached out for her, part of him hoping his touch would heal the wound.

"No, don't fucking touch me. I'm leaving now. The research on Charity is in the file." Theresa opened the door. "And Nick?"

"Yeah."

"Unless you want to drink from a straw the rest of your life, stay the hell away from me."

The door slammed shut.

~*~

Nick thought about chasing after Theresa, to tell her he was sorry, to tell her he loved her, to hold her, but he knew she was right. He hadn't told her MaryLou was alive. And he didn't tell her because he did still have feelings for MaryLou. When he thought she had died in the fire Nick had been devastated, moping around for weeks, then months, feeling a part of him had been lopped off. When he got MaryLou's email confirming she was alive, the possibility of a life with her became real to him again. Then the weeks turned into months and he questioned whether the email had been a hoax. Now MaryLou turned up alive and in Austin. And he's driving away Theresa, who actually had seemed to want to be in his life, because of a woman who can't be bothered to contact him, just to let him know she was still breathing.

His eyes scanned the file Theresa had prepared. Screenshots of Facebook pages talking about the Ferrari, the lobsters, and the dangling Dodge. He noticed Theresa had left the browser open to Charity's Facebook page and apparently Charity had friended Theresa. Nothing on the explosion or last night's shooting in the news feed. Maybe Hoyt was right about the governor gunning for him. Then he clicked on the most recent posting to see a thumbnail image of what looked like Hoyt running bare butted down a hallway with a caption, "Carbon spewer runs, but he can never hide." Charity must have stolen all of Hoyt's clothes and towels while he was in the shower at the hospital in the last two hours. He couldn't help but like this woman.

He clicked around a bit more, checking out the photos of her victims and then noticed a photo she took just this morning before Hoyt's hospital streaking episode. A sunrise, with downtown Austin in the distance to the south.

Wait. I know this spot. I came here with Sarah once for a romantic weekend and we had the same view. The Renaissance Hotel.

He couldn't believe it. Was it possible Charity had taken a photo of the sunrise from her room at the Renaissance Hotel? He checked his gun, grabbed his keys and headed for the door.

Time to finish this business up and get Hoyt out of my life.

Let's Make a Deal

Theresa confirmed what Nick knew about his business partner when he called with the lead on Charity. She took in the information like a pro and told him to pick her up at her apartment on the way to the Renaissance Hotel. They drove in Nick's El Camino through light, afternoon traffic to the Arboretum—a complex of shops, restaurants, office buildings and the hotel nestled among trees on a hillside overlooking the city.

"Do you really think she would give away her location so easily Nick? She's been very careful."

He glanced over at Theresa, grateful she had compartmentalized their relationship, or what was left of it.

"Well, sometimes people get so confident they start to make mistakes. Anyway, it's the only good lead we've had so far."

Nick pushed past the speed limit as much as he dared, not wanting to waste time being pulled over by the police. When they reached the hotel, he parked near the front door of the modern white fieldstone and glass structure. They both got out of the car, ignoring the bellman, and walked swiftly into the foyer.

Nick gently grabbed Theresa's arm to slow her down. "She may be armed, Theresa. I don't think she'll try anything, but we need to be careful."

She pulled her arm away. "I can take care of myself, Nick." With a mischievous smile, she grabbed Nick's hand and dragged him with her to the reception desk. A woman behind the wood and granite counter greeted them.

"Welcome to the Renaissance Hotel. Checking in?"

Theresa took a step forward, speaking before Nick could stop her, a slight slur in her voice as if she may have had one too many margaritas at lunch.

"Hi. I don't believe this. I managed to leave my room without a key and now I'm locked out."

"Yes ma'am. What is your room number?"

"That's the thing, see. I checked in and then met this *precious* man." Theresa glanced over at Nick, rubbing his arm as if he was Aladdin's Lamp. He nodded acknowledging they were together. She leaned in conspiratorially toward the receptionist. "We met at lunch today over margaritas."

The receptionist offered a knowing smile, Theresa apparently not being the first semi-inebriated lovebird to cross her path on the job.

"I think I found my soulmate. He's just so, well..." She teared up. "I'm sorry. You probably don't want to hear about my love life. Anyway, I've lost track of everything—my key, my room number. I even left my cell phone in the room and I never go anywhere without it."

"Do you have a photo ID?"

"Purse is in the room too. Maybe you could walk us to my room and once you open it for us, I can show you my license. Would that be okay?"

"I don't know ma'am. Our policy is designed to protect our guests."

"Well, I'm a guest and my soulmate is standing right here. My future is in your hands. Protect me."

The receptionist looked at Theresa, then to Nick and back to Theresa. Nick could see her defenses melting away at the thought of being the one to play cupid.

"I suppose there's no harm if I go with you and you show me your ID once you have your purse. If it was me, I'd just let you in the room, but the hotel does have policies."

"I completely understand. The reservation is for Charity Swenson. Thank you." She wrapped an arm around Nick's, snuggling in. "Thank you so much."

In the glass elevator Nick watched the atrium fall away as his "lover" clung to him as he wished she would want to do in real life. The receptionist tried to avert her attention, but occasionally Nick would catch her glancing over, their eyes meeting and Nick smiling in a "how does a guy like me get a fabulous woman like this" kind of way. He wondered how obliging the receptionist would be if Charity was in her room and they had to draw their weapons. In the back of his mind he had imagined sneaking into the hotel, finding her room number, picking the lock, and waiting in ambush. Arriving on the ninth floor, the receptionist motioned for the couple to go through the open elevator doors. Theresa gave Nick a shove through the door, then careened into the receptionist.

"Oh, excuse me. I'm a bit of a mess. I should know better than to have more than one of those margaritas."

Nick watched Theresa's plan unfold.

"It's okay. Let's just get you settled back in your room."

They turned down a walkway overlooking a huge atrium on one side and the hotel rooms on the other. The receptionist led the way.

"Is this starting to look familiar to you?"

"A bit," Theresa put a hand on the railing to steady herself, "although all of these floors look pretty much the same to me."

The receptionist stopped at room 929. "Here we are." She fumbled around her pockets, her face shifting from consternation, to frustration, to embarrassment. "I seem to have left the key back at the desk."

"Oh my. It was such a long way up here and for you to take the time…"

"No. No problem. I'm happy to help." She searched pockets again, not believing she had left the card nine floors below. "Well, I'm going to have to go and get the key card. Maybe I need one of those margaritas."

"It could happen to anybody. I guess we should just wait here for you?"

"Yes, if you don't mind. I'll just be a few minutes."

Once the receptionist had walked back to the elevators and begun her trip down to the first floor, Theresa produced the key card.

Nick reached for it. "Aren't you a crafty one."

Pulling the card back from his grasp, she slipped it into the lock until the sensor light glowed green, then turned the handle and pushed the door open. "Skills, Nick. Skills."

Nick followed Theresa into the room, closing the door and locking the deadbolt behind him.

Charity sat on a sofa in a track suit, looking up from a copy of *VeloNews*, in bemused shock at her unexpected guests

"Nick?"

"Good afternoon, Charity. Sorry to barge in on you like this, but I don't think either one of us has been completely upfront with each other."

Nick sensed Theresa moving to his side, checking out the room for possible weapons and escape paths. Charity stood, tossing the magazine on the coffee table, her eyes focused on Nick.

"Yes, Nick. You lied to me. I don't like liars."

Theresa turned her back to them as she checked out the bathroom. "Yeah, he's a liar. True enough."

Nick gave Theresa an annoyed glance, then turned his attention back to Charity. "I have never lied to you, Charity. However, you failed to tell me you were engaged in making my client's life a living hell."

Charity glared, her mouth a thin line. "Now that completes the circle."

"Circle. What are you talking about?"

Charity clenched her fists. "How was I supposed to know Barry's murderer would be a nice guy with ecological sensibilities? Threw me off my game. I almost decided not to make you pay for the pain you've caused. But then I got to thinking. The kind of man who would kill a defenseless dentist is also the kind of man who would lie about his concern for the planet as a strategy to get to me. And now you tell me a stinking, carbon spewing, sonofabitch is your client. I should have offed you at the trailer."

"Barry's murderer? Barry Swenson?"

"Yes, Barry Swenson and don't act like you don't know what I'm talking about."

Theresa stepped over to a laptop computer open on the desk. Charity took a step towards Theresa, then stopped when Nick's gun appeared. Urgency tinged her voice. "Get away from there. That's private property."

Nick motioned to Charity. "Why don't you sit back down, Charity."

Theresa tapped on the laptop's keyboard. "We're friends on Facebook, you know. Pearl Schultz."

"You're Pearl?"

"Not my actual name, but yeah, I'm Pearl. I've been following your exploits. Quite imaginative." Theresa clicked through various documents, while Nick kept his gun pointed toward Charity. "What's this? A file with Nick's name."

"Don't open it."

Nick moved to look over Theresa's shoulder. "Why not, Charity?" Theresa opened a document called *Strategic Plan* in the *Nick Sibelius* file. Under the header *"Kill the Bastard"* was a list of activities, some with one or two sentence summaries of results. Under *Explosive Device?* she noted

"Someone apparently wants Hoyt to suffer as much or maybe more, than I do. They failed. My work continues."

Under *Shoot Him* she outlined hacking into Hoyt's corporate computer to get his personal schedule, and a diagram of the Littlefield Building roof.

Nick looked past the laptop to Charity. "So it was you in the Littlefield building shooting at Hoyt?"

She snorted a muted laugh. "Hardly. Why would I want to kill Hoyt?"

"So you weren't at the window with a rifle?"

"No, I was there. I was aiming for you."

"Are you a really a bad shot or did you have second thoughts?"

Charity crossed her legs, shifting her gaze away from Nick, then fumbled with a coaster on the table. "Bad shot. Do I look like someone who sits around shooting high-powered rifles?"

"You know what I think, Charity?" Nick holstered his gun. "I think you're not the type to murder people. I think you want to do right by your brother, but you're not a killer, at heart."

She had found another coaster on the table, stacking it on top of the other. "Maybe."

"Two things are going to happen here, Charity. First, you're going to stop harassing Dan Hoyt. I don't know what he did to warrant your attentions, but it needs to stop. And second, you're going to leave town and promise to never come back."

Theresa looked up from the computer. "Leave town? Nick, we should give her to the police."

"Normally I'd agree with you, Theresa, but I'm thinking Charity wouldn't let a little jail time get in the way of her continuing to harass Hoyt."

"You're damn straight. Hoyt tried to run me down in his fancy Ferrari. He deserves everything he's getting and more."

"What if he apologized to you?"

She frowned, crossing her arms and shaking her head.

"Nick, she's a sociopath. You're going to cut a deal with a nut case?"

Charity glared at Theresa. "Listen up little Pearl Schultz. I'm not crazy. I'm standing up for all the cyclists out there who are maimed and killed every day. And you don't see me living a lie, using fake identities online. Who's the sociopath now Pearl?"

Nick stepped over to her, sitting on the arm of a lounge chair. "What if he provided some kind of restitution? Gave to your favorite charity?"

"My Bicycle Safety Association?"

"Maybe a charity that's a little less confrontational."

"Well, I do support Wheels 4 Life. They provide bikes to people in Third World countries."

"So if Hoyt gave ten thousand dollars to Wheels 4 Life, would his donation get him off the hook?"

"Make it one hundred thousand."

Theresa shook her head. "One hundred thousand. She's a nut case, Nick." Charity gave Theresa a look capable of bending rebar.

Nick glanced over to Theresa and then back to Charity. "Hundred thousand's pretty steep, Charity."

"I think he can afford it. He could sell his carbon spewing Ferrari as scrap."

"You did destroy a two hundred thousand dollar car. The other option here is I bring in the police. I don't think you'll get much cycling time in prison."

Charity leaned back in the sofa with a resigned sigh.

"Okay. He makes a ten thousand dollar donation and I'll take him off my list."

"Good, Charity. That's good."

A knock on the door reminded Nick the receptionist must have gotten a key. Theresa moved to the door. "I've got this, Nick. Finish up and I'll meet you back at the car."

Before the receptionist could get the key in the lock, Theresa swung the door open.

"Oh, thank God you're here."

"Ma'am, is everything alright?"

"Alright?" Theresa turned in the doorway, blocking the receptionist's view into the room. "He's married." She screamed, "You son of a bitch!" Turning back toward the receptionists, tears streaming down her face, Theresa moved them both out of the doorway. "She's in there now. They wanted me to do some sort of threesome. If my mother…" The door clicked shut, leaving a mumbling sound of Theresa's sobbing diatribe. Charity raised her eyebrows and looked back at Nick. "Is she your girlfriend? Because if she is, you've got a handful."

Nick sat across from her. "She's my partner and I suppose she is a handful."

"No, I think she's more than a partner. Hell, all you have to do is see the two of you together. It's a yin and yang thing."

"While I'd like to sit around and chat, Charity, I think we have more important things to discuss."

"Like what?"

"Like, what are we going to do about us?"

"If you think you can buy me off, forget about it. This is a blood thing."

"Who was Barry Swenson to you anyway?"

"My twin brother. We were separated at birth and I was adopted by a couple who moved to Australia. Barry stayed in the States."

"So the two of you were pretty close, I imagine."

"We would have been, but I never met him. I mean, we were infants when our parents were killed in a car accident. Then the adoption happened and we never reconnected."

"Then how did you find out about Barry's death?"

"I moved to the States about five years ago, even changed by name from my biological parents' name, McDuffy, to Barry's last name, Swenson. You know, to feel more connected with my only blood family. I had been meaning to look Barry up, but there was an accident and some other issues. Anyway, I never reconnected. Then I read in the news Barry Swenson had been killed by an ex-cop, by you. I may not have known Barry, but I'll be damned if I'm going to stand by and let somebody get away with murdering my brother."

"I didn't kill him, Charity."

"Right. The denial of a condemned man."

"Barry had an illegal toxic waste dumping scheme going and had gotten himself involved with a very bad man named Jayson Moore. Barry kidnapped a Homeland Security agent who was investigating Jayson and when I showed up to rescue her, Barry had a gun. The agent shot him in self-defense. I know he's your brother, but I'm telling you the truth."

"That's your story, Nick? All I know is you walked out of his house and Barry was dead."

Nick stood, Charity's eyes defiant. "If I am the kind of man you say I am, Charity, I'd kill you right now, stage the death as a suicide and walk out the door free and clear."

"How would you pull that off?"

Nick looked around, pondering the possibilities. He walked over to the closet, pulling out a plastic laundry bag.

"I could strip your clothes off, put a bag over your head and make it look like a case of autoerotic asphyxiation. The newspapers love a sex story."

He tossed the bag aside and pulled out the iron. "Or I could tie this cord around your neck and the tie the other end around the hangar bar. I wouldn't have to hold your feet off the floor for very long before you'd be dead." Charity shifted uncomfortably on the sofa, one hand at her throat. He stepped into the bathroom, coming out with a hairdryer. "I could put you in a bathtub filled with water along with this hairdryer and plug it in. Pzzzttt. I know it's a bit of cliche, but trust me, you'd be dead. Of course the simplest thing will be to just take you into the atrium hallway and toss you off the side when no one is looking. How many floors up are we?"

"Nine."

"Yeah. Ninety, a hundred feet to hard marble floors? Should be high enough to do the job."

"You said 'if I was that sort of man'. What sort of man are you?"

"Your brother pointed a loaded weapon at a Federal agent with the intent to kill. I'm sorry about your brother, but if you do the research, you'll learn he was not the kind, gentle dentist you make him out to be."

She sat on the edge of the sofa. "Yeah, I did check into Barry after I ran into you at your place. You were right. Our separation must have weighed heavily on him, driven him mad with pain and rage, which made him a toxic waste dumper. But there's one discrepancy I don't understand. If what you're telling me is true about the agent who killed Barry, why do the papers and the police report say you pulled the trigger."

"How did you get a police report?"

"Just answer the question, Nick."

"I lied to the police to protect her, to protect the agent."

"What's to protect? Wasn't she just doing her job?"

"She had a brother also involved in Barry's scheme."

"Yeah, I've met him. Junior."

"You've met Junior? Well, she killed Barry to protect Junior and then ran away with him. Aiding and abetting a felon is not something a Homeland Security Agent wants to be caught doing. She died in a fire trying to help him escape and Junior, as I guess you know, was arrested and is serving time in the State Penitentiary."

"And why did you try to protect a Homeland Security Agent committing a felony? What did she promise you? Money? Did she have something on you?"

Nick hesitated, then said, "I loved her."

"You risked everything for love?"

"Yeah."

"Damn. Didn't see that coming. I hope somebody loves me that much at least once in my life." Charity fell back into the sofa, as if the idea of Nick risking all for love weighed her down. "So you didn't kill Barry, you're a good person, and you're not going to kill me. What *are* you going to do?"

"Charity, you know I could kill you now, be done with you and walk away. Or at the very least, have you thrown in jail. But instead, I'm going to leave trusting you to do the right thing. For your part, you're going to stop harassing Hoyt and leave town—today. Do we have a deal?"

Charity met Nick's gaze, finally nodding. "Yeah, we have a deal, Nick. But if I find out you're lying to me about Barry, I'll come after you and I will have learned to shoot by then." She smiled. Nick had never seen a genuine smile from her before.

"Sounds fair enough, Charity."

~*~

Nick walked out of the hotel to Theresa, who was waiting for him in the parking lot. Together they headed back toward Theresa's apartment.

"Am I going to read about a redhead found dead at the bottom of the ravine outside the Renaissance Hotel, Nick?"

"Nope. She's leaving town today."

Nick summarized his conversation with Charity, explaining the deal he had negotiated with her.

"You know Hoyt won't be satisfied with your deal, Nick?"

"He'll get used to it. He has nothing to gain by getting revenge and peace of mind in settling with her."

"Even if he agrees to the deal, I still don't understand how you could let her go. You're saying she tried to kill you, and you just let her go?"

"Look, I'm not a cop anymore. She acted out of love and duty, Theresa. I can respect that."

"Nick, she didn't paper your lawn. She tried to kill you."

"I've been betrayed a couple of times myself, so I can certainly understand her rage. If she went to jail, she'd just get out in a few months or a year and go after Hoyt again. This way Hoyt is rid of her. And besides, you never know when you'll want a sociopathic eco-terrorist as a friend."

"You really think that nut job won't go after Hoyt, just because she gave you her word?"

"Charity, in her own way, has a strong ethic. Yeah, it's a twisted morality, but she does live by a code. And now she has new information."

Trepidation filled her voice. "Nick."

"So you'd be upset if she killed me?"

"Of course I would. What kind of stupid thing is that to say?"

"Well, the last conversation we had you were reaming me out for not having told you about MaryLou. Whether she's alive or dead, whatever happened between us is long over, Theresa. I don't know how else I can say it."

"I believe you Nick. I think it was just the shock of hearing you had known all along she might be alive and didn't tell me. I understand you were trying to protect her and you can protect someone without still being in love with them."

"So we're good?"

"Yeah, Nick. We're good."

Nick reached across to touch Theresa's hand, which she gave up to his grasp. Pulling up to her apartment, Nick wanted to lean across, give her a kiss, and pronounce his love, but decided not to press his luck. Instead, he said, "Now that we've got Hoyt sorted out, I guess we'll have a little down time until we get our next client."

"Down time sounds good to me, Nick. See you in the morning."

Nick drove away, a smile creasing his face. They had delivered successfully for their first client, which also meant an influx of cash to the new business. And if the success of the business weren't enough of an excuse for celebration, his relationship with Theresa appeared to be moving in a positive direction. He looked forward to a beer or two, watching the sun set and the moon rise over Texas. All he needed for the day to be absolutely perfect was a good storm to bring everything back to life.

Resurrection

As he drove up to his trailer, Nick noticed a Porsche parked out front and the trailer lights on. Whoever it was either had a key—and he didn't recall giving anyone a key—or had broken into his trailer. He doubted anyone with serious ill intent would have left the car in plain view, unless of course, the guy felt so confident he didn't bother to hide his car. Nick pulled his Glock from the glove box just in case, approaching the trailer at an angle, crouching to see underneath it. With slow, deliberate movements, he made his way to the trailer door, pausing there to listen for any sound which might give his adversary away. He put a hand on the door handle, turning it slowly. The door opened a few inches. He paused, taking in a deep breath, then flung the door open, gun at the ready.

MaryLou stood in the kitchen, a glass of red wine in one hand, the same long hair and hazel eyes which had captivated him, now watching him with undisguised humor.

"Nice entrance, Nick. Very testosterone-y." She took a sip from her glass.

He looked at MaryLou, the woman he had loved and lost in her fiery escape. The photo must have been real. The woman standing before him, who he had grieved over for so long, stood in his kitchen. Nick's chest tightened, he couldn't breathe. He wanted to scream, to shout for joy, to send her flying through the wall, to hold her close, feel her warmth once again.

"You're...alive."

Her lips parted in a slight smile, but her eyes stayed focused on the Glock Nick had pointed directly at her heart.

"Yes, Nick. I'm right here. Why don't you put your gun down?"

"Why don't you tell me where the hell you've been? Why don't you tell me why you left me hoping you were alive and thinking you were dead?"

"We had a special moment together, Nick—"

"Special moment? That's what it was, a special moment?"

"Nick, we don't have time to go through all this. I was on an assignment, I did what I had to do. Now you need to put the gun down."

"What I need to do? You lying, betraying bitch."

MaryLou stopped smiling. "Nick, I'm with Homeland Security and we have a situation here. Now you can either help me, and I hope you will, or get the hell out of the way."

"Homeland Security? What could possibly be happening in this town for Homeland Security to send one of its spooks?"

"Nick."

"You know I loved you? I really loved you. I would have given my life for you."

"Nick."

He moved a step closer, shifting his aim to her head, the muzzle pointed directly into one of her hazel eyes. She stared right into the barrel.

"And you left me hanging in the breeze. I even covered for you shooting the dentist, told them I did it."

"I know."

"Why am I supposed to believe you now? All you've ever done is lie to me."

"Nick, put the gun away. I know I hurt you." She reached for the gun with a hand, pushing the weapon down. "I didn't mean too. I didn't mean for that night to happen."

"You mean the 'fuck the local guy so he won't get in your way' night?"

She stepped toward him. "No, I mean the night I let my guard down. I let you in." He let her touch his face, a confused mix of anger and desire roiling in his gut. "I know I've hurt you, but my job doesn't allow much room for somebody like you. We shared a beautiful night. Let's not argue with the little time we have together."

She stroked his arm, releasing the Glock from his grip, setting the gun on the kitchen table. She kissed his neck, his cheek. Nick relaxed into her scent, her touch. He wanted her. His body wanted her. Her hand slid down his chest, his stomach, to his crotch becoming hard against her touch. He had loved her so much and then she had broken his heart. He wanted to meld into her, but the pain endured over the last year left him suspicious. He put his hands on her shoulders and took a step back.

"Why didn't you tell me where you were? All these months I've been hoping you were alive and thinking you might be dead."

"I know. I'm sorry, Nick."

He had rehearsed in his mind what he would do if he ever saw her again. She would beg for forgiveness and he would turn his back on her, let her feel the pain of losing him this time. But before he could stop, he found himself caught up in her hazel eyes, the curve of her breasts, the slope of her hips to her long legs. He scent took him back to the night they had been together. Without knowing how, his arms embraced her, taking in the softness of her skin, the heat of her body against him. He hovered just beyond her parted lips, when she moved to him, relaxing into his grasp.

"Why did you leave me, MaryLou?"

"Please, Nick. Just hold me." She pulled his shirt out of his pants, fumbling with the buttons as she kissed him.

"I loved you, MaryLou."

She loosened his belt. "Just make love to me, Nick."

On her knees now, she pulled at his pants.

The part of him, the crazy part pounding in his head who wanted this woman kneeling before him outvoted the reasoned part of him who knew she was trouble. He pushed her to the floor, devouring her like a starving man dying of hunger. The love making turned violent and raw. Somewhere along the way, they managed to stumble into the bed. He used his strength to overpower her, bend her to his will, until they both lay sweaty and spent.

In hindsight, he knew he should have stopped. Pushed her away. Told her to go to hell. But once he held her in his grasp, the train got away from him, crashing through any obstacle getting in the way, knowing the ride could only end in disaster. Nick got up, pulling his clothes back on.

"We're not going to do this anymore, MaryLou."

She smiled. "I think we already did, Nick."

Her loveliness still stunned him. Lying now on her stomach, long, dark hair cascaded down her back to the soft roundness of her rear end punctuated by two dimples.

"I want a woman I trust. Someone I can love. Not whatever this is."

She rolled over and rose to a seated position, wrapping her arms around her knees.

"Well, Nick. Fucking good sex. That's what *this* is." She stood, picking up her panties and bras on the floor between them. "We're good together, Nick. Isn't that enough?"

"MaryLou, why are you here? What do you want?" Nick grabbed the rest of her clothes off the floor, tossing them at her. "You've got one minute to tell me what you're doing here and then you're out."

She found her glass of wine, taking a long drink. "You've changed, Nick."

"Yes, I've changed. Think you had something to do with it. Now why are you here?"

She picked up his Glock, inspecting the weapon. "Do you ever clean this? God, I'm surprised it shoots."

"MaryLou..."

"I need your help, Nick. It's important."

"You show up out of the blue, and because we have sex, you expect me to just turn on a dime, follow your lead right into hell again?"

MaryLou broke Nick's gun down with the unconscious and effortless motions of practiced hands. "Nick, I can do this myself, but together we have a real chance at stopping Izzy Zydeco from whatever he has planned."

"Izzy Zydeco. Hoyt's business partner?"

"Yes. He's one of these whiz kid high tech CEO's. Has a company in Austin. We also have some intel about a connection to Los Diablos Tejanos. We're not sure what he's up to, but the Diablos are involved with Zydeco in some way. I know you're doing a small investigation job for Hoyt, so I'm thinking your connection might be helpful to us."

"So I'm just supposed to trust you?"

She looked up from the Glock. "Well, yes."

Nick paced the small space of the trailer. "I trusted you before. Remember, LouLou?" He used Junior's nickname for her like a blade thrust in her direction.

"We're not going to go back through this—"

"The hell we are. The woman I met, the woman I made love to, the woman I—"

"Nick, the sex is great. I love being with you too, but you're blowing this all out of proportion."

He stepped toward her. "No, I'm not. You know I'm not. In bed I know you felt what I felt. I trusted you. And you ended up being a goddamn covert operative here to keep your dumbass half-brother from getting himself killed. You murdered a suspect right in front of me and then left me to take the fall for the dentist. Am I wrong, MaryLou?"

She let out a breath as if calming herself before speaking, her hands now reassembling the gun on the counter. "Nick, I don't expect you to understand or approve of what I've done in the past. But what I do know is we've got a guy out there with some crazy ass scheme and it has something to do with your client, Hoyt. I need you, Nick."

"No you don't. You definitely don't need me, MaryLou. Thanks for cleaning my gun." Nick threw open the trailer door.

"Nick, Hoyt needs to look dead. To gain Zydeco's trust I had to pretend to kill him."

A piece fell into place for Nick. "The explosion."

"Yes, the explosion."

"You do realize you almost killed me too, don't you?"

"I wanted to scare Hoyt, not kill him."

"I don't believe you. I think you intended to kill Hoyt just so you would be solid with Izzy for your cover, and if I died, well, collateral damage happens."

"Look, Nick. If Zydeco doesn't believe Hoyt died in the explosion, he'll be coming after me and your boy, Hoyt. So I don't care how you do it, but Zydeco has to think Hoyt died. This investigation has gone on too long and there's too much at stake to back away now."

"Pretend to kill Hoyt? What you're really saying, MaryLou, is I need to make Hoyt disappear or you'll kill him, just so you can get to Zydeco."

"Think what you need to think, Nick."

"I knew you were a bit twisted, but I guess I never really knew you at all." He turned his back, grabbing a bottle of Johnny Walker and a nearby glass off a bookshelf. "Don't let the door hit your pretty ass on the way out!"

The Water's Fine

Nick knew he should have gone directly to Hoyt's place as soon as MaryLou left the trailer the night before. Clearly Hoyt hadn't told him everything. But he had slammed down several shots of Johnny Walker before he left civility behind and just drank right out of the bottle. Getting drunk was foolish, but in the moment, he wanted to numb the pain more than he needed to be in control. The headache, the haze, the pasty mouth, all told the story when he woke from the floor to a 5 AM alarm. The governor. He had called the governor's office the day before to get some time with her, primarily to rule her out as one of his suspects. The only time she had available was 6AM at the Barton Springs Pool during her daily swim workout. *Shit.*

With a pair of swimming trunks, as requested by the governor, a handful of aspirin, and a very strong black cup of coffee, Nick made his way, in light early morning traffic, to Zilker Park. Barton Springs, a natural spring-fed pool, had been a gathering spot in Austin for a hundred years. Nick had been there a few times over the years, especially recalling with fondness the topless female sunbathers who occasionally populated the hillside rising from the green blue water when he was a teen.

Parking by a stone bathhouse he noticed three black SUVs making up Governor Adamson's entourage. Having been relieved of his gun by security, he walked down steps to the side of the pool, watching a lone figure smoothly move through the water, her hands entering with barely a splash, and the vee of a small wake forming around her.

A suit in dark sunglasses, cowboy boots, and hat, stood beside him.

"She wants you to put on your trunks and join her."

The thought of the initial shock of icy water and the throbbing of his head left Nick less than enthusiastic. "Really? Can't I just talk with her when she's done?"

"Tight schedule today. It's either take a swim or go home. Your choice."

Nick turned to go back up the slope to the bath house.

"We're all men here. Well, except for the governor, of course. Just drop your shorts right here."

Too tired and hung over to fight or care, he stripped down, pulling on

134

a loud pair of red floral trunks he had purchased a few years ago for a trip to Hawaii. Diving in, the cold water felt like thirty below, but after the initial, breathtaking shock, the cold seemed to suck the pain right out of his head. And the haze of the morning had definitely lifted. He waited for her to swim by, joining her briefly, then trailing her to the deep end and returning, his lungs burning, to the shallow end almost three football field lengths away. They turned and the athletic governor, wearing a black swim cap with GOV in two inch high white letters on either side, a pair of black goggles with yellow tinted lenses and a one piece swimsuit, which looked like someone had made two lycra Texas lone star state flags and sown them together for gubernatorial swim wear, paused to speak.

"Nick Sibelius?"

"Yes, ma'am."

"Race you."

And with those words the Governor had taken two lengths, splashing water at him with her powerful kicks. Nick decided he had been trailing behind this woman enough, taking in a deep breath and then powering into his stroke. However, each time he looked up, she had several more body lengths on him, until at the wall, she gave the appearance of someone who had finished so long ago his arrival was an afterthought.

She leaned away from the wall, as if she intended to do another lap. Nick measured out his words in the gaps between his gasps for air. "Governor. We need. To talk. Urgent."

She lifted the goggles off her eyes, moving them to her forehead. "How can I help you, Mr. Sibelius?"

Nick took in a few deep breaths. "I believe you know Dan Hoyt."

"I've heard of him. Developer?"

"He introduced me to you yesterday when you were having breakfast with him."

"Oh, yes. Of course. Mr. Hoyt."

"Governor, normally I'd be happy to beat around the bush with you, but the current situation requires me to cut to the chase."

"Situation?"

Nick ignored her question. "I understand from Hoyt the two of you have had a relationship for the last two years."

Her tone shifted dramatically. It passed through Nick's mind she was quite capable of pushing him under the water until he was dead. "I will publicly deny it. What do you want?"

"You misunderstand. I'm not blackmailing you. I'm trying to keep someone from killing Hoyt."

"Someone's after Daniel?"

She had turned soft in a flash. If she kept this up, Nick thought he might get motion sickness.

"Yes, and I think it may have something to do with your business arrangement with Hoyt, with Daniel."

She turned hard again, suspicious. "What did he tell you?"

"This works better if I ask the questions."

"Get over it. What did he tell you?"

"He said you helped him get the votes for the project and the easements for both the plant and the pipelines."

"Again, publicly, I will deny it, but yes, you are correct."

"And Los Diablos Tejanos? How do they fit into the plan?"

"The drug cartel? I don't know what you're talking about."

"I've got information linking Hoyt to Izzy Zydeco and the Diablos. Surely if you're in business, and if I may be so bold to say, in bed with Hoyt, you'd know about Izzy and the cartel?"

Governor Adamson ripped her swim cap and goggles off her head, hurling them to the deck. The killer shark appeared, yet again.

"Listen to me, Sibelius, and listen good. I only took this meeting because I know you're working for Daniel. You tell him if he's gotten me entangled with the Diablos I will personally pull his testicles up through his throat and shove them where his eye balls used to be. My God. I'm in the middle of a presidential campaign. If the press gets hold of this it will take me off message for several weeks to clean it up. I cannot afford to lose weeks of this campaign because of some little prick."

"Yes, ma'am."

She grabbed the deck and effortlessly popped herself up on the sidewalk. One of her security detail held open a white terrycloth robe, which on the governor reminded Nick more of a prize fighter's robe than a pool coverup. Before Nick could get out, she stepped to the side of the pool, her immaculately manicured toes positioned right by his hands. He looked up to the Amazonian prize fighting female goddess-warrior presidential candidate towering over him.

"One last thing, Sibelius. You tell Hoyt to clean this up—now. And if he doesn't straighten out this mess, then he better be dead. Because as God is my witness, I will stomp his ass so far into the ground the only evidence of his existence will be a wet spot."

"Yes, ma'am."

He watched her walk away, surrounded by four men in dark suits. It didn't take a psychotherapist to know the Diablos and Izzy were a surprise to her. Nick pulled himself out of the pool, shivering as he made the long walk back to his clothes. Hoyt had not been honest with him. If the man wanted to be breathing in the next few days, he better start telling the truth.

Linebacker

Dried off from his swim, and dressed, Nick went back to the hospital to see Hoyt. If someone like MaryLou had an eye on him, then Hoyt had not been telling Nick the whole truth, if he told any truth at all. Having learned the hard way in Pflugerville, a covert Homeland Security agent roaming your turf predicts the shit storm to come, as surely as the gusty, humid Gulf winds foretell lightning and rain. When Nick got to Hoyt's room he discovered the man had checked himself out, probably trying to evade Charity's next attack. The last place Hoyt should hole up would be his house on Island Palms, which is why Nick drove as quickly as his El Camino would take him to the house. Arriving at Hoyt's home, still expansive in spite of the garage lying in charred ruins, Hoyt's white pickup truck sat parked in plain view.

Hoyt answered the door barefoot in some baggy boxer shorts and a Bahama tee shirt with a bourbon in one hand and a smoldering cigar in the other. The pungent odor of Hoyt's favorite Cubans filled the foyer as if a priest had just walked through with a silver censer filled with choice Cuban tobaccos.

"Ah, my protector. Come on in, Nick."

Nick stepped through the door, waving the thickest part of the smoke away from his face. "Self-medicating, Hoyt?"

"This?" He looked at his smoldering cigar. "Yeah. Want to join me?"

"We have some talking to do."

"Oo...sounds serious." Hoyt attempted to make quotation marks in the air as well as a person with a bourbon in one hand and a cigar in the other can do.

"Yes, Hoyt. It's serious."

"We better sit down then. I wouldn't want to be serious standing up. Hell, I'm having trouble just standing, much less standing seriously."

Hoyt had definitely been home long enough to have more than one double bourbon. Nick took the drink out of Hoyt's hand, setting it on a nearby table, then plucked Hoyt's cigar out of his other hand.

"Hey, my cigar!"

"You can finish it after we talk. Now go over to the sofa and sit."

"I'm not your f-fucking employee, Nick."

"You're going to need an employee to feed you liquids if you don't sit down right now."

"Okay, okay. Jeez. So damn serious all the time." Hoyt plopped on the sofa, a nonchalant smile on his face.

"What are you not telling me, Hoyt?"

"I don't know what you're talking about."

"That's really how you want to play this? Someone tries to kill you by blowing up your garage and you want to sit there acting like you don't have a clue?"

"It's that crazy Charity bitch you told me about. Seems to me if you're as good as you think you are, then she wouldn't be a problem anymore."

"Charity didn't blow up your garage. Someone else is after you. Who?"

"I honestly don't know, Nick. I mean, I'm a pretty high-profile guy."

"Who are you doing business with these days? Any major partners involved in your water deal?"

"Nobody. I learned to not let anyone have too large a percentage—"

"How about Izzy Zydeco? He's a principal in the deal, right?"

Hoyt shifted nervously. "Izzy? Yeah, so what?"

"Is there a reason your partner would be after your ass?"

"Well, maybe. But he wouldn't be interested in killing me."

"Izzy Zydeco? You've got a multi-billionaire partner with a history of busting your balls and you don't think he might have a reason to see you dead?"

"He's just providing some cash for the deal."

"Then why are federal agents sniffing around, Hoyt? What's going on? What are you not telling me?"

"Federal agents? Look, he screwed me over on my condo deal and set it up so I'd have to use his money for the water deal. That's all there is to it. I don't see why he'd want me dead."

"I completely agree, Hoyt. Why would he want you dead? If he kills you he only takes over a water project covering the entire state of Texas worth billions of dollars. No reason at all."

"But we're business associates. You really think he'd kill me to get control of the business?"

"Seems a little extreme, but all I know is someone wants you dead. Is there anything else you're not telling me?"

"No, no that's it."

Hoyt sat there fidgeting, eyes darting around the room, the fingers of his right hand unconsciously tapping on the sofa.

"Hoyt, tell me about this deal you have with Izzy."

"He's just a financial partner who will get a percentage of the profit based on his investment."

"What else?"

"What else? What is this, the damn Inquisition? Are you going to take me to the dungeon and torture me?" Beads of perspiration appeared on Hoyt's forehead. The calm and collected salesman had some cracks in his tailored, entrepreneurial suit.

"Why are you so nervous, Hoyt? Am I asking too many difficult questions? Having trouble coming up with convincing lies to tell me?"

Hoyt stood, face flushed. "I think we're done here, Nick. You've overstayed your welcome. In fact, you're fired."

Nick sat calmly, watching Hoyt move from denial to fear and now to a tenuous flash of anger. He figured despair would be showing up in the next thirty to sixty seconds.

"What are you staring at? I told you to get the hell out. You think you can just come in here and push me around. Well you can't. I'm Dan Hoyt, damn it! This water project is the deal of a lifetime. A lifetime! I can't believe someone's trying to kill me. Kill *me*." He sat back down on the sofa, his head in his hands. "Look, Nick. I didn't mean what I said. I just can't believe this is happening. I'm not up for being killed over this. But I have to know you can protect me. I mean, do you really think Izzy's a killer? Jesus. I don't know. I suppose it's possible, but I don't think I can tell you. what's going on If he finds out and what you say is true..."

"Hoyt."

"What?"

"Take a breath."

"But if you're right?"

"Breathe."

Hoyt stopped talking, and took in several deep breaths, which brought some color back to his face. Nick noted a slight tremor in Hoyt's hands.

"He wanted to do a deal with the Diablos Tejanos. Something about using the pipeline to move drugs. I told him I wouldn't do it."

"But?"

Hoyt held his head in his hands. "But when we couldn't meet the project deadline on the desalination plant, I needed Izzy to help make the governor and our other investors believe we were up and running."

"So you cut a deal with Izzy to let him use the pipeline for the Diablos."

They both sat in silence, Hoyt still holding his head and Nick astonished how such a publicly successful businessman can be such a total idiot.

"I tell you what Hoyt. The combination of Izzy and the Diablos is like kicking a fire ant bed and then shoving your face into the mound. What part of murderous drug cartel failed to register in your mind?"

He lowered his hands, looking up at Nick, with eyes on the edge of tears.

"I know. I just wanted this deal to go through. Desperate times require—"

"Desperate measure, I know, Hoyt. Only this desperate action is going to get you killed."

Hoyt wiped his eyes with his hands, sighing. "I can't believe Izzy is a murderer. So, what's the plan? Kill him before he kills me?"

"No, Hoyt. I'm a private investigator, not your personal hit man. I'll watch him, see what I can find out. In the meantime, you're going to disappear. I assume you have panic room among the thirty-plus rooms in this place?"

"Not here, but at the compound, yeah. State of the art. Independent filtered water and air supply, home theater, satellite communications, wet bar—"

"Yeah. I don't need the sales pitch. Go to the compound and lock yourself in the panic room. Don't stop for a beer and nachos and don't bring anyone with you."

"What? How long am I supposed to be locked away in a dungeon?"

"You have two options here, Hoyt. You either lay low for a few days, maybe a week, in a dungeon suite with a home theater and a wet bar, or you can choose the second option."

"I suppose the second option involves hiding me away in jail or something?"

"No, Hoyt. The second option is death. Permanent death."

"I bet you were a star on your high school debate team, Nick."

"Middle linebacker—All-State. So, which is it, life or death?"

"Persuasive argument. I choose the home theater and wet bar."

Hoyt Is Dead

Over the years, first in the CIA and now in Homeland Security, MaryLou had come close to death. But not since Barry Swenson had raped her in high school had she ever felt so defenseless inside of Izzy's virtual game. Pulling off the gaming body suit in the dressing room, she wasn't really surprised to see the bruises and welts from Izzy's "virtual" assault on her. He was bright, he was vicious, he was unpredictable, and when this assignment was done, he'd be dead—one way or the other. She couldn't believe she had let him surprise her, overpower her so easily. Outwardly she had forced a facade of empowered rage with Izzy. However, deep inside, a frightened little girl haunted her.

When Izzy had demanded she terminate Hoyt, MaryLou considered her options. Killing Hoyt would be the easiest thing to do. Killing a civilian in the cause of national security would be a difficult sell and potentially set off a political shit storm if not contained quickly. However, Nick Sibelius being in the mix created the greatest impediment to a simple, clean kill. No matter what she did, he would know and wouldn't stop until he had hunted her down. But she needed Izzy to believe in her, to trust her. What she hadn't counted on was Hoyt pressing the remote button so close to the garage door.

Not ready to give up on her plan, she had followed Hoyt to the Four Seasons Hotel. Just avoiding Nick, she waited for Hoyt's limo hoping the opportunity to take him out would present itself. Instead, some amateur started shooting from a rooftop. An ambulance had picked up Hoyt. He was alive, but he was screaming something about being shot and bleeding to death, so hope sprung eternal. Besides, killing him in a hospital room would be easy. Just a little medication error and the deed would be done. Having stolen a lab coat and badge from a careless intern, she stood behind a small gathering of nurses having a good laugh watching a patient on YouTube—Dan Hoyt—running stark naked down the hall. In the midst of the frivolity she discovered he had run bare butted from the hospital over an hour before she had arrived.

As a last-ditch effort, she took a chance on convincing Nick to keep Hoyt out of sight, for old time's sake—not that they had much in the way of 'old times'. She had connected with Nick one wonderful night over a year ago. Hell, for a few days, she thought she had fallen in love with the guy and was prepared to leave the agency. In hindsight, the whole episode was pretty unbelievable. Apparently her emotions around her half-brother, Junior, and the guy who had raped her when they were teenagers, were stronger and more disorienting than she had imagined. Fortunately, she had come to her senses in time to save the mission.

Now, a small voice in the back of her mind argued her tactics were underhanded. However, a much stronger, professional voice drowned out the weak chatter. The love Nick felt for her, an emotion she had cultivated in him, was an asset she could use as leverage to get the job done. She hadn't counted on Nick turning her away. She could only hope Hoyt would keep out of sight and Izzy would stay wrapped up in his own empire-building and not pay attention to the news. If Izzy discovered Hoyt was alive, her cover would be blown and her only choice would be to kill Izzy, hoping his death stopped whatever destructive plan he had going.

She knocked, opening Izzy's office door to see him sitting behind a desk consisting of a glass top resting on brushed steel legs. His desktop was completely clean, except for an iPad. Two walls were solid glass with views of sandstone cliffs rising from Lake Austin and the Loop 360 suspension bridge. A third wall had four large flat screens combined to create on huge picture covering most of the wall. She expected to see world stock market reports, but instead the giant screen offered a live satellite image of the earth. The room held no books, knickknacks, awards, or family photos. The sterility of the space gave the office an artificial feel opposite the effect of his virtual game environments. He rose, walking around the table to greet her as she entered. He hooked his left arm around her waist, his face almost touching hers. MaryLou wanted to shove a gun into his chest and pull the trigger, but she fought back her anger, even as she felt his disgusting breath against her cheek, her ear, her neck. His lips just grazed her earlobe.

"So good of you to come by, MaryLou. I've missed you."

She stepped away, but he held her firmly, leaving her slightly off balance. She imagined throwing a quick punch to his groin and a quick thrust of her knee into his face, crushing the bridge of his nose into his brain. He'd be dead before he hit the floor.

"It's good to see you too, Izzy."

"Is it? Is it, really? That's good. Sometimes I think of you, MaryLou. Soft, naked, vulnerable. I think we both know how quickly terrible things can happen."

"Yes. Terrible things."

He released his grasp on her waist, walking back to his desk.

"What can I do for you? Another round of *Guns n' Drugs*? Or do you have some good news for me?"

"Good news. Hoyt's dead."

"Excellent. Sit down. Tell me all about it. I want to hear every last detail of his demise."

MaryLou sat in a leather and chrome chair across from Izzy.

"I planted a bomb in his garage. He died in the blast."

Izzy sat back, his fingers drumming on the glass top.

"That's it? No screaming, burning flesh, the sound of eye balls popping in the heat? Come on, MaryLou. The details."

She wasn't sure if he was testing her, or if he was a crazy sociopath, or both.

"I set the explosive to detonate when he pressed the garage remote to open the door. He died not only from the blast, but the shrapnel from the door tore him open. I could see him aflame, trying to open the door, then screaming. A hideous sound, like a wild animal being eviscerated alive. Black smoke billowed from the wreckage, the air pungent with burning tires and fuel." *I should turn this into a screenplay.* "He's dead, Izzy."

"An eviscerated wild animal. I like it." He banged a palm on the desk top for emphasis. "I like it, MaryLou. You're working out just fine. Much better than my last associate."

"What happened to her?"

"Him. He made a promise he failed to keep. Once he finally came through, I had to let him go."

"Fired him?"

"Terminated him. Gave him the old heave-ho, but I'm sure someone will pick him up in the next week or two."

"Good. It's a tough market out there right now."

"Life or death, MaryLou. Absolutely cutthroat. But enough about the past. Let's talk about the future. Since you've gotten yourself bloodied, if you will, I'd like you to go with me to meet one of my other business associates."

"What, do you need me to hold your laptop for you?"

Izzy smiled, but his eyes narrowed enough to let MaryLou know her sarcasm had hit a nerve.

"Not that kind of business associate. More of the kill you if you turn your back on him type. Do come armed."

"Always."

Here, Piggy

Nick made sure Hoyt packed some clothes and other necessities, then drove away to the compound before he left to have a conversation with Izzy Zydeco. On the way, he considered giving Theresa a call to let her know their case was not as completed as they had hoped, but he told himself she needed a break. He'd do some legwork, figure out what Hoyt really had going on with Izzy, and if needed, bring Theresa in. Of course, he knew she didn't need a break. Nick just didn't want to face her after sleeping with MaryLou. *What was I thinking? I get around that woman and just go stupid. Theresa's not an idiot. She'll figure things out, even if I don't tell her.* He willed himself to push his feelings about Theresa into a compartment. He needed to focus on one thing right now: Izzy Zydeco.

Nick didn't have much of a plan in mind other than walking into Izzy's office and confronting him directly. Izzy would, of course, deny everything, but Nick knew he'd learn a lot from how Izzy responded to his questions. Once at the corporate office, he noticed MaryLou's Porsche parked nearby. He waited, not wanting MaryLou in the mix when he had his one-on-one with Zydeco. An hour later MaryLou came out of the building with Izzy Zydeco at her side. What was she playing at? They got in her car, driving south. He followed at a discreet distance as they picked up State Highway 71 toward Bastrop. Soon they were driving among stands of pine trees, until the Porsche turned onto a dirt road. Nick had to drop back farther, partly because he didn't want to be spotted and partly because the old El Camino kept bottoming out on the crown of the dirt road, but he still managed to follow the dust cloud MaryLou's car kicked up. Given his old car could barely keep pace with a low-slung sports car on a dirt road, he put having Charlie get him some new shocks on his mental to-do list. Coming to a locked gate, he pulled off the road, hiding it partially behind some brush.

Luckily, the Porsche only drove another quarter mile, so Nick followed on foot and hid in a stand of mesquite and oak fifty yards from them. He could see a pipeline ground angling up to a platform and then disappearing back underground. MaryLou and Izzy stood by the platform with two men. They spoke for maybe two minutes, then one of the men used a socket wrench to remove the bolts covering a section of pipe intersecting the main pipeline. He called for his partner and together they pulled a large metal object, the diameter of the pipe and maybe three times the diameter in length, from the opening in the pipe. Setting the object on the platform, they pulled out a package. There were some congratulatory shouts, a high five between the two men and then one of the men crashed over the platform safety railing, followed immediately by the delayed sound of a single gunshot. Nick drew his weapon, but knew he didn't have a shot at that distance and he had only open ground between himself and the pipeline. The other man raised his hands in the air, the package having been tossed to the ground when his partner fell. Izzy, who had fired the first shot, spoke to MaryLou and then with his gun trained on the man, climbed the ladder to the platform. He pistol-whipped the man who held his arms up protectively, sending him crumbling to his knees. Izzy continued to beat him, finally resorting to repeatedly kicking him as he now lay prone on the platform. He dragged the man to the edge, rolling him off where he landed in a heap on the ground. The first killing took MaryLou by surprise, but surely she would intervene if Izzy tried to kill the second man. Izzy resealed the pipe and then came back to MaryLou, who had kept her weapon trained on the other man the entire time Izzy had been on the platform. Some words were exchanged, then he fired once, twice into the first victim. The second man had somehow gotten to his knees, crawling away toward an SUV parked fifty feet from the platform. Izzy walked over to him, put two bullets in his head and the man slumped to the ground dead. Izzy walked back over to MaryLou and kicked the other dead man, screaming and then shooting several more times into the body.

They walked back to the Porsche, Izzy now on the phone, as MaryLou opened the driver's side door. He got in, but MaryLou remained standing by the door, then turned to look directly in Nick's direction. He couldn't imagine she could see him, but she looked anyway, as if some sonar bearing had gone off in her head. Then she got in the car and drove away.

He let sufficient time pass for MaryLou to have gotten back to the highway, then made his way over to the platform and the dead men. The one by the car had two bullet wounds in the head and would be hard to identify from the beating Izzy had inflicted. The other man, a twenty-something Latino with rattlesnake boots and a Diablos tattoo, lay in the dirt with three shots to the chest and couple to the head. Definitely dead. He didn't have a wallet, but Nick found a book of matches from a men's club called Loaded 4 Bare. Why would Izzy kill two Diablos members and get so crazy violent? They clearly were in on his plan with the pipeline, which must entail moving drugs. But why the fireworks? And what was MaryLou doing, really? Would a Homeland Security Agent, even a covert agent, stand by while some whack-job killed two people? If she was trying to get Izzy to trust her, the price was high, so the prize must be something quite significant.

What are you playing at MaryLou?

After gathering what he could from the dead body he climbed onto the platform. Nick knew nothing about pipelines or what the platform could possibly be used for, so he pulled out his phone, googling "pipeline." He read through a Wikipedia reference not finding anything explaining the platform, when he came upon an odd link to the word "pig." The page opened to a picture of the object, a pipeline inspection gauge, he had seen the men retrieve from the pipeline. Izzy had apparently used the pig to transport a package of some kind. Hoyt's pipeline plan included Austin, Houston and San Antonio with a longer-term plan for Dallas and even El Paso. Izzy must be moving drugs, weapons, or something else illegal through the pipelines using pigs to ferry the goods. Nevertheless, the pig still didn't explain Izzy killing members of the cartel.

He pulled the matchbook back out of his pocket. The front showed a naked woman bending over, back side facing him, as she looked back between her legs, her breasts hanging like plump fruit on either side of her face, and two revolvers blasting away. On the back he found an address for a place a little farther east of Bastrop on 71. If he was lucky, the Diablos Tejanos hung out at the club and he might be able to get some insight into Izzy. That is, if he survived the conversation.

~*~

Driving Highway 71 past Smithville, the face of a pretty young woman with a come hither look filled a billboard advertising *Loaded 4 Bare*. And if a motorist had any doubt, a large yellow arrow pointing down to the club underneath the sign urging passersby to "Get Loaded." Nick coasted into the parking lot filled with a number of motorcycles, pickups and a few tricked out low riders. Normally walking into the hornet's nest of a drug cartel would not be a healthy choice. However, he hoped he could drop Izzy's name here and there and maybe be seen as an ally to the Diablos and find a way into Izzy's operation. He knew he was being reckless, but his intuition told him whatever was happening was going to happen very soon and in a very big way.

The bouncer, a large Hispanic man, 350 pounds and six foot-three, sat on a bar stool by the door. As Nick walked up, the man stood. "Twenty bucks cover."

"Must be a good band."

He stared at Nick without breaking his neutral expression.

"Ladies. No band. Twenty bucks."

Nick pulled a twenty out of his wallet, handing the bill to the doorman. "Izzy around today? Izzy Zydeco?"

"Why do you ask?"

"Not that's it's any of your concern, but I've got some unfinished business with him. So have you seen him?"

"Do I look like your social secretary?"

Even in the middle of the day, the club was dark, loud music blaring, naked women pole dancing on the stage while men sat watching and drinking. He walked over to the bar and was about to order a drink when he felt someone step in close beside him. In his peripheral vision, Nick could see the guy had the advantage by height and weight and he smelled like he had forgotten to shower the last couple of days.

"You don't want to be drinking here, *cabron*."

"Really? I thought I came in here for a drink."

"Leave."

Nick looked back to the bartender. "Dos Equis."

The bartender responded with open palms communicating, "Sorry, but I can't serve you."

The big guy moved in closer. "What part of leave don't you get, asshole?"

"How about this? You tell me if Izzy's here and I'll leave."

"How 'bout this, *cabron*? You leave now or you wish you never came in." He grabbed Nick with both hands by the shirt, pulling him close enough for Nick to feel like the man had shoved Nick's head into a nasty, rank hole of stale beer and rotted nachos.

Nick looked the large man in the eyes, smiling. "Do you really want to do this amigo?"

"You're not my friend, asshole."

In one smooth movement, Nick thrust his arms between his attacker's, impacting the man's chin with both fists, while simultaneously crushing his knee into the large man's crotch. Having broken the hold, he stepped to one side, grabbed the back of the man's head, and slammed his face hard against the bar, the bridge of the big man's nose crushing on impact. Beer bottles flew as he crumpled to the floor, now covered in shattered glass, beer, and blood. Nick turned away from his attacker only to see the bouncer holding a gun at point blank range directly at his chest. Realizing he had picked the wrong time and place to fight a Diablos member, he raised his hands in surrender. The man's moans could just be heard over the thumping music, the naked showgirls not pausing for something as mundane as a fight among clientele.

Nick shrugged. "Sorry. We just had a little disagreement."

"Yeah, so I saw. Something about this Izzy guy you keep asking for?"

"Just a personal disagreement."

The bouncer motioned with his gun for Nick to turn around. "Come with me, *hijo de perra*. We'll see what Tigre wants to do with you."

They pushed through the crowd, the muzzle of the bouncer's gun jabbing Nick toward a door. Up some stairs Nick walked into an office. Two, two men sat on a leather sofa engaged in a video game playing out on a large flat screen. On another leather sofa, two young women curled up together with board expressions. A tall, thickly built muscular man covered in tattoos of guns and skulls bench pressed an impressive amount of weight, maybe three hundred pounds, while one of his foot soldiers spotted him. He pressed the bar up, then dropped the bar bell into its resting place. Rising, one of the girls came to him and proceeded to towel him off. He let Nick stand before him while she finished wiping him down like an SUV in a car wash.

He looked disinterested. Maybe a bit perturbed about a white man on his turf. "Who are you?"

"Nick Sibelius."

"I understand you're looking for someone named Izzy. I've got the name right, don't I?"

The weightlifting Tigre sounded educated, unlike everyone else he had met since he walked through the strip club's doors. There was something about the guy that seemed familiar.

"Yeah. Izzy Zydeco. Do I know you?"

"You just met me."

Nick couldn't quite place him, but the image in his head involved burnt orange-white football uniforms and a guy who could drill a quarterback right into the ground. "Did you play for UT? Linebacker?"

He smiled, obviously enjoying the lingering fame of his college career, which Nick remembered as being pretty damn outstanding. "Yes. Those were good times."

"And now you're the leader of a major cartel. How did that happen?"

"It's all about teamwork and leadership." The girl finished buffing Tigre and went back to her position with the other girl on the sofa. "So what about this Izzy?"

"I understand you're doing some business with Izzy."

"And how is my business your concern, Nick Sibelius?"

The two guys at the video game had stopped, either to listen to the conversation, or more likely in Nick's mind, to kick the crap out of him when Tigre gave the word. "I think he's gotten my client in over his head."

"Your client. What are you, an accountant?"

"Private investigator. I think my client didn't realize his business partner, Izzy Zydeco, had an arrangement with you."

"You seem to know a lot about my business. Who's your client?"

"Confidential information. I'm sure you understand."

"I understand. Still, who is your client?"

"So you are in business with Izzy?"

Tigre glared at him.

Nick knew he couldn't back down. Not now. Not in this place. "I'll take that as a yes."

"You don't like living, do you, Nick Sibelius?"

"Actually I do. In fact, I'm willing to make an exchange. I'll give you some information about Izzy Zydeco I'll bet you don't know and you'll let me walk out of here."

"How about you tell me what you know, then we'll see what state you'll be in when you leave."

The two large guys perked up at the mention of potential mayhem.

"Tigre, you mind if I call you Tigre? Do you really think I'd walk in here all on my own? If I don't walk out the door, there will be hell to pay and you'll be doing the paying."

A gun pressed against Nick's back, a voice behind him speaking. "Do you want me to take him out back and pop him, boss?"

Tigre looked at Nick, the unfeeling look of a wild predator determining if he wanted the kill now or later.

"Tell me what you know and it may go well for you. Otherwise, I'll leave you to my associates."

The girls were doing lines of coke and the image of some guys in an alley with machine guns, dead bodies sprawled here and there, sat frozen with the word "pause" in the middle of the video game screen.

"I saw Izzy earlier today at a pipeline insertion point near Bastrop. I believe two of your men were there to test moving drugs with pigs."

Tigre offered a dismissive laugh. "So far you're telling me things I know." He stopped laughing. "Things that get people killed."

"Do you know that Izzy murdered your men and stole the drugs?"

An eye-twitch, Tigre's only reaction, gave Nick all the information he needed. Izzy had betrayed Tigre.

"Goodbye, Nick Sibelius."

The bouncer grabbed Nick by the collar, pushing him out the door, down the stairs, and toward another door opening into the back lot of the club. They stood in the empty lot beside a large blue dumpster.

"On your knees, asshole."

"You know, the name *is* Nick. How would you like it if I called you asshole all the time?"

"On your knees."

Nick looked on the ground beside the dumpster, noticing a piece of rebar protruding just a few inches from underneath. Blocking the bouncer's view with his body, he got on his knees, his right hand grasping the heavy metal bar.

"I told you to leave, but you just wouldn't listen."

"Well, in all fairness, I asked you about Izzy and you failed to mention you knew him."

"I failed to mention him?"

Nick inched the steel rod out from under the dumpster. "Yeah, you failed. If you had told me you knew Izzy from the get go, all of this nastiness could have been avoided."

"Well, asshole, you won't have to worry about anything much longer."

"I suppose you're right."

Feeling the gun at the back of his head, Nick flipped onto his back, swinging the steel bar with ferocious precision at the bouncer's gun hand. The man screamed at the steel crushed his hand, gun flying across the asphalt. Nick planted a foot viciously in the bouncer's knee, the crunch signaling he had hit home. The bouncer toppled to the ground. Nick jumped to his feet, aiming one more savage kick to the fallen man's face, slamming his head with a thud against the dumpster. Nick grabbed the bouncer's gun and ran around the building to his car.

Only a few minutes after leaving the parking lot, one of the trucks from the club, a big double-dually Dodge pickup, appeared in his rear view mirror. They might simply be patrons leaving the club or they could be Tigre's men sent to finish the job. As a test he sped up to eighty then slowed to fifty, the truck staying about five hundred feet behind him the entire time.

Coming on the small town of Smithville, he took the exit, hoping to lose his pursuers in the gridded streets of the town. The truck followed him off the highway. Nick turned toward town, accelerating into a back street until he hit a dead end. Taking a hard right, the rear end of the El Camino sliding away, he regained control and sped down a road with a railroad to his left. The Diablos truck kicked up dirt, tires smoking as it made the turn and then accelerated, rapidly closing on him. Realizing he couldn't lose them on a straightaway, Nick began a series of sharp turns, using the grid of the town to slow down his adversary. He turned north, rushing toward an intersection just as a car drove across his path. He slammed on the brakes, the tail of the El Camino fishtailing, then slamming into the side of the other car. Looking left he could see the truck coming toward him, the driver of the other car yelling obscenities. He jabbed the accelerator with his foot, tires smoking as they struggled to gain traction. He pulled into an ally, then turned again crossing two more streets. Nick raced down the street, the truck filling his rear view mirror, when ahead of him, a garbage truck stopped, blocking the road. He swerved, bouncing over the curb, then plowed through several lawns and then back on the street, turning again, wondering how long the old El Camino would be able to keep this up. Just before he hit another dead end, he checked the mirror. The Dodge was not behind him anymore. He took a turn out of Smithville onto a small state road and seeing a sign, turned in to the Smithville airport. If he could find an empty hanger he could hide for awhile until the Diablos had given up the chase. Driving into the airport he opened the gate and took a small dirt road to a set of aged, rusting metal hangers. He cut through the lock with a pair of cutters he kept behind the passenger seat—standard private investigator gear—then pulled at the heavy door which creaked and groaned open. Two high-winged planes, both Cessna Skyhawks, shared the hangar with just enough room for Nick to fit his vehicle in between them. He backed in, shut off the engine, and breathed a sigh of relief.

Even though Nick let Tigre know Izzy had betrayed him, Tigre still wanted Nick dead. Probably Tigre didn't like anyone outside his control knowing his business. Nick couldn't imagine what Izzy had going that would include screwing over a drug cartel. However, getting out of this alive was the more immediate matter. He couldn't call the police. They would stop some guys in a truck who were just riding around. He had, however, just broken into a hangar containing two airplanes. Before he could think through his next steps, the rumble of the Dodge's big engine broke the momentary calm.

Nick ran to one of the planes. No keys. He went over to the other. The door opened. The owner had left the keys in the magneto switch. Ideally, he'd do a preflight and check the fuel, but all he could do right now was hope the tanks had enough to get him to Austin. He had never started a plane inside a hangar, but he had no choice. The aircraft engine roared to life, the sound multiplied many times over by metal hangar walls, dust and dirt flying everywhere. Nick hoped the Cessna's propeller would not strike the ground as he taxied over a dip at the hangar entrance. Once clear of the hangar he kept taxiing toward the short Smithville runway. He didn't have the time or luxury to check the wind, only knowing he needed to be on the runway as soon as possible. The Dodge slowed on the tarmac, clearly trying to determine if this plane had anything to do with their quarry. They raced away toward the hangars and Nick gunned the engine to taxi as fast as he dared. Stopping at the beginning of the runway, he hoped he could remember how to fly. He had been working on his pilot's license until the divorce a couple of years ago put those plans on hold. He had soloed, but he had only about thirty hours. The Dodge swung wide around the hangars, clearly having spotted his El Camino and put the pieces together. He lowered the flaps twenty degrees, held the brakes, then pushed the throttle in full. His pursuers raced toward him and he could see gun flashes from the windows. Releasing the brakes the plane lurched forward. Bullets exploded on the tarmac all around him. He didn't have a headset, so he could hear the metallic sound of lead penetrating the plane's aluminum hull. The plane lifted into the air, Nick holding a shallow angle of ascent, opting for distance from his pursuers over altitude.

Once at a safe distance he climbed to five thousand feet, turning off the transponder so he'd be invisible to traffic control. He would have to sort out the matter of stealing this plane, but not right now. In this moment he needed to find a non-towered airport, or better yet, an isolated grass landing strip. Fortunately, the plane's owner had a sectional map in the cockpit and after studying it briefly, Nick found what he needed—a private strip.

He altered course just as the engine quit, the drone of the motor replaced with the quiet whoosh of wind over the wings. Apparently the owner hadn't refueled after the last flight or bullets had ruptured one or both wing tanks. He quickly went through what he remembered of the emergency landing procedure, but after a two-year hiatus, he couldn't be sure if he was hitting all the points and didn't think to look for a checklist. Assuming he was going down, he shut off the fuel valve and looked for a landing spot. Below him he could see a two-lane road, a pasture with cattle grazing, and a cornfield. The road looked empty, long and straight, so he pointed the plane's nose in its direction, descending.

Less than fifty feet off the ground, he had the the plane aligned with the road. Trees lining the fields on either side rushed past, when a hay truck crossed the road right in front of him. He instinctively pulled on the yoke, lifting the nose and delaying the descent just enough for the truck to pass underneath. However, with the stall warning horn screaming, the nose abruptly dropped the ten feet to the ground at sixty miles per hour, slamming into the road, shearing off the prop and nose wheel. The last thing Nick remembered was the sickening screech of tearing metal.

~*~

"Are you okay?" A disembodied voice of a woman broke into Nick's consciousness.

"What?" He opened his eyes to a deep blue sky.

"I can't believe you tried to land your plane on the road. Did you run out of gas or something? I pulled you out, well, you helped a little. Didn't know if your plane was going to explode or something. You know, they always explode on TV, so that's why I wanted to get you out of there. You okay?"

"Yeah, just, just a little shaken up."

He sat on a grassy shoulder, the plane twenty yards away. The woman standing over him kept talking, adrenaline driving her on.

"I'd say shaken up at least. I can't believe you survived, I mean, look at your plane. You really crunched it into the ground. Thank goodness you were wearing a seatbelt. I didn't know they had seat belts. I mean, it makes sense. I just hadn't seen the inside of a little plane until you showed up. Are you sure you're alright? You look a little disoriented."

He glanced toward the plane, nose down with a collapsed landing gear and a sheared wing. Must have hit a telephone pole. "I think I just need a few minutes. A few minutes of peace and quiet to get my thoughts together."

"I totally understand. By the way, I called 9-1-1, so somebody should be here soon. You just hold on tight."

"I'm okay. Really."

Nick looked at his middle-aged, rather overweight, Good Samaritan. In other circumstances he would be very grateful for her assistance, but today, with Izzy Zydeco planning something terrible enough for MaryLou to be involved, the Diablos trying to kill him, and his client Hoyt the target of an assassin, he didn't have time to be helped.

"Can I borrow your car?"

"What?" She looked at him as if he had just spoken in a language foreign to her. "Darling, the only thing you'll be borrowing today is a hospital bed."

Nick grabbed her arm firmly, pulling himself to a standing position. "I do appreciate your help, but I have a situation. I can't hang around for the EMTs to arrive. Do you keep your purse in the car?"

The woman, who only a moment ago wouldn't shut up, now stood, mouth agape. Nick limped over to her car and found the keys in her purse. By the time he got back to her, she was standing, arms crossed, frowning.

"This is how you treat people who help you? Steal their car?"

Nick handed her the purse. "Normally, no. And I'm not stealing your car, only borrowing. I'll be in touch to get your car back to you and compensate you for your trouble."

As he walked back to her Corolla, she yelled, "Compensate? What do you mean, compensate? I don't understand. What's happening?"

Nick started the car, then raced past her. A mile down the road he passed, an ambulance rushing the other way to the scene of a plane crash.

Connections

Nick's mind raced as he drove backroads toward Austin. Things weren't adding up in his mind and he didn't like the feeling. Hoyt had said Izzy wanted to gain a toehold in Los Diablos Tejanos by using the pipeline to transport narcotics across the state. The governor, responsible for the easements and political lubrication to make the pipelines happen, had no idea Izzy or the Diablos were in on the deal. But when Izzy had a meeting at a pipeline pig insertion platform in what must have been a test run, he went all psychopath on the two Diablos members, killing them. Not exactly normal practice for building a good working relationship with your partner, unless, of course, the plan was to take over the cartel. A man would have to have balls the size of Goodyear blimps and an armed force capable of taking over a small country if he planned on starting an all-out war with Tigre and the Diablos.

And MaryLou. She just stood there while Izzy gunned down both of those men. She either was never the agent she purported to be or something significant enough to warrant the deaths of two men was in the works. What reason could she have for allowing those murders? Nick knew there had to be more to this.

He pushed the Corolla hard toward JVI, hoping MaryLou would return there sometime tonight with Izzy. His luck held and her Porsche sat parked by the entrance. She wouldn't be expecting him in a Corolla, so he was able to park at a far corner of the company lot where he could see her car. Forty-five minutes passed before MaryLou walked out of the building toward her car. He let her drive past him and then followed from a discreet distance all the way to South Congress and the San Jose Motel. He parked a block away, walking quickly to the hotel to see her enter Room 3.

She answered the knock on her door, a look of pleased surprise in her eyes.

"You're becoming quite the detective, Nick."

"May I come in?" He placed a foot in the doorway.

"How did you find me?"

"Followed you."

"From JVI?"

"Yes, may I come in? We need to talk."

She thought for a moment, then stepped aside to let him in.

Nick looked around the minimalist decor of her room. "What's going on, MaryLou?"

"You were there, weren't you?"

"Was I there when you participated in the murder of two people? Yes, I was there."

"I knew it. I just had a feeling you were hiding up in that stand of trees. Look Nick, walk away from this. You've done your part with Hoyt. Walk away."

"Too late."

MaryLou took a step toward him, touching his arm with her hand. "No it's not, Nick. Walk away."

Nick moved away from her, inspecting an abstract painting on the wall. His best guess was a tiger eviscerating a lamb. "I've got a client with a target on his back because he's gotten entangled with a drug cartel and a psychopath. I can't walk away. Besides, you're not telling me the whole story. What is Izzy doing with the Diablos?"

"Sure I am, Nick. Why do you think Izzy killed those guys? He *is* crazy, but he wants to be the head of the Diablos."

"What does any of this have to do with Hoyt? And does every mission you take involve murdering people?"

"I didn't want to get you involved, Nick."

"I am involved, MaryLou. I watched you stand by and let Zydeco kill those guys. So you better start talking to me or I'm going to make your life difficult."

"Yes. I see that." Nick could see her doing tactical calculations in her head about sharing information with him before she proceeded. "Okay. We've been watching Izzy Zydeco for some time now. He made some unusual connections in the Middle East and Latin America while developing *Guns n' Drugs* and his latest, *Mujahid Death Match 1.2*. Then, he went out of his way to destroy Hoyt's condo project, only to come back as his business partner in a massive desalination plant and pipeline grid. Odd pair, don't you think?"

"So Izzy went to a lot of trouble to worm his way into Hoyt's water deal. Where do the Diablos come in?"

"We thought he was generating some off-the-books revenue by using the pipeline to transport drugs for the Diablos. But after his performance today and my conversation with him after, he doesn't want to partner with them. He wants to destroy the Diablos and take over their drug business."

"I don't know, MaryLou. You'd think if someone went to the Diablos saying he wanted to kill Izzy Zydeco, the Diablos would be all over it. Probably give the guy some extra ammo and maybe even a couple of thugs to help out."

"Yeah, maybe."

"Well, I offered and they came after my ass. I had to steal an airplane just to get away from them. It was almost as if they had orders from Izzy to kill anyone asking questions about him. Doesn't add up, does it?"

"So you're thinking he only wants to have the appearance of a war? Possible. Of course, the cartel is famous for killing anything that moves."

He looked at MaryLou, sensing the conversation had flowed far too easily. She had to be withholding something.

"There's more, MaryLou. What else? You wouldn't have let Izzy murder those two over some drugs. What's going on?"

She met Nick's gaze. Then, with a shrug, she shook her head. "Fine. A few months ago we began tracking a man named Jonah Martin, a programmer with the Department of Defense. Izzy met him in Germany and hired him to help develop one of his games, *Mujahid*. Then Jonah made contacts with sources who could supply him with radioactive materials. Earlier this week he dropped off the grid. Then yesterday his body was found in a dumpster under the 360 bridge, which, as you know, is only a few hundred feet from JVI. He had trace levels of radioactivity on his clothes and skin."

"You think Jonah supplied radioactive materials to someone and was then killed to keep him from talking. And you think Izzy had something to do with it?"

"I don't know for certain, but from what I've seen of Izzy up close so far, killing Jonah Martin would not be out of character. And I wouldn't be too surprised if he had a plan for a some radioactive material. I thought he might contaminate the Diablos' drug shipments to drive them out of the business. Given your experience with the Diablos today, I'm thinking he might have something else in mind."

"So Izzy is using the Diablos as a diversion. A diversion from what? This must have something to do with Hoyt and this water business. I take it you're in tight with Zydeco?"

"After today, I'm his trusted associate."

"Good. I'll work the Hoyt angle. If either of us comes up with something we call each other. Agreed?"

"This is a Homeland Security mission, Nick."

"MaryLou, because of our long, trusting relationship I'm going to pretend you didn't say that. Besides, I'd hate for the photos I took of you helping Zydeco murder two men today get to the local and national papers."

"You're bluffing."

"Try me. We either work this together or you're going down. Your choice."

Her lips curled into an irritated smile. "You've become a real bastard, Sibelius."

Nick moved toward the door, turning the knob to let himself out. "Well, I suppose it's hard to really know a man after only bedding him a couple of times. So long, MaryLou." Nick closed the door and walked back through the courtyard. Its fountain, shut off because of the drought, stood partially filled with stagnant water.

~*~

Nick drove to the office hoping he wouldn't be face-to-face with Theresa. Not right now with so much happening and so many unanswered questions. Even though they were business partners, this first case was clearly spiraling out of control and he didn't want Theresa in the middle of the mess. Unfortunately, her loaner car sat parked by the front door. Would she know he had slept with MaryLou? He needed to tell Theresa about Tigre, MaryLou, and all the rest. Or did he? He wasn't altogether sure why he went to bed with MaryLou and he didn't want to screw up what he had developing with Theresa.

Well, Theresa doesn't need to know, and besides, I don't have to explain my personal life to her.

He walked into the office hoping to get the conversation focused on the business at hand instead of MaryLou. Theresa greeted Nick as he walked in the office door, "Hi, Nick. Where have you been all day?"

Nick described following Izzy to the pig insertion platform, the murdered men, and finding, and then running, from the Diablos.

"So I tracked down MaryLou to find out what she wasn't telling us."

"And did you find her."

"Well, yes."

"At JVI?"

"Uh, no. I followed her to her hotel. Turns out she's withholding information from us."

"So you questioned her in her room, I suppose?"

"Does it matter where I questioned her, Theresa? We talked. Okay?" Nick felt defensive, guilty.

"Don't get your chaps in a bind there cowboy. Just wondered. Seems to be a sensitive topic."

"What do you want to know, Theresa? You want a blow-by-blow or can I just cut to the chase?"

She looked at him with a blank expression. "How about a blow-by-blow."

Nick felt himself sinking in quicksand with no easy escape. A look of recognition passed across her face.

"You slept with her, didn't you." Her words were not a question and Nick's silence only confirmed her hunch.

"Dammit, Nick."

"It's not what you think."

"It's not? Let me guess, you used your guile and charisma in bed to force her to reveal state secrets. Something like that?"

"What do you care, anyway? You said we were done." Nick didn't know why he was taking the offensive. He wanted to take each word back as he spoke.

"Of course I said we were done you stupid sonofabitch. What, you think I'm going to stand around while you lie to me about your old girlfriend? But instead of crawling back to me and begging for mercy, what do you do? You fucked her. God, I knew this was going to happen to me again. Goddamn you."

Nick didn't understand what was happening. Theresa stood before him in tears. He thought she had written him off. And now she once again stormed out of the office slamming the door with such force the walls shook. No matter how good the sex had been, he knew sleeping with MaryLou was a mistake. She wanted a sex buddy, not a relationship. A relationship with MaryLou, no strings attached, didn't appeal to him because he wanted—he needed—a partner. A real life partner. Something he thought he had with his ex until she broke her commitment to him. Yes, he wanted a partner and he sensed he might have one in Theresa.

Part of him wanted to follow after her, but he decided instead to go check on Hoyt. He told himself he had a responsibility to his client, but he knew the truth. He knew he had lost Theresa and he didn't want to confirm the reality yet.

Thirst Quenching Plan

Izzy Zydeco sat in his office, laptop open on the desk in front of him. Several images had been thrown up on the large flat screens. A market report showed VGI up five points and trading at $347 a share. The next sales report for the quarter should make his investors happy. *Guns n' Drugs* continued to sell strong and projections for *Mujahid* estimated two million units next quarter. He had someone in Dubai who wanted him to invest in a solar energy project. But what interested him the most was a live feed from Hoyt's compound that he had his team covertly install when he partnered with Hoyt on the desalination plant. In general, Izzy never liked to have a business partner, preferring a more autocratic style of leadership. So if he had to have a partner for strategic reasons, he certainly wanted to know what they were doing at all times. Take today for example. His dearly departed partner, killed in a horrific explosion described in glorious detail by his new trusted associate, MaryLou Perkins, stood in his panic room, picking out a movie to watch. Izzy picked up the laptop, slammed it shut, and then hurled it at the screen which fractured on impact.

~*~

Theresa let her phone ring a few times, unable to pull away from her anger with Nick for being such a bastard. Over the last several days she had let herself imagine the two of them together, only to be smacked in the face with MaryLou—the ghost and now, the real thing. The incessant ringing drove her to finally pick up the call. A low, gravelly voice came on the line.

"Hello, Theresa Soliz?"

"Yeah."

"I have information you might be interested in about Izzy Zydeco."

"Who am I talking to and how did you get this number?"

"My name is not important. Zydeco is planning a terrible terrorist act and I can give you the information you need to stop him."

"What's the information?"

"Not over the phone. Do you know the abandoned control tower where the old Mueller Airport used to be?"

"Yes."

"Meet me there in thirty minutes."

Before Theresa could respond the caller hung up. Her initial instinct was to call Nick, but the idea of talking to him right now, even with a good lead, did not appeal to her. No, she would follow this one up, and if anything came of it, then she'd get in touch with Nick.

The old airport had once been the main airport for the city. Now much of the runways, the terminal and hangars had been supplanted by a master-planned community, complete with ponds and running trails. The tower, a piece of 60's architecture, had been saved from demolition. The structure, with its blue porcelain paneling flaring toward the sky, stood alone in an open field of broken rubble and tall, golden grass.

Driving through the Mueller neighborhood, she slowed to a stop near a parked Audi sedan next the abandoned tower. She stepped out of her car, keeping the door open as a shield. Just in case. A very large man stepped out of the sedan. She could see another man in the back seat.

She nodded to big man walking toward her. "Afternoon."

He didn't acknowledge her greeting, continuing to approach her.

"So you have some information for me?" She reached behind for her gun, but kept it holstered.

"Yeah. I do."

She couldn't believe how massive this guy was. Standing an arm's length away from him, his hands alone looked like giant pie tins.

"Okay, I'm listening."

Before she could react, one of those pie tins smacked her across the face, knocking her to the ground away from the car and almost into unconsciousness. Woozy, she struggled to her feet, fumbling for her gun, but something akin to a large tree plowed into her stomach. She flew a couple of body lengths, landing with a thud on the hard ground. Her ears rung, she couldn't take in a breath. The giant picked her up like a small animal and tossed her painfully into the Audi's trunk. He bound her hands behind her back, then slammed the trunk lid.

~*~

A few hours after Nick left MaryLou, Izzy called her to say he'd be by shortly to pick her up for another small job. Within fifteen minutes his Audi appeared. She got into the back seat with Izzy, Puck driving them south on Congress past the lunch trucks, the shops and restaurants, and the burnt, charred remains of a store which had caught fire a couple of nights before. The big news story in Austin centered on the drought and the city's desperate shortage of water. The day of the fire, city water pressure had been so low that fire fighters had been unable to put sufficient water on the blaze. Puck took 71 to Capital of Texas Highway, stopping at a service station for gas and something to drink. Puck stepped out of the car to refuel and Izzy went in for the drinks. MaryLou called Nick.

"I'm with Izzy, Nick."

"Where're you going?"

"Don't know. He's been unusually quiet. I may need your help."

"I seem to remember you saying you had it all under control."

"Do you have my back or not, Nick?"

"I don't know. Are you planning on killing Hoyt?"

MaryLou hit the end call button as Izzy came back with two opened bottles of water.

"Here's some water, MaryLou. Man, this drought just dries me out. It's hell on my skin."

"You moisturize, Izzy?"

"Yes, I moisturize. A man in my position can't afford to look old and wrinkled. Cheers."

He tapped his bottle against hers and they both took drinks of cold, clear water. Puck pulled back out onto the highway past JVI and the 360 bridge, north to the Ranch Road 2222 exit.

"So what's the plan, Izzy? Are you trading your job as a game developer to be the head of a drug cartel?"

"What do you think MaryLou? Can you see me leading the Diablos? Dealing in drugs and death?"

"I can see it, but I'm not sure why you'd want it. This water deal will make you wealthy without all the risks."

MaryLou felt weak, her breathing shallow, her body removed from her. The last time she felt anything like this she had spent the next week sick with the flu, vomiting into a toilet.

Izzy continued speaking, his voice distant and muffled, as if from the far end of a tunnel. "Very perceptive. Well, you'd find out anyway. The Diablos are just a smokescreen. My real play here, as you said, is the water. But I'm not content to bid against the Lower Colorado River Authority and all these municipal utility districts. If I'm in the water business, then I'm in to dominate the water business. Today, you're helping me establish a significant barrier to market for my competitors."

MaryLou, her lips having difficulty forming words, slurred, "Whabarah?"

"What barrier? Radioactive contamination. I imagine if my competitors' water glows in the dark, I'll be winning the bids. It's quite tragic. These terrorists. There's no stopping them." He put a hand on her thigh. "Are you feeling okay?"

No she didn't feel okay. She felt encased in jello, her senses dulled.

"Yes, I'm sure you're feeling a little odd right now. I spiked your water with a narcotic to take the edge off, make you easier to manage. Oh, don't worry. You're not going to die. At least not yet, Agent Perkins. You don't mind if I call you Agent Perkins?"

Panic gripped her as she fought her body to respond, to move, to get away from Izzy. But the more she fought, the less she cared.

"This is a big day for you, Agent Perkins. You're going to be responsible for the most heinous terrorist act to occur on Texas soil. Your people will wonder how they let you fool them. You—a terrorist mole in their midst. And now, because of you, the people of Austin will have no drinking water for decades. Over a million people in the metropolitan area without water. You are an evil one."

She spoke as if in a dream. "I am evil, Izzy. Evil. Evil, Izzy." She giggled at the sound of her words.

The countryside shifted from cedar-covered hills and cliffs to browned-off Hill Country to the concrete expanse of Mansfield Dam holding back Lake Travis. Puck came to a stop at the center of the dam. Her door opened and then the world moved around her body as Puck carried her to the edge of the dam, Izzy at his side.

"I suppose you're wondering how I discovered your true identity? Simple really. I have cameras in Hoyt's house and compound and office. Never can be too cautious with a business partner. You lied to me you little vixen. Lied to Izzy Zydeco. No one lies to Izzy Zydeco and lives to talk about it. I trusted you. I gave you opportunities a lot of people would kill for. Apparently, you weren't willing to kill for me. Imagine my surprise after you told me how you burned Hoyt to a crisp and then I see him in his safe room, picking out a movie for his home theater. A dead man watching movies. Amazing. So I had you thoroughly vetted. Quite a disappointment, Agent Perkins."

She looked out over the side of the dam to green lake water and jagged rocks hundreds of feet below.

"No, Izzy."

"What?" He laughed. "Oh, you're not going to die so easily dear. Puck, put her right there by the case."

Puck propped her in a seated position against a railing, handcuffing her to a metal suitcase he must have dragged out earlier.

"You really are a deceitful little bitch." Izzy hit her. Hard.

Izzy winced, the impact of his fist on the now unconscious MaryLou leaving his knuckles aching. He stepped over to the car, punching a number into his cell phone.

"Hoyt?"

Yeah. Who is this?

"It's Izzy. Are you okay?"

I suppose. Just a bit rattled. I've got somebody gunning for me. I've been shot and bombed—

"Yes…I think the powers that be don't like the competition."

Somebody blew up your garage too?

"No, but like you, I'm the target of an assassin."

Assassin! Holy shit, Izzy. Who do they work for?

"I don't know who's after us, but they're bringing out the big guns. They definitely want to stop us from dominating the water business in Texas."

Well, whoever they are, they're going to have a pretty damn hard time getting to me in my panic room. Reenforced walls, steel doors, even a secure air supply. I'll just wait 'em out.

"Yes, about that. I got an anonymous email—I'm assuming it's from our assassin—with a picture of you *in* your panic room. Can you believe it, Hoyt?"

What? But...how?

"I know. I can't imagine how they'd have pictures from a secure panic room, but they do."

Ah, shit, shit, shit—

"My advice is not to trust anyone. I know you hired Sibelius, but Hoyt, think about it. Since he's been around you've been attacked, shot, bombed. You've got to get out now."

I don't know, Izzy. Nick has gotten me out of some tight scrapes. He could help you too.

"No, Hoyt. Don't tell him. I don't know if he's involved or not, but why take the chance?"

So what am I supposed to do?

"Meet me at Mansfield Dam. Take the turnoff from 620. When you get to the gate, park your car out of sight and walk across the dam. I'll meet you."

I think I get hiding the car. Keep the bad guys from finding us. But why Mansfield Dam?

"We'll be able to see anyone approach from all directions. Trust me. This is the safest place to meet. I'll have a plane readied nearby for us to disappear for a few weeks until all of this gets cleared up. Maybe the Bahamas. Sound good?"

I do like the beach. I meet this really hot mamacita, if you get my drift—

"Excellent. See you shortly."

Izzy ended the call and walked back toward Puck who had been standing near a just conscious, MaryLou.

"What an idiot. He'll be here within the hour. Puck, get the other one out of the trunk."

Puck stepped over to the car and lifted Nick's partner, Theresa, out of the trunk, dropping the bound and gagged woman onto the pavement ten feet from Izzy. When Izzy approached, she tried to kick him, but he easily sidestepped her.

Izzy sneered. "You are a feisty one. All I need now is your partner and

Hoyt here and I'll have a clean sweep."

Theresa rolled, as if escape was remotely possible. Izzy gave her a quick kick to her gut, which left her curled in a fetal position, her breathing taking on a panicked rhythm.

"Move again, and I'll have Puck break a few ribs."

He stepped back over to MaryLou, her right eye swollen shut, her left eye tracking him.

"My sweet Agent Perkins. Don't worry, sweetheart. This is the beginning of a wonderful thing. And I do apologize if you're uncomfortable being handcuffed to a nuclear device. Think of it this way, my dear. Once the bomb goes off, you won't feel a thing."

On the Run

During the long drive from his office to Hoyt's compound, Nick tried to focus on the business at hand, but Theresa kept creeping into his thoughts. She had called earlier, her picture and name coming up on his screen, but he didn't answer. He just wasn't prepared to say goodbye—not yet. If he ever got another chance with her, he'd let her know how sorry he was for everything and how he was falling in love with her. Nick paused over the thought. Yes, he was falling in love with her.

Lost in his thoughts, Hoyt's big Hill Country house almost seemed to appear out of nowhere. Nick left his El Camino parked near the front door and entered the compound, calling out Hoyt's name, but heard no response. Downstairs he pressed the intercom for the panic room. Hoyt didn't answer. He knocked on the steel security door and stood in front of the camera so Hoyt would know who was doing the knocking in case the intercom wasn't working. Still no answer. Nick punched in the access code on a nearby keypad. As the door slid open, Nick could see a sofa littered with pillows and tortilla chips. A half-empty glass of bourbon sat on the coffee table. He scanned the space looking for some clue about why Hoyt had left.

He punched Hoyt's number into his phone, but all he got was voicemail. He put a hand on the flat screen TV. Warm. He must have had the TV on, maybe watching a movie. He didn't leave in a huge panic. Either the idiot went out for more chips or someone lured him out. He had taken the time to turn off the flat screen and set his drink on the coffee table. Then Nick noticed a small, blank pad of paper by the glass. Hoyt had pressed firmly enough to leave an imprint of his writing. Nick found a small scoring pencil by a putting machine, rubbing the lead across the pad to reveal Hoyt's writing. Mansfield Dam.

Why would Hoyt leave the safety of the panic room for Mansfield Dam? Unless, of course, MaryLou had somehow convinced Hoyt he needed to go there. A perfect spot for a sniper to kill a wealthy Texas developer in order to maintain her cover.

Dammit, Hoyt. I told you to stay right here. If I don't get to you first, MaryLou will kill you. You're just collateral damage in her world.

Fortunately, Nick had a way to find Hoyt. He had set up his client's cell phone with a GPS locator before sending him off to hide in the panic room, in case the man didn't follow instructions. He pulled out his

165

phone, tapping the screen several times.

He's on 71 heading north towards Austin.

Then he noticed Theresa's voicemail and hit the play button.

"Nick. Theresa. Got a call from someone at JVI who says he has have some information for us regarding Zydeco and Hoyt. Sounds like you're right about Hoyt still being in danger. I'm going to check it out." She paused long enough for Nick to have almost deleted the message. Then she continued, "Look, I know things have been confusing between us. After we finish up with Hoyt, let's talk. Other than sleeping with dead girlfriends, you're a good guy, Nick. I've been hurt before, so this whole MaryLou thing…anyway, I'll see you later."

Still in the safe room, Nick sat on the sofa, knocking a bottle of water over, the clear liquid spreading across the coffee table, then dripping onto the floor. How could everything go so wrong so quickly? Clearly, MaryLou planned on killing Hoyt and yet, against Nick's precautions, Hoyt had decided to leave the safety of the panic room and walk right into her line of fire. Now Theresa, whose heart must be broken because he can't keep his dick in his pants, had gone off on her own following some lead involving Izzy. She was being her usual, fearless gung-ho self. Only this time she didn't know she was walking right into the arms of psychopath.

Nick shouted, his voice reverberating within the safe room walls. "Goddamn it! Is anyone ever going to listen to what the hell I'm telling them?"

He picked up Hoyt's glass, hurling the drink at the wall, the glass exploding into shards. This was just like Houston, when his wife cheated on him and he lost his edge and then his job. Just like Pflugerville, when he found himself in a twisted path of death and pain. He did the best he could, but forces outside his control took over in a crazy swirl like a dust devil across a desert floor. Chaos ruled and he kept being swept into the fury. He walked over to the bar, finding a bottle of whiskey and a glass, then poured a tall drink of the golden liquid. His heart screamed at him to numb the pain, the confusion, the helplessness. As he brought the glass to his lips the whiskey's smokey aroma enveloped him. He pulled MaryLou's picture out of his wallet, a tattered, folded print of the picture she had sent him almost a year ago proving she remained alive. She had betrayed him, broken his heart and now planned on killing his client and probably Theresa, if he didn't intervene. He picked up a lighter on the bar, lit the fumes of the whiskey and then held her picture to the flame. Nick watched MaryLou disappear in the ash, now floating on the tainted whiskey. He would not give in to MaryLou. He would not give in to the chaos. He would wrap his arms around the dust devil and strangle the holy shit out of it—or die trying.

The Only Good Partner Is...

Right after Izzy's call Hoyt had punched in the code, opening the door to his panic suite. He was not about to sit there and wait for someone to kill him. He didn't even bother with the elevator down to the garage, taking the stairs instead. Seconds counted after all. Hoyt didn't trust Izzy Zydeco as far as he could spit and Hoyt never could spit very far. But when Izzy called, saying he feared for both of their lives, Hoyt knew in his gut for once, Izzy was speaking the truth. Sure, he had proven over the years to be a heartless and brilliant competitor who almost put Hoyt out of business. However, putting someone out of business is one thing. Being the target of a corporate assassin was something of a different order.

He scanned his cars for the right vehicle to make a daring escape. The Bentley seemed too ostentatious and the Shelby left him exposed to the elements. Hoyt had seen enough TV dramas to know this kind of trip often resulted in a cross-country car chase. He keyed in the code for the key safe and pulled out a set of keys with a large fob imprinted with the Land Rover logo. Once in the car, he started it up and raced out of the garage.

Hoyt knew in his heart you don't become a successful entrepreneur without being able to accurately read people. He could tell in Izzy's voice the fear he had been feeling these last few days had also crept up on Izzy. The idea Nick Sibelius was somehow a tool of the assassins seemed a bit of stretch until Izzy had pointed out, and rightly so, that most of Hoyt's trauma started when Nick showed up in his driveway. Yes, the car had been trashed beforehand, but maybe Nick paid off his mechanic to bring him in under a false pretense. *The crafty, underhanded, sonofabitch.* Hoyt had bought the whole deal, even giving Nick's accomplice a code to the panic room. They maneuvered him just where they wanted him—in a locked, secure, kill zone.

He drove his Range Rover, not wanting to use the Bentley or the Shelby for this task, just in case evading assassins involved off-roading. He'd get the car picked up later. For now, the idea of escaping to the Bahamas with Izzy sounded like a foolproof plan. They'd still be able to work the water deal remotely and who knows—maybe having some time together they'd form a real connection. Hoyt imagined the combination of Izzy's ruthless business sense and his entrepreneurial vision. They'd be unstoppable.

As instructed, he pulled his car off 620 onto the two-lane road which used to convey traffic across the dam. He parked to the side of the road at the chain-link gate before the dam. A chain securing the gate had been cut. So Hoyt pushed it open slightly and began the long walk across. This was the only part of Izzy's plan which didn't make much sense. Why walk out onto the middle of a dam? When he finally reached Izzy, he couldn't quite make sense of the scene before him. If front of him, Izzy stood casually by his car with a look that reminded Hoyt of a cat's satisfied smirk, mouse tail dangling from its mouth. To his left, the massive Puck stood by a metal suitcase. And oddest of all, a couple of women sat by the suitcase with their backs to the railing. When Izzy finally spoke, Hoyt expected the mouse to pop out of his mouth first.

"Glad you made it, Hoyt. A helicopter will be picking us up in a few minutes. Just gave them a call."

They shook hands and then walked toward the suitcase, Izzy letting Hoyt take the lead.

"What are we doing out here, Izzy? Shouldn't we be walking to the pick up site?"

"Yeah, we'll get out there shortly."

"What are these women doing here? Izzy, what's going on?"

Izzy pointed a small black box at Hoyt, which sent to barbed wires at point blank range into Hoyt's chest. The intense pain of 80,000 volts coursed through his body. Convulsing, he fell to the pavement.

"Sorry, Hoyt. But I didn't want to put a bullet in your head quite yet. I've got something very special planned for you."

Hoyt tried to move, to fight back, but his muscles wouldn't cooperate. Izzy waited for the effects to wear off. After a few minutes, Hoyt spoke up.

"Izzy, what the hell?"

"You see those two wires attached to barbs embedded in your chest?"

Hoyt looked at the wires running from a small box-like thing in Izzy's hand to two small blood stained spots on his salmon colored polo shirt.

"Yeah, I see them. What are you doing? I thought we were partners."

"We are, Hoyt. We are. I'm just adjusting your role in the partnership."

"What?"

"Do exactly as I say, and I won't zap you again. Disobey me and you will be writhing on the ground and soiling yourself. Do you understand what I'm saying to you?"

"Yeah. Sure, Izzy."

Puck stepped up, pulling Hoyt to his feet. A woman with a battered face sat handcuffed to a suitcase and to the railing, and another woman, the hot chick who worked with Sibelius, sat next to her bound and gagged with duct tape.

"Sit down by the case." Hoyt sat on the other side of the case as Puck then cuffed his wrist first to the metal suitcase and then his other wrist to the railing.

"Dammit, Izzy. What the hell are you doing? I thought we were escaping together."

"Have I disappointed you?"

"You sonofabitch. Let me go, dammit!"

"You're staying right where you are Hoyt. You crazed terrorist, you."

"What are you talking about?"

"I'm talking about the dirty bomb you're attached to. Enough explosives to put a sizable hole in this dam and sufficient radioactive material to contaminate the water supply for years."

"What?"

"You heard me, Hoyt. You and your accomplice over there," he nodded in MaryLou's direction, "have some crazy plan, which unfortunately for the city of Austin, you will successfully execute. The destruction of the dam will, of course, create an immediate need for water in the city. A need which I am now positioned to meet with the first of many desalination plants and the pipeline grid. When your letter gets published in all of the Texas and national papers, people will see you as the twisted psychopath you are, rambling on and on about the environment and they'll see me as the victim of your lies."

"Izzy, don't do this. We can make plenty of money without destroying the dam."

Izzy shook his head, disappointment in his voice. "And you call yourself an entrepreneur. You have no vision, Hoyt. Don't you see? Sure, blowing up the dam creates some immediate cash flow, but what happens when the LCRA repairs the dam? Back to the status quo. We can't have that now, can we partner? But if the waters of the Colorado River prove undrinkable for years, well now. I think we have the foundation of a very profitable long-term business. Plus I own the drug transport business for the Diablos and any other drug dealing organization requiring distribution in the state."

"Come on, Izzy. Don't do this man. Look you can have the whole business, pipelines, everything. Just let me go."

"I am very disappointed in you, Hoyt. You'd sacrifice the well-being of a million people as long as you get away safely? I'll bet your slut of a governor would be disappointed in you, too."

"Izzy."

"No one's going to vote for an ex-governor, who allowed a massive terrorist action to happen on her watch, become president. She doesn't deserve to be president."

"What does this have to do with Franny, uh, the governor?"

"Enough talk. Time for you to fulfill your obligations in our partnership."

Izzy stuffed a rag into Hoyt's mouth, wrapping duct tape over the gag and around his head. He flipped an external switch on the side of the suitcase, then stepped back as if admiring his work.

"Goodbye, my friends. May your atomized remains be the foundation for a new Texas."

~*~

Nick flew down the highway, his latest rent-a-wreck vibrating in protest to the speed, until he arrived in the town of Bee Cave. Checking the GPS on his phone, he confirmed Hoyt had definitely gone to Mansfield Dam. He surmised MaryLou had maneuvered Hoyt into position for the kill and he hoped his thinking was wrong. If MaryLou had lured Hoyt to Mansfield Dam she must be planning to shoot him, or probably better, in terms of evidence, toss him over the side of the dam. Hoyt wouldn't be the first distraught entrepreneur, visions of grandeur crumbling around him, to end the misery with suicide. He pressed the accelerator, urging every last horsepower out of the beater Chevy Nova's straining engine. Car horns blared as angry drivers swerved out of his way. An RV pulled out of a rest stop directly in his path forcing Nick to slam on the brakes, the car skidding to the shoulder just missing the it, his tail clipping an SUV. He raced up and down the steep hills, fighting to keep control on the sweeping turns.

Approaching the dam, Nick turned into Mansfield Dam Park, rushing past cars towing ski boats on trailers ready to leave after a day of skiing, until he got to the entrance of the road running the length of the dam. He accelerated once again, crashing through a barrier fence, driving toward a car and several people at the center of the dam. As he closed in, Izzy's Audi faced him. Both Hoyt and MaryLou were seated on the ground, each with arms handcuffed to a large, metal case. Izzy held Theresa up as a shield, his gun pointed at her temple, her hands bound, her mouth and eyes covered with duct tape. Nick came to an abrupt stop about fifty feet away.

He opened the door, stepping out and keeping his gun concealed from Izzy.

"Izzy? What's going on?"

"I know you've got a gun, Sibelius. Throw it on the ground and I won't put a bullet in your girlfriend's head."

"Not my girlfriend."

"Oh, so then you don't mind if I kill her."

"I didn't say that. Let's slow this down a little. I'm just here to keep Hoyt safe."

Without warning Izzy fired at MaryLou, concrete exploding inches from her body.

"Dammit, Izzy." Nick had his gun up now, aimed at Izzy's head, wanting the shot, but Izzy already had his gun back at Theresa's temple. "Let's talk about this."

"Enough talk, Nick. Step away from the car and throw your gun down or she's dead." He screamed, "Do it!"

Nick stepped out from behind the door, holding his gun by a thumb and finger, then tossed it to the ground a few feet away.

"I'm here, Theresa. I'll fix this. Trust me." He glanced over to MaryLou. "You okay?"

"Great, except for this asshole who keeps shooting at me."

Izzy waved his gun impatiently at them. "Are we through with the chitchat? Are we? Because I'm conducting some very important business and all of you people are getting to be a real pain in the ass. Now turn around and get on your knees."

Nick thought about complying with Izzy's request, but he knew neither he nor Theresa would live if he did. Diving for his weapon, he rolled coming up to a kneeling position. Izzy, enraged, fired at MaryLou, who cried out as the bullet ripped into her leg. Nick stood, ready to take the shot, but Izzy had again placed his gun at Theresa's temple. With an arm around her, he dragged her toward the Audi. Nick followed them, his gun trained on Izzy, waiting for him to let his guard down for a moment.

"Put the gun down Nick, now. Unless you want MaryLou to bleed out and your girl here to get a bullet in the head, throw the gun down."

Izzy punched Theresa's temple with the muzzle. Nick raised his hands in surrender, tossing the gun to the ground.

"Kick it over to me. Do it."

Nick kicked the gun toward Izzy and out of his own reach. Izzy pushed Theresa in the car, then picked up Nick's weapon, firing as Nick rolled away. Izzy stood at the passenger side door.

"I'd kill you now Nick, but I kind of like the idea of you suffering a little more before you head off to oblivion."

Izzy got into the car, gun still pointed at Nick with his free hand out the window. As soon as the car started Nick ran toward them, but with tires squealing, the car raced past him.

"Theresa. Dammit!"

Nick ran to MaryLou. Blood pooled around her wounded leg.

"I'll call 911, MaryLou. You're going to be okay."

"Nick. You can't." She spoke weakly, her breathing labored. Using his belt he tied off her leg to slow the bleeding. Nick called for the police and an ambulance then moved to Hoyt, tearing the duct tape gag from his face.

"Ahhh. Sonofabitch. Damn it hurts."

"The police and an ambulance will be here shortly. I'm going after Izzy."

"Wait, Nick."

"Hoyt, you'll be fine."

"No I won't. I'm attached to a goddamn dirty bomb. That sonofabitch is blowing up the dam and destroying the water supply for the entire city."

"A dirty bomb. He used those words?"

"Is there something about this metal case I'm cuffed to that you don't get? Yes, he said it's a bomb. A dirty bomb. He's got some crazy idea to be some kind of water czar. And he's got a real burr up his saddle about the governor. Don't know what it's about, but he's willing to do a shit load of damage to make her suffer."

Nick looked at the suitcase. He had assumed it belonged to the LCRA, holding some equipment they used to monitor the dam and had just served as a convenient tie-down point for Hoyt. A bomb. At best the police were ten minutes out and a bomb squad would take even longer.

MaryLou confirmed the truth of their predicament. "It's a bomb, Nick."

Nick knew each second he delayed diminished Theresa's chances for survival. But if the container held a bomb, he couldn't walk away. Nick took a deep breath, resigning himself to the situation.

"Yeah. Okay. I'm going to open the lid."

Hoyt barely kept his panic at bay. "Wait! Do you really think you should be messin' with it? No offense, but I didn't know you were some kind of bomb expert."

"I'm not."

Nick knelt beside the case and opened the lid slowly. Relieved to still be among the living, he looked at what appeared to be a timing mechanism with wires leading to a package wrapped in duct tape sitting on what he figured must be some kind of lead lined case filled with radioactive material which would vaporize in the explosion.

"Looks like we do have a bomb, MaryLou. Do any bomb work in the Agency?"

"Took a class. What have you got?"

Hoyt interrupted. "She took a class. Great. You don't know what the hell you're doing and she took a class. Can't we just wait for the professionals?"

The timer flashed 2:00, 1:59, 1:58. A numerical keypad that included an off and on button sat below the timer display. Nick pushed the "off" button. The timer countdown moved to the top right corner of the display, replaced by the words, "Enter Code."

Nick's mind raced for a response. "Six numbers. Birthdate? Do you know his birthday, Hoyt?"

"Jesus, you're going to do this."

"His birthdate. Now."

"Its June. He had a party just a few weeks ago."

"What day, Hoyt? What day was the party?"

"It was on a Wednesday night. Twenty-third, I think. He was thirty, so that would be 1970."

Nick entered 062370, 230670, 700623, 702306, but each time the screen flashed "error." The clock counted down, 1:01, 1:00, 0:59.

MaryLou asked, "What about his social security number?"

Hoyt dropped his head back against the railing, closing his eyes in despair. "His social? Shit, we're dead! Oh God, I don't want to die. This is all a big mistake. I shouldn't be here."

"Hoyt, shut up. Forty-five seconds, MaryLou. Any more ideas?"

Hoyt opened his eyes. "Wait."

"Hoyt, there's no time for your pity party right now."

"But I think I know what it is. The code. Izzy always throws a party every year to celebrate his first breakout game."

Nick watched the timer. 0:24, 0:23, 0:22.

"What, Hoyt? What's the game?"

"*Et tu Brute.* Players would plot and carry out the assassination of Caesar. It was a huge hit."

0:15, 0:14, 0:13

A memory of Mr. Hancock's history class from high school flashed in Nick's mind. "The Ides of March. March 15. 0315. We need two more numbers."

0:09, 0:08, 0:07

MaryLou called out, "44 BC."

"What?"

"Caesar was murdered in 44 BC."

0:03, 0:02

Nick punched in 031544.

0:01

Then the screen flashed, "disabled."

All three remained motionless, the reality of averting death by only one second slowly sinking in. Hoyt spoke first, as sirens approached.

"Did you do it? You did it? Sonofabitch. Don't tell me I don't know how to pick a security team. Sonofabitch. You did it! Damn. Cuttin' it kind'a close though. But hey, we're alive. Sonofabitch."

Nick had crawled back over to MaryLou, blood soaking her jeans and staining the ground. Her skin had a pallid cast, her breathing shallow and labored.

"MaryLou, come on. Stay with me."

Her lips parted in a faint smile, pulling Nick toward her with her free hand.

"Go."

He leaned over, kissing her forehead, then rose, running toward his car to give chase to Izzy.

Hoy, shouted, "Hey, where the hell are you going? You can't leave us here on a goddamn dam attached to a load of radioactive material. Hey, listen to me. I pay your salary you sonofabitch. Nick!"

Nick didn't hear the rest of Hoyt's pleading diatribe. He had to find Izzy and Theresa and he knew exactly where to look.

Mujahid Deathmatch 1.2

Given the ego, Nick figured someone like Izzy would assume his plan worked and would act like nothing had happened at all. Which meant Izzy took Theresa to the JVI offices. Nick parked behind Izzy's Audi on the drive, in front of glass entrance to the JVI building. Nick took his Glock and several ammunition clips, walking to the glass front doors. Locked. A security guard at the reception desk, visible from the front door, keyed the intercom.

"You need to use your badge."

"Don't have a badge. Let me in. It's extremely urgent."

"Sir, no badge, no entry. If you want to get approval for a guest pass you'll need to call the number posted by the card reader."

"Look, I know this sounds crazy, but if you don't let me in someone's going to die."

"You need to leave the premises. The police are on their way."

Nick really didn't want to get into it with this guy, probably an off-duty cop working for a private security firm. But he also wasn't about to let company policy keep him from getting to Theresa. He stepped back, firing two rounds into the door, shattered glass exploding across the foyer. The security guard, a look of desperation in his face, yelled into the phone until the muzzle of Nick's gun pointed at his forehead left him speechless.

"Do you have cuffs on you?"

"You don't need to do this. The cops will be here in a few minutes. If I were you, I'd get the hell out of here."

"Well, you're not me. Cuff yourself to the leg of the desk."

"Come on."

"Do it. What floor is the executive suite?"

The guard got on hands and knees to cuff himself to his desk. He hesitated before answering, "Third."

"I hope you're telling me the truth, because if I have to come here to ask you a second time—"

"Fifth. My mistake. Fifth floor."

Nick took the elevator to the fifth floor. Gun at the ready, he raced past the Danish Modern furnishings looking for Izzy & Theresa. Past another reception desk and down a hallway, he found a door with the name 'Izzy Zydeco, President and CEO' written in large gold block letters. He took a breath to slow his heart rate, then slowly turned the door lever into Izzy's office. Empty, except for Izzy's sparse modern furniture and the bank of flat screens on the wall.

Turning to leave, a larger than life image of Izzy appeared on the screens.

"Good to see you again, Nick. I've heard so much about you from our mutual friend, MaryLou. Dead, is she?"

"Cut the crap, Izzy. It's over. Your plan's a failure, the bomb didn't explode. There's no point in holding Theresa. Let her go."

"The bomb didn't explode? My, my. And you had something to do with it? I figured you for a big, dumb ex-cop, but apparently your IQ is a bit higher than a crustacean. How did you figure out the code?"

"Ides of March. Your game."

"So you're a fan. I suppose there's poetry in having a fan thwart my plan." Izzy sounded more amused than angry, as if the bomb, MaryLou, and Theresa were just part of an elaborate game.

"It was Hoyt. He knew about the Ides of March."

"Now that just pisses me off. He's supposed to be my partner and what does he do? He gives you the code to the bomb."

"I wouldn't be too hard on him, Izzy. You did have him handcuffed to the thing. Now, how about Theresa. Let her go, Izzy. Let her go and I'll let you walk."

"What a generous offer, Nick. But no. I don't need you to *let* me do anything. So here's how this is going to play out. Come to the gaming room. It's in the basement."

"And why would I go to the gaming room?"

"Because you want to see her alive, Nick. You've got two minutes or I put my gun in her mouth and pull the trigger."

"Izzy, let's talk about—"

The screens went black. He had two minutes to find the gaming room. Stepping out of the suite he could see the numbers increasing on the readout above the elevator. Someone was coming. The guard must not have been bluffing about the police. He had to get to Theresa before the police, otherwise he knew Izzy would kill her. Nick threw open the stairwell door, sprinting down the metal steps two and three at a time. Hearing the metallic clang of feet coming from the first floor, he crashed through the third floor stairwell door and into the hallway. The elevator had made it to five. He hit the down button, waiting for the elevator to come to him. The clanging in the stairwell got louder. The guys on the fifth floor must have noticed the elevator descending. The elevator doors opened just as a SWAT member slammed open the stairwell door, his assault rifle pointed at Nick.

"Police."

Nick dove into the elevator, pounding on the button marked 'B,' as automatic fire filled the hallway. The door shut and Nick sat at the back of the elevator hoping he wouldn't have to choose between saving Theresa and shooting a police officer. A bell rang, and as the doors opened, he realized he had made it to the basement. Across from the elevator was a black, steel door with a biometric lock. He didn't have a security clearance at JVI, but given Izzy's desire to have him come to the gaming room and the fact the elevator skipped several floors to deliver him here, he imagined Izzy had control of the building and would let him enter. He placed his palm on the pad and the security door clicked open. Stepping through, he let the door lock behind him knowing Izzy's trap would also keep the police away.

He walked into the lounge room as Izzy's voice filled the space.

"Glad you made it, Nick. And with twenty seconds to spare. Very nice."

"Okay, I'm here, Izzy. Now let Theresa go."

"Not so fast, Nick. Don't you want to play the game destined to take the gaming world by storm? It's called *Mujahid Death Match 1.2*."

"What happened to *Death Match 1.1*?"

"Old technology. 1.2 uses my new cutting edge virtual game space and sensor tech. Very sophisticated and very realistic. I think you'll be quite impressed."

"I'm not really a gamer, Izzy. So if you don't mind, I'd like to just get Theresa and leave you to your own devices."

"Not a gamer? Ah, see, that's the thing. With my new technology, everyone's a gamer. You'll see. *Mujahid* is reality. Now go put on a body suit and a visor. You'll find a suit your size in the adjacent dressing room."

"Izzy, enough of the games. Where's Theresa?"

"You think I'm playing games, Nick? Is that what you think? Theresa, what do you think? Are we playing games?"

Nick could hear Theresa's voice, weak and more vulnerable than he had ever heard her.

"Izzy, you don't need to do this. Let me leave with Nick."

A clanging, not a gun, something else, like a sledge hammer filled the space. And then Theresa's jagged scream tore into Nick.

"Goddamn it, Izzy! You sonofabitch."

Theresa sobbed in the background.

"The body suit, Nick. Now."

Nick strode into a small changing room, a black body suit hanging from a wall hook. He donned the suit and a visor, walking out through the lounge and lounge into the game room as instructed by Izzy.

"Excellent, Nick. So here are the rules. Your objective is to locate and save your partner before you are both terminated by insurgents. If you remove the visor or your body suit, she dies. If you are mortally wounded, she dies. You have ten minutes to complete the mission. If you run out of time, she dies. Oh yes. If you fail to make forward progress, in other words, if you don't play the game, she dies. Sound fair?"

"You're a lunatic."

"How disappointing, but if you want me to kill her—"

"No. No, Izzy, I'll play. Let's get this over with."

The large black room flickered and Nick had to fight a falling sensation as the game setting came on line. He found himself outside a mud brick one story building surrounded by a ten foot high chain link fence with coiled razor wire around the top. In his hand he held a M-16 rifle, a watch counted down from ten minutes on his left wrist. The air, dry and dusty, a dog barking somewhere in the distance. Voices whispered on the other side of the door. Kicking the door in, he scanned the room, firing at a man raising his weapon, hesitating at two women. He told them to leave, motioning with his gun for them to go out through the door. The two women argued with him, yelling in a language he didn't understand, when one pulled a pistol out of her robes, firing into Nick's side. He returned fire, killing them both. But the damage had been done. His right side felt like someone had impaled him with a fiery iron and then twisted it for maximum effect. He reached for his wound, discovering his torso remained intact, the excruciating pain being caused by the game's interface with his sensory body suit. Nick almost pulled off the suit, but remembering Izzy's threat, he knew he'd have to live with it.

At the far side of the room, an open doorway led to another room. Laboring to breathe with the pain, he moved into the room, a family huddled in the corner. He went through to a back yard surrounded by a mud brick wall. A shrill scream came from an adjacent house. Willing himself to move in spite of the pain, he heaved himself onto the wall. A gun fired, as a searing pain exploded in his right leg. Falling to the ground on the other side of the wall, he lay still for a moment, struggling to force his mind to ignore the signals coming from the suit. Then he crawled to the door and cover. He had to think. Izzy would not set up this game so he could win. But how do you win a game you know is rigged for you to lose? Nick took a deep breath. Awareness let a smile crack his now parched lips.

"Theresa. How you doing?"

"Don't Nick. Get out of here." She sounded weak and in pain.

Nick stood, listening carefully to Theresa's voice.

"No worries, Theresa. Izzy tells me this is just a game."

"Nick. Please. Go."

"Have I ever told you how much I love your coffee?"

Nick almost had a bead on her.

"My coffee?"

"Just admit it. You know I love your coffee."

"You…you hate my coffee. You're always… always pouring it out, as if I…I don't see you do it. Nick."

That was enough. Honed in on her voice, he closed his eyes, and then against everything his body and his brain told him, he ran as fast as he could toward the sound. His body exploded in pain, as if his arms and legs shattered into a hundred pieces, his abdomen and chest eviscerated, his mind screaming. Plowing head first into Izzy, Nick took him to the ground. But blinded by the pain, he couldn't keep Izzy from slipping away from his grasp.

"You lose, Nick."

A foot forcefully hammered into Nick's side. His body, screaming with pain, didn't register the cracking rib, but he heard the pop of fracturing bone.

"Now I'm going to kill you and your girlfriend."

A huge man, the one who had been driving the Audi, stood over him.

"Why do you want to kill us, Izzy?"

"Why? You interfered with my plan. I was supposed to have been the sole distributor of clean water for the state of Texas."

Nick crawled over to Theresa. Her hands each impaled with a spike hammered into the wall. Tears rolled down her face, but her eyes held a fierceness.

"Not to mention how you interfered in the destruction of my dear mother, goddamn her to hell."

"Your mother? What are you talking about?"

"Yes, my mother. She didn't have time for me. Wouldn't acknowledge me. Even when I created the greatest gaming company the world has ever seen." Izzy held his arms out, Nick uncertain if the gesture referred to the vastness of his vision or in imitation of self-styled crucifixion at the hands of his mother.

"All of this because you're pissed at your mother? Unbelievable."

"Here's the deal, Nick. The vest around your girlfriend's chest is not virtual. And the code to stop the vest from exploding is on this piece of paper. But as you can see, between you and the paper is Ah Pucah, the Mayan God of death. You've got…let's see." Nick, how much time do we have?"

Nick checked the timer embedded in his suit ticking down the ten minute time limit. "Less than two minutes."

"Right, less than two minutes to get the paper and use the code to disarm the bomb. Security code 031544, disengage program."

Nick ripped off the visor, the Middle Eastern scene dissolving into the black walls of the sim room. Theresa sat against a wall, her hands impaled with actual spikes.

"I'm going to leave you to it, Nick. It's been a nice challenge." He turned, and with a nod to Puck walked to the far corner of the space. A door opened at Izzy's approach and he slipped away.

Blood streamed down Theresa's arms from the spike wounds in her hands, her body shaking from fatigue, fear, and pain. She raised her head, her voice only a whisper. "Nick, don't let him. He's too dangerous. You've got to stop him."

"Not without you, Theresa."

Nick flung himself at Puck, but the large block of a man didn't budge. He picked Nick up, throwing him across the room. Nick tried again to hit him, but Puck easily absorbed each punch, grabbing Nick again and hurling him against Theresa. Puck walked over to cover the slip of paper with his shoe, arms crossed and smiling. Nick looked at his watch, 1:20, then to Theresa.

"I'm sorry, Theresa."

"What are you doing? Ahh!"

He moved the spike impaling her hand back and forth as she screamed in pain.

"Nick...he's coming."

Nick turned to see Puck advancing. He had to get spike free.

"Just a little more, Theresa. Trust me."

Straining against the spike, Theresa screaming in pain, he freed the metal shaft from the wall and her hand. Her arm fell to side, blood pooling around her hand. With the hammer Izzy had used in one hand and the spike in the other, Nick approached Puck. The big man moved forward with the confidence of a Mayan God.

"Hey Puck, heads up."

Puck stepped towards Nick, glaring. Grasping the spike by the point, Nick threw the metal shaft end over end, the pointed end crushing Puck's eyeball before impaling itself several inches into his brain. As if a puppet master had taken a lunch break, the large man flopped to the ground. Nick limped as fast as he could to retrieve the paper, returning to Theresa with only seconds to spare.

"I hope this works, Nick."

He looked into her eyes, red from torture, but still beautiful to him. "Just in case." He input the code on the vest timer, then kissed her gently on the lips.

Into the Future

Charity liked Nick Sibelius. Yes, the carbon spewer let the MaryLou woman kill her brother, Barry, but he had stopped to help a cyclist, not once, but twice. Besides he had a nice butt. And she couldn't forget he could have handed her over to the police. She still didn't understand why he let her go. In a perfect world, Charity imagined the two of them would have been insatiable lovers, but he was with another woman, Theresa. *A carbon spewer who helps cyclists and is loyal. Damn.*

So, she felt a little bad about not doing things exactly the way Nick had spelled them out. Namely, she was supposed to get the hell out of town and never be seen or heard of again. In her defense, she had stayed in Austin a few days longer just to check out Nick's story about Barry. To her profound dismay, Barry Swenson had been a carbon spewer and toxic waste dumper, not to mention a dentist with more malpractice suits lined up against him than the number of teeth in his head. The very thought that a blood relative would be insensitive to the planet was so abhorrent, she made a vow to change her name back to her adoptive parents' name, McDuffy, as soon as she could secure a lawyer.

She wanted to thank Nick for clarifying her familial connections and frankly, to get one more look at his butt before she left town for good. Not knowing any other way, Charity followed Nick around. Some would unkindly call her method "stalking," but she preferred "observing." After the business on the dam, she followed him over to a corporate office on Lake Austin. SWAT teams surrounded the place, but then a man emerged from a steel trap door obscured by a stand of trees near the parking lot at the bridge. Izzy Zydeco. A famous carbon spewer if there ever was one. He drove big cars, rode in corporate jets, and was a business partner of her #5, Dan Hoyt. Zydeco could be her #6! He looked like he was heading out of town anyway, so she decided to "observe" Izzy for a few days.

When she heard the news the commotion on the dam had been about a dirty bomb Izzy had planned to detonate, well, her mission took on a crystal clarity. Izzy may have fled to the isolation of West Texas, but as far as Charity McDuffy was concerned, Izzy had come to the end of his career as an enemy of Mother Earth.

~*~

Theresa, in a white bikini, sat on a beach lounger, a large grass umbrella shading her. "I'm beginning to think I could spend the rest of my life right here on this beach."

Nick sat beside her, watching deep blue waves roll in and crash on the white sandy beach of Isla Mujeres. "I'm up for it. Nothing in Texas to pull us back."

Theresa flexed her hands, something he noticed her doing after the bandages had been removed. A broken bone, some minor nerve damage, but the doctors had told her she'd have ninety percent of her motion and feeling back by the end of the healing process. Even though the Feds told him to back off, Nick packed a bag, ready to go after Izzy himself. However, Theresa asked him to stay and after the incident in Izzy's sim room, he couldn't bring himself to leave her alone.

"Would you like another beer, Theresa?"

"Sounds perfect."

Sipping cold beer, Theresa pulled up the news she had downloaded on her phone. "I haven't seen the news in days. I wonder if the rest of the world is still spinning or if it's just you and me on a beach."

"Don't forget Pedro keeping us supplied in cold beer and margaritas."

"Okay. You, me, and Pedro. Hey, look at this, Nick."

She passed her phone to him. Nick read the story, filed the week before, out loud.

NAKED TERRORIST CAPTURED

Austin, TX - Virtual game entrepreneur, purported drug cartel leader, and alleged terrorist, Izzy Zydeco, has been captured, FBI sources revealed today. Zydeco is believed to be responsible for a plan to detonate a dirty nuclear bomb experts say would have destroyed Mansfield Dam, contaminating Austin's water supply. At approximately 1 pm CST, Zydeco was found naked, tied on his stomach with bicycle tire tubes to an air mattress, floating on Lake Travis. A local resident, Jimmy Masters, found the alleged terrorist while skiing on the lake. "I thought it was a dead wild hog or something. But when I got up close, I saw this white dude with a bunch of bicycle spokes sticking out his (buttocks) and the words 'Bunyip Food' tattooed in two inch letters on his back. I hear he's some kind of terrorist drug dealer. If I had known, I would have run his (buttocks) down myself." An unnamed Homeland Security source described Zydeco as a sleeper with ties to an Afghanistan terrorist cell. The source believes a leader of the cell, code named Bunyip, punished him for failing in his jihadist mission. The suspect has been charged with terrorism, conspiracy to commit terrorism, and public nudity.

Unnamed sources for the governor's office revealed Governor Francis Adamson played a "key and heroic role" in a Homeland Security operation to dismantle Zydeco's Diablos Tejanos drug cartel and Bunyip Terrorist activities. The governor called for Zydeco's swift trial and execution as a terrorist during a presidential campaign stump speech in Iowa earlier this week.

Theresa laughed. "Charity rides again."

"Yeah. At least he won't harm anyone else. And I suppose Hoyt is happy to know his dysfunctional friend is behind bars."

Nick scrolled to a follow up story.

GOVERNOR GAVE BIRTH TO LOVE CHILD TERRORIST

Austin, TX - In a morning press conference, Zydeco's legal team announced a connection between Izzy Zydeco and presidential candidate, Texas Governor Francis Adamson. DNA evidence provided to the Attorney General's Office has proved Zydeco is her illegitimate son. Records indicate Adamson attended a political junket in New Orleans while serving as a state representative nine months prior to the date of birth on Zydeco's birth certificate. Zydeco alleges he is the product of a love tryst between Governor Adamson and Cajun musician and fast food crawfish entrepreneur, Alphones Babineaux. When asked about Adamson's call for their client's execution, Zydeco's lawyers said, "He (Zydeco) is not an international terrorist or a drug cartel leader. Our client is simply a son crying out for a mother who denies him."

In an impromptu press conference, Governor Adamson, in tears, appeared to back away from her execution comments. She took full responsibility for having not revealed the truth about her son, but argued like all Americans, he needed to take responsibility for his actions. "Mothers are the backbone of this great country. All you mothers out there, if our overreaching federal government starts prosecuting you for every little felony your children commit, where will it end? I am categorically opposed to the federal government persecuting the Mothers of America. I challenge my opponent to join me in condemning such practices. As for my own dear child, sending him to prison for the rest of his life is both the loving thing to do as a mother whose child has shown sociopathic tendencies and is a danger to the community, and the responsible thing to do both as an American, and yes, as your future president. God bless Motherhood and God bless the United States of America."

Governor Adamson continues in the presidential race with planned fundraisers in North Carolina and New Hampshire over the weekend.

Theresa took a long drink from her beer, then tossed the empty bottle to the sand by her chair. "Like mother, like son."

"Yeah, I think if they take a closer look at the DNA from both of them, they'll see little sociopathic genes."

"I'll give her one thing. She got me off the hook for borrowing that plane and the car."

Theresa raised an eyebrow. "Oh, you *borrowed* the plane."

"Yes. Extenuating circumstances."

"Is the governor covering the repair costs too?"

"She's not that generous, but I think she knows if Izzy had succeeded, her political life would have been over."

"What if she becomes president?"

He let out a long breath as he contemplated the consequences. "I guess that's why we have term limits."

They both sat quietly, letting the news sink in and the surf soothe them.

Theresa spoke first. "Do you wonder what MaryLou is up to right now?"

"What on earth made you think of MaryLou?"

"The news story. Izzy. Just wondering."

After getting Theresa out of JVI in one piece, Nick had checked to see what hospital MaryLou had been taken to. Homeland Security, as well as state and local officials, claimed Hoyt was the only person found on the dam. There was no other woman. Typical MaryLou. However, this time, he didn't bother to check his email for evidence of her continued existence. His mind, and more importantly his heart, had moved on. Nick stood, offering a hand to a woman he found himself loving more each day.

"Come on. Let's take a walk. And no, I don't wonder what MaryLou is up to right now. She's in my past and I'd like to keep here there."

They stood at water's edge, surf washing over their ankles, the sand slipping away underfoot. Nick leaned into her, touching his lips to hers, tasting her sweetness mixed with beer and salt. He pulled back, nose-to-nose, her hair drifting in the ocean breeze.

"You're my future, Theresa."

ABOUT THE AUTHOR

Richard Hacker, after living many years in Texas, moved to Seattle, Washington. He may be wanted by authorities for transporting Texas BBQ across state lines. His writing has been recognized by the Writer's League of Texas and the Pacific Northwest Writers Association.

www.richardhacker.com
Follow the author on Facebook: www.facebook.com/RWHacker
Twitter: @Richard_Hacker

ALSO BY THE AUTHOR

KILL'T DEAD OR WORSE

After a murdered partner, a cheating wife, and a lost job in Houston, Nick Sibelius sets up a private investigation business in a small Texas town hoping to find some peace and maybe himself. When two lovers disappear and a fisherman turns up dead, he finds himself drawn into a web of crime and deceit involving MaryLou, a beautiful woman with a mysterious past; Junior, a failed farmer whose best intentions seem to always result in a dead body; and Barry, a sociopathic dentist turned illegal toxic waste entrepreneur with a violent right wing agenda. When the felon who killed Nick's partner in Houston joins forces with Barry, Nick must not only stop the toxic waste dumping while finding his client's missing daughter, but keep from being killed in the process. In the end, MaryLou's dark secret will either save him or kill him -- whichever comes first.

A full-flavored Texas novel worthy of your attention!
Hacker masterfully weaves his plot through the cultural fabric of the Lone Star State. A smart novel chocked full of great characters.
Brian Braden, *Underground Book Reviews*

Available now at **Amazon.com**

Preview the Next Nick Sibelius Novel

Buzzard Bait
Secessionists, Drones, & Serial Killers: Nowhere Else But Texas

Nick Sibelius Series, Book 3

by R.W.Hacker

Lake Hazard

Nick leaned back in the cockpit of a rental sailboat, admiring a very fine, bikini-clad ass. Death wasn't on Nick's mind. Theresa, his partner in business and, over the last few months, in life, made her way across their boat's sparse deck. With line in one hand, she fed loops until only a few feet remained, then twirled it around the center of her coil to make a neat package. Nick kept them sailing generally on course, but he found the small gold bracelet on her left ankle, the tuck of white bikini panties between those round, muscular butt cheeks and her dark, straight hair tumbling down her back, to be quite distracting. When a wake from a bass boat racing past at high speed slammed into their sloop, he initially admired Theresa's athletic form flipping gracefully overboard. She hit the warm water of Lake Travis with a ferocious smack.

He yelled over the roar of three hundred Evinrude horses. "What the hell! Slow down!" The boat, lost in its own engine spray, sped away like some giant buzzing water insect.

"Theresa!"

Having focused on the offending boat, Nick had kept sailing on, which meant Theresa was somewhere behind him. He searched the water, making out her head fifty yards away.

"I'm coming around!"

Nick tacked and the sails fell limp, then gathered air, flapping loudly. Theresa, who learned to sail as a young girl, had talked him into going out today. Nick's entire sailing career consisted of a single outing on a twelve foot Sunfish at camp in high school. Sailing a twenty-eight foot sloop with a mainsail and whatever they call that triangular sail in the front, left him with a steep learning curve. Not the optimum conditions for saving your girlfriend from drowning.

As he turned, he kept an eye on Theresa, then watched in disbelief as another bass boat raced toward her. Frantically waving, he yelled at the boat. "Stop. Turn away! Stop!" It missed her by only a few feet, then passed Nick, its wake leaving him grasping for a firm hold.

"Theresa!" *I can't see her.* Did he hit her? Oh, God. "Theresa!" He saw a flash of white. Her bikini. *Screw this.* Nick dropped the sails and dove in, swimming in the direction he last saw her. He stopped, treading water to scan the lake.

"Theresa!"

A splatter of water.

He raced toward it, each stroke an explosive splash. Part of her head rose above the surface. He closed the fifteen feet between them, slipped an arm around her chest, and rested her back on his hip.

"You're okay. I've got you."

"Nick." She gasped, coughing. "What...happened?"

"Let's get back first."

He got them to the boat's stern, slipped a life preserver on her and, with some effort, hauled her onboard. Blood dribbled down her forehead.

"Goddamn fishermen. Jesus." Nick pressed a cloth to her head, already imagining the terror and anguish those fishermen would experience from his vengeance.

Theresa smiled, placing a hand on Nick's. "My own fault."

"Your fault? You've got to be kidding me. Those assholes came through here at a hundred miles an hour."

"Yeah, but I should have been wearing a life vest. Anyway, I think I hit my head on the boat as I went overboard."

"Maybe you should be in a life vest, but those guys shouldn't be racing through here like hell on a hydroplane either. When we get back to the marina, I'm going find those bastards."

"Nick."

"What?"

She smiled, then winced. "Thanks."

He touched her cheek, leaning in to kiss her. "I believe rescue is part of my job description with you." They never talked about Izzy Zydeco impaling her with spikes to a wall or Nick fighting a blood match against a huge adversary to free her while Izzy made his escape, but the pain of those experiences left an imprint on both of them.

She pulled herself up, pausing as if to realign her senses, then stepped down into the hold.

"What are you doing?"

"Ice."

"Let me get it for you."

She turned, only her head visible. Swollen and bruised skin surrounded the gash on her forehead, still seeping blood. "I've got it, Nick. Just make sure we don't get run over by a cigarette boat or something."

A mixture of relief and anger swirled inside Nick's gut. If she'd been killed...How could he let his guard down, after all she'd been through? And the jerks on those boats. Clearly they didn't care about anyone but themselves. *Well, I'll make sure they remember this day.*

"Hey, move over."

Nick, lost in his thoughts, hadn't noticed Theresa back on deck. "You doing okay? Maybe you should let me get us back to the marina."

She pressed a plastic bag wrapped in a towel to her head, taking the tiller from him. "I'm fine, Nick. How about if I steer and you follow my every command."

Given he didn't know what to do with the sails, her plan did make sense. However... "Or I could fire up the outboard and you could kick back with your ice pack."

"We came out here to sail. I'll be damned if I'm going to let a couple of fishermen mess up my day. Now get ready to come about."

They sailed up the lake, then tacked back to the marina. Theresa expertly maneuvered the boat into a slip. The marina office, a small wood building on a floating dock, held an assortment of fishing, boating, and skiing gear. Stuffed striped bass, blue gill and crappie hung on walls, each posed to celebrate the epic struggle of man versus fish.

A gray-haired man in his late sixties, wearing a green gimme cap emblazoned with a large mouth bass leaping out of blue water, sat behind a glass counter filled with reels. "How can I help you, young man?"

Nick laid the boat keys down on the counter. "Just turning in our boat. By the way, we had bass fishermen flying around us like they were at NASCAR. Knocked my girlfriend right out of the boat and then almost ran her down."

He let out a sigh. "Yeah. Striped bass."

"What do you mean?"

"We've got a big striped bass tournament goin' on this weekend." He laughed, shaking his head. "Some of these folks will kill their kin to get a lunker. So I'm not surprised. Those ol' boys put some big engines on the back of them bass boats. Crazy fast, tryin' to beat each other to the best spots." He paused, concern etched on his face. "They didn't damage my boat, did they?"

"Well, no, but like I said, my girlfriend took quite a fall."

He relaxed, leaning back in his chair. "That's good. Not good about your girlfriend, mind you. But good about the boat."

"They were moving so fast I didn't get a registration number, otherwise I'd call it in."

The man took the keys, chained to a bright yellow float, and hung them on a board crowded with other boat keys.

"Well, the tournament's being held at the Mansfield Dam Park. I'll bet if you remember what the boat looked like, then you'll find the guy there. He's got to bring his catch in if he wants to win."

"I tell you what. If I find 'em, that will be the last damn fish he'll catch for years to come."

~ * ~

Nick climbed back into his pickup. Theresa, now in cut-offs and a tee, along with a clean bandage on her forehead, pulled a brush through her hair. She smiled at Nick.

"Don't let the bandage put you off there, cowboy. I can think of quite a few things we can do that don't involve my head."

Nick glanced at her and put the truck in reverse. "Glad you're feeling better. I'll definitely take you up on the offer, if you're sure about your head."

"But?"

He shifted into first, pulling away from the marina parking lot. "We have one stop to make, then we'll head on home."

Theresa looked out the window, then back to him. "Nick, I know what you're thinking."

"You don't know what I'm thinking."

"You want to find the bass fisherman who bounced me off the boat. And let me guess—you want to kick the crap out of him. Am I close?"

Damn. Bullseye. He kept his focus on the road, not wanting to give her the satisfaction. "No, I just want to talk to him. Help him gain a deeper appreciation of water safety."

He could feel her eyes rolling. "Right. Mr. Coast Guard's going to school him. Nick, leave it."

"I'm not a dog, Theresa."

"Leave it alone. Look, neither one of us saw a registration and we definitely didn't see a face. How do you think you're going to identify the guy?"

"I'll know."

"Nick."

He looked over at a slight pink tinge staining a portion of her bandage. "I'm not going to let someone hurt you."

"You mean, hurt me again, don't you?"

Nick gripped his steering wheel so tightly his knuckles turned white.

"That's what you mean, Nick. You still think it's your fault about what that psycho Izzy did to me."

He reached for her hand, feeling the ridges of scars left by the stake Izzy had driven through her palm. He should have been there. He should have protected her.

"Nick, you came for me. You saved me from that bastard."

"I know." She didn't get it. She couldn't. He had failed to keep his Houston PD partner alive, he'd let his buddy Quen almost get blown up, and he barely got Theresa out. Nick had sworn to himself he'd never let anyone take the people he loved away from him, ever again. "I know, Theresa. I just wish I could have gotten there sooner."

"You got there soon enough." She squeezed his hand, but he kept on driving to Mansfield Dam Park. Some good old boy with a rubber worm was about to wish he had never been born.

~*~

Nick expected to find a few guys in lawn chairs drinking Shiners by an awning for the weigh-ins. Instead he found a bustling crowd gathered at the park, country music from a local FM station blaring, food venders lined up selling turkey legs, tacos, beer and funnel cakes dusted in confectioners sugar, a stage for the weigh-ins and photos, a mobile fishing trailer charging five bucks for kids to catch perch with bamboo poles, and an assortment of vendors selling everything from folding camp chairs to lures to fishing vests and gimme caps. At the center of activity sat a gleaming new eighteen-foot bass boat painted metallic red, with a sign proclaiming the boat came with the latest in fish-finding technology, ergonomic seats, and huge outboard engines complete with electronic ignition.

Walking through the crowd with the smell of hot dogs and funnel cakes wafting in the air, Nick made his way to the information table. A volunteer in a Texas Bass Roundup tee shirt smiled up at him, but his eyes focused on the armadillo struggling to haul in a big bass across the woman's well-endowed chest. A perky ponytail of blonde hair stuck out of a hole in the back of her Roundup ball cap.

"Howdy. How can I help you?"

"I'm looking for one of the competitors."

"Sure. What's the name?"

"Uh, that's the thing, I don't know the name. Just saw him pass by."

She chuckled knowingly. "A fan, eh? Well, they do all come back here to weigh in their catches. So I imagine if you stick around, you're bound to find him."

"You don't do any GPS tracking or anything like that?" Nick tried to keep his eyes up, but the armadillo was having quite a battle reeling in the bass on her chest.

"Are you kidding? Some of these guys would kill for their precious fishing spots, honey. They sure as hell aren't going to let us track 'em with a GPS. You fish?"

"Yeah, some." Nick looked around the park, feeling a bit defensive. "But not like this."

"Well, take your normal fisherman. By normal, I mean a guy who likes to drink beer and sits waiting for a fish that may or may not ever strike. When he catches one, he does a little jig, has another beer, then sits in a boat waiting for another fish that may or may not ever strike. When he runs out of bait or fuel or, worst case scenario, beer, he comes to shore with his catch and at least one tall tale about the fish that—"

"That got away?"

She dismissed the notion with a wave of her hand. "Oh, hell no, honey. They got away in the old days. Now the biggest fish in the pond is the very one, for the sake of the environment, he caught and released. So you take this normal fisherman and you give him a financial incentive, carbon fiber rods and a three hundred fifty horsepower engine. Do you know what you've got?" She stood, hands on hips, waiting for his response, the armadillo still in the fight of its life with the bass on her chest.

"No ma'am, I'm afraid I don't have clue."

"A damn psychofishinlunatic. That's what you've got."

"I don't understand. If you feel that way about fishing, then why are you here?"

She teared up. "'Cause my husband, well, my ex-husband Harlan, died from his addiction to fishing. I guess I do this to honor his memory. He lived to fish, but my Harlan, he was a good man. Besides, my current husband's in the tournament."

Through the tears, the ponytail, the ball cap and makeup, Nick now recognized Harlan Jones's ex-wife, Dolores. He'd interviewed her after Harlan turned up missing, then floating dead in Junior Pendleton's pond. "Dolores. Ms. Jones, I didn't recognize you."

"Sorry?"

"Nick Sibelius. I spoke with you after your ex, after Harlan, was reported missing."

She cocked her head, taking him in. "Oh, yeah. I remember you. Nick. I guess I should be thanking you for putting Junior in prison, but knowing the two of them, I can't help but figure it was some sort of weird accident."

"Yeah, you've got a point. But Junior's in prison for quite a few more things than drowning Harlan."

"I suppose he is. Well, if you're looking for one of the competitors, like I said, he's bound to show up here, so stick around."

Gubernatorial Jacuzzi

Governor Francis Adamson nestled down into the hot waters of a rooftop jacuzzi, watching sporadic snowflakes dance in a cold Colorado mountain breeze before plummeting to their deaths like so many fairy kamikazes. Only her head protruded above the bubbling surface, her short red hair damp from steam and snow melt, the rest of her naked body luxuriating in warmth and the gentle massage of strategically placed jets. Closing her eyes, she transported herself into the embrace of past lovers. A development entrepreneur who did this wonderful thing with her toes. The college-aged daughter of a well-known Senator, whose tongue, during the last legislative session, worked a magic this jacuzzi could never emulate. And her personal pilot, who took her up into the clouds even when they weren't in her gubernatorial King Air.

If only sex, her third favorite thing after power and money, helped her career. Instead, it always seemed to muck things up. She lost her first bid for President, mostly because her stupid bastard of a son, Izzy Zydeco, decided to become some kind of domestic terrorist in the middle of the political silly season.

Izzy. Now there was one for the books. She had actually loved the guy who helped create Izzy, a fellow law student at the University of Texas. The sex wasn't outstanding, but this was love, not pay for performance. After knocking her up, he convinced her to keep the kid, then left a month before the birth because a child would "slow him down." No shit.

All of her youth she dreamt of becoming a state Senator, a governor, and yes, President of the United States. But at the age of twenty-three, even she knew having a child out of wedlock, which was nice talk for saying your kid's a bastard, would torpedo her political quest before she got out of the gate. As soon as Izzy took his first breath when she birthed him in her apartment, alone with no witnesses, she made sure to distance herself from him. She drove to New Mexico, called social services, and told them she found an infant seat resting on the hood of her car when she went into the local Albuquerque Walmart to buy Slim Jims and tampons. Using a fake ID with a false name and address in Little Rock to misdirect the authorities, she drove I-10 east toward Austin, never looking back.

Opening her eyes, foaming water tickling her nose, she lifted a leg up until her deep red French painted toenails splayed against the bare chest of her most recent lover, Bruce Reynolds. She smiled as he took her size six foot in his warm hands, nibbling her arch in his mouth. Not as good as her developer toe-sucking lover, but not bad. She had known him for several years as a financial donor to her campaigns. He started small. A few hundred thousand here, a few hundred thousand there. So she decided he needed a more personal reason to fund her campaign.

Sex wouldn't do it. She had already tried campaign fucking earlier in her career. Men had an annoying ability to compartmentalize their bank accounts from their love lives. In her case, she endured six months of boring sex with a man old enough to be her father, but he had financial resources she hoped to capitalize during a run for state representative. Not only did she have to fake her orgasms, but she learned too late his desire for his "sugar pie" didn't directly link to his offshore accounts. No, experience had taught her she needed to target a guy where he lived, which with money guys and politicians had everything to do with power and surprisingly little to do with pussy.

Bruce Reynolds, a lawyer by training, had purchased two hospitals in Abilene with family money, fired everyone in both facilities, closed one up and rehired a staff from the laid-off pool of past employees. Declaring his new hospital the flagship of an emerging empire in healthcare, he also bought some office space downtown, slapping up a big sign. The Mesquite Ridge Healthcare Corporation had been born. Since then, he had spread east to Dallas, Oklahoma City, Little Rock, Birmingham on down to Tampa and Miami like some terrible, great wildfire consuming every healthcare facility in its path. In short, the man was loaded and she planned on relieving him of a large chunk of wealth. She couldn't offer up hospitals since he had already ravaged most of those in the state, but her research revealed a unique interest. He not only believed strongly in the for-profit healthcare model, he also fervently hoped for the resurrection of what he considered to be the state's God-ordained destiny, returning to its glory as the independent and sovereign Republic of Texas.

At first she couldn't believe anybody felt strongly about Texas becoming its own nation. Sure, she railed against federal money and intervention, but that was politics. If Texas left the Union, it would be surely and irrevocably fucked. During her presidential bid, she took the opportunity to offer up some conservative candy, calling for the secession of Texas from the Union. Yes, it was over the top. No, it wasn't taken seriously by anyone but the late night comics. But if Bruce was a rabid rebel of the Republic, a call by a standing governor for secession would give him an erection Viagra would never be able to match.

To her delight, he called within twenty-four hours. The lovemaking, damn. She should have called for secession earlier.

"Did you mean it, Fran? Are you serious about the Republic?"

She straddled him, her hips pulsing in rhythm with his, hoping for her third orgasm, but who was counting. "Absolutely. But I can't succeed without your help." She dug her nails into his chest hair.

"Anything, Frannie. Anything."

Exactly what she wanted to hear.

The first few months of their new relationship had gone according to plan. His desire to see a Republic come to fruition was so strong, he even set up, in the event of his death, an offshore account. He kept the passcode in a safe deposit box at the National Bank in Houston. Of course, she planned on having access to his wealth well before any of it flowed to the Caymans. However, she soon realized a dyed-in-the-wool revolutionary, especially a capitalist like Reynolds, would expect results. She wasn't about to let him have his Republic, but he had to think she would. In discussing the necessary elements of a successful military, they had landed on the notion of air power as the key. No matter what they did, if the new Republic's leadership didn't control the skies above Texas, they'd never be able to hold off the Americans, or the Mexicans, for that matter.

Air power. How perfect. She figured Bruce would spend years trying to figure out how to acquire and hide aircraft and weapons. Long enough for her second well-financed campaign for President. Then she would, in a noble act of patriotism, bring Homeland Security down on her traitorous longtime friend like the wrath of God. This was the stuff of made-for-television movies and second term Presidents.

"But if you're President, Frannie, why would you allow Texas to break away?"

"Oh, but that's the beauty of our plan, Bruce. Imagine the President of the United States calling for the independence of Texas. We'd both get what we want the most."

She came back to the present when Bruce slipped her graceful arch slowly from his lips, his feet adroitly exploring her hither parts. "I have news for you, my dear."

She looked up into a dark sky. The snow had stopped falling. "Another hospital acquisition?"

"Nothing so mundane. No, I'm putting the first step of our strategic plan into place."

Crap. This was supposed to take six years, not six months. "You've put an air force together in six months? How could you possibly have enough aircraft and resources in place in this short a period of time?"

"You sound angry. I thought you'd be pleased. You're not having second thoughts, are you?"

She pulled her foot, cold in the night air, back under water. "No second thoughts. I just want to be sure we have what we need to be successful."

"Maybe a demonstration."

Great. He wants to have Republic of Texas F-16s fire missiles at a refinery? Maybe the capital? "No demonstrations, Bruce. We don't want to give away our one strategic advantage. Right now, no one knows about our movement. We need to keep it that way until we're ready to strike."

He moved toward her, squatting to keep his shoulders under the water. "I don't know. Maybe it's time to raise the Republic's flag. A demonstration might help some of the naysayers shift into our court."

"No demonstrations. Not as long as I'm governor. We go when I say we're ready to go."

He ducked under the surface, barely visible in the bubbling water. His lips circled around her right nipple, doing the little nibbling thing he did. Her heart beat faster, her body prickling with desire. She placed her hands on his head, shoving him down, past her stomach, between her legs. Even though he stood over six feet tall, she knew the strength of her thighs, tempered by distance running, swimming, and cycling. She could easily hold him under and end this little game. Her legs tightened around him. He strained to pull his head away, his hands struggling for leverage to part her thighs. If she killed him, the police would be involved and Bruce had an annoying ability to capture a win from the jaws of defeat. She could see the headline. *Governor Adamson's Pubic Hair Found In Dead Healthcare Executive's Mouth.*

Spreading her legs, she let him pop to the surface, gasping. "What the hell, Frannie?"

She rushed to him, a hand stroking his face. "I'm so sorry. You're just so...incredible. I forgot you were under water."

He continued panting, but a slight smile parted his lips. "It's okay. I understand."

How have men been in power all these centuries when they all lead with their dicks? "No demonstrations, right?" She kissed him, then hugged him, making sure her breasts had full contact with his chest.

"No demonstrations. I'll just have to remember the scuba gear for next time."

She ran her nails down his back. "Mmmm. Tanks, hoses, masks. I love it."